BLUE MOON BAY WITCHES
1

SIERRA CROSS

Cover Design by Arcane Covers
Interior Formatting by Qamber Designs

FANGS and FRENEMIES

CHAPTER ONE

BLUE MOON BAY'S "antique" cast-iron streetlamps were brand spanking new, but you'd never know it to look at the hideous things.

Our town's latest bid to charm tourists, the lamps blazed with an eerie orange glow that only stoked my anxiety as I sped past Ocean Street's deserted bistros, yarn shops, and taffy stands at dawn.

Come hex or high water, I could *not* be late for work again.

Not today, when Grandma Sage was counting on me to bake a very special wedding cake. Raspberry crémeux, three tiers of it, draped with glossy fondant. A cake that had to taste like heaven and look pretty enough to grace a magazine cover. Literally, since our bride's swanky reception would be featured in *Oregon Coast Bride*.

But the baking was ... well, cake, compared with the *other* task Gran expected of me. Like her own grandmother before her, she imbued each wedding cake with a signature magical marriage blessing. As her apprentice witch, it was my job to assist with the spell.

A tough spell that called for deepest focus.

Bleary eyed, I guzzled milky coffee from the to-go cup balanced between my knees. No doubt binging Netflix last night, cuddled up with my new boyfriend, was a bad life choice. But Bryson and I had only been dating since summer, and the feel of his strong arms wrapped around me melted my brain every time.

I was still daydreaming about Bryson's soft, full lips when Trixie, my ancient VW Rabbit, hit a red light at the corner outside Java Kitty Café.

"Check them out, doll," she exclaimed, speaking telepathically straight to me. "How come *their* parking lot's full at six a.m. while I'm sittin' alone in our dinky lot? What are they putting in that coffee? Cocaine?"

"I don't know, Trix." Just the sight of Java Kitty's pink neon sign—a smug cat outline with winking eyes—sizzled my blood. Ever since their grand opening a month ago, the trendy new café had been a real burr in my boot.

I'd made a point of avoiding the place. Wouldn't want to look like I was spying on the competition. But here we were, stuck at the light, and it was hard not to peek through the window ... seeing as how the entire wall *was* window.

Sleek design, I must admit.

Inside, morning shows lit up jumbo flat-screens on the wall behind modern, white counters. A smiling barista, gliding by on a Hoverboard, offered nibbles from a pastry tray.

My stomach sank. No wonder they were picking off our customers. What chance did we have against a Hoverboard?

"Now that is how it's done, dollface." Trixie sounded way too impressed. *"You might want to take notes."*

I gritted my teeth. "More driving, less chatting, please."

Trixie went silent, so silent I could suddenly hear the engine. Her primitive spirit was hardwired into the car, though, so I could still sense her sulking.

If experience held, she'd drive passive-aggressively for the next mile and then go right back to yakking.

It was times like this I bemoaned not having a cat for a familiar, or one of those cute owls.

Trying to calm my nerves, I turned my gaze back to the street. The blasted light was yellow again.

"I'm late," I begged the car. "I can't play games with you this morning."

"Ugh, fine," Trixie huffed, and floored it.

Just as her front wheels entered the intersection, a flash of khaki uniform appeared on Java Kitty's patio. I registered the buzzed black hair and achingly perfect proportions of Deputy Elliot James, whose hawk eyes clocked me from behind his to-go latté cup. *Et tu, Elliot?*

Trixie slammed on the brakes. They screeched. I yelped as hot coffee lurched into my lap, scalding my stomach through my knit top. It rivered down my jean skirt and onto the floormat.

Elliot was at my side in a hot second. "Hazel."

How'd he fly over here so fast to ticket me? And Trixie, that traitor, was lowering her drivers' side window for him without even asking my consent.

"Already know what you're going to say." I folded my arms miserably over my coffee-soaked sweater. Hex my life, my first traffic ticket ever. "But please note that I did stop, before I *fully* ran the red light. Better late than never, right?"

"I'll take that under advisement." His sharp, nearly black eyes looking too amused for my taste. "It's not like you to bend traffic rules. Or any rules."

Great, so he was going to twist the knife and make fun of me too, by alluding to my dorky rep in high school? Yeah, I'd earned a Good Citizenship award all four years. So?

Weirdly, my high school crush—the brooding loner in the back row who got no awards—was the one to enter law enforcement.

And now he was enforcing laws on me.

Something in Elliot's expression shifted as he took in my sleepy, coffee-covered self. "Something wrong?"

"Not at all." Other than dying of embarrassment. And lateness. "I just need to get to work."

His expression seemed to snap back to normal. "Yes, you do."

He gestured to the road, and the sheer relief of it hit me.

"You're not giving me a ticket?"

"Not when the people need their muffins and scones and … I don't know, little breakfast cakes," he added with a completely straight face. "Godspeed, but don't speed."

He thought he was so above it all with his low-carb lifestyle.

"We serve great lattes too," I called pointedly after him as Trixie tore off like a mike drop.

I drove the rest of the way to work drenched and coffee stained. As Trixie tucked herself into my reserved spot behind the bakery, I silently cursed the Third Vow of a Green Witch, "Thou Shalt Not Use Magicks to Augment Thine Appearance."

The first two were way more reasonable.

"Thou Shalt Not Use Magicks To Commit Murder." Well, duh.

And "Thou Shalt Not Use Magicks to Cause A Person to Fall in Love."

I wasn't a monster.

I just didn't see why conjuring a clean, dry outfit should get me turned into a toad.

Ok, not literally, these days. I'd only be forbidden to practice Green Magic for a year and a day, which was an embarrassing inconvenience. Modern Green witches were chill compared to vampires and shifters, who still ordered executions at the drop of a hat like it was the Middle Ages.

Or so I'd heard. No one we knew hung out with vampires or shifters. Gran always said they were secretive creatures, which I took to mean they didn't organize pancake breakfasts. Like the Green Witch Association monthly meetup, where I'd won Trixie in a business card drawing last year.

I was bending over the utility sink in the bakery's back room, wringing out my sopping skirt, when the savory scent of Granny Sage's rosemary-cheddar-scallion scones baking in the oven wafted in.

"Hazel dear, you're late again."

I looked up to see Gran gazing with intense concern from the kitchen doorway. Embroidered toads danced on the sleeves of her cotton dress. Her white hair—silvered on the ends like a raincloud—hung over one shoulder, twisted into its usual side braid. She frowned at the wet spot on my skirt.

"No, I didn't pee my pants, before you ask." I squeezed the bottom of my sweater like a sponge. "My coffee spilled in the car, because of … um … a bad driver."

"Dang tourists." Gran tsked, hands on her generous hips. "Ruining the town is what they're doing. Probably demon spawn, half of them."

Of course she'd blame the tourists. That was her catch-all insult for newcomers to Blue Moon Bay. Or those whose parents had been new. Yep, Gran could be a touch small minded when it came to her beloved hometown.

I bit my lip and tried not to think about the fact that Bryson was a newcomer to the Bay himself. Thanksgiving was only a few weeks away, and I still hadn't introduced him to my family yet … not even to Gran. She'd never approved of any of my boyfriends. And, one by one, I couldn't help but notice, they'd all turned out to be prize jackwagons. Jackwagons who dumped me and broke my heart. Her judgment was like a cosmic pronouncement.

Please, oh please, let Bryson break the loser chain.

"Sorry I'm late, I'll start mixing up the cake batter right away." I hung my purse on its wooden peg between two old broomsticks (ceremonial, not for transport) and offered a placating smile. "We should be ready to start the blessing spell by 10 AM."

"About that, Hazel dear … you can take it off your to-do list." Grandma Sage blew out a sigh, and guilt slithered through my guts.

"You don't think I'm up to helping you with the big spell?" Crap, had I been screwing up worse than I thought? I'd be the first to admit I'd been erratic lately, walking around dreamy and absent-minded, showing up late. It's just that I'd never had a healthy and happy relationship before.

"It's not that."

Gran cleared her throat and looked away, like what she was about to say was painful. My stomach plummeted. I was her granddaughter, apprentice, and sole magical heir. But that didn't make me immune to getting fired.

"We'll be skipping the spell," she said.

My head snapped back in surprise. "Skipping, as in, no one's going to bless this marriage? We're leaving things up to chance?" My voice had pitched up. I couldn't believe what I was hearing.

Gran shrugged vaguely. "It's not like the bride and groom will ever know anything's missing."

"Not the point." Ordinals, nonmagical people, never knew about our spells, but they still benefited from them. Everyone in town did. "A happy marriage lifts up everyone around it," I began. "You're the one who taught me—"

"Yes, well, not *every* union can be harmonious." Gran's voice turned sharp. "Some must be below average, by definition."

I frowned. What had gotten into her? "But if we have the power to make things better, then we owe it to the people of Blue Moon Bay—"

"That's what I'm trying so desperately to avoid telling you, Hazel dear." Gran exhaled. "I don't have the power. Anymore."

I stared at her in confusion. "What are you talking about? You're the most powerful witch I know. You *poof* into work every day while I still drive a car."

Which wasn't at all embarrassing, I told myself. Sure, Gran had mastered teleportation spells at twenty, but not every witch could be Gran. Between the bakery and having a love life for once, who could find the time to curl up with a six-hundred-page grimoire? At this rate I'd have to put up with Trixie's prattle for another decade, but hey, work life balance.

"You practically shine with magic," I finished, getting back to Gran. "It's intimidating."

"Oh, honey, I know all that." She waved her hand at me like I wasn't getting the point. "The magic's still inside me, I'm just having trouble getting it out these days. When you get to be my age, casting is a struggle. Lately even minor spellwork leaves me stiff and aching. It's been happening for a while, but now it's progressing quickly." She smiled sadly. "Soon it will be your time to shine."

A chill ran down my back. Gran was over eighty, but she didn't look it. Didn't act it either, most of the time. Her magic couldn't be fading. I was nowhere near ready for her to retire. For me to take over.

For the sign outside to read "Hazel's Bakery."

"I tried one of those trendy 'living room refresh' spells last night," Gran confessed. "Broke into hives. Worse, when my furniture rearranged itself, it looked dull and sterile, like a dentist's waiting room. I half expected to see a tropical fish tank and stacks of *Us* magazine."

"You're scaring me, Gran." I shivered. "I thought we'd have more time."

I'd meant more time with me as her apprentice. Not, you know … on Earth. But with sudden horror, I remembered that Gran's own mentor, Granny Marge, had passed away soon after bequeathing her the business.

Gran was all the family I had, not counting the rest of my family. Which I didn't.

I'd been born to an elegant Beige Witch mother who drooled over Bottega handbags and was forever wringing her hands at what she called my fashion blindness. At least she had my two stylish sisters to console her, and my clueless Ordinal dad to dote on them.

Meanwhile, I had Gran.

What would I ever do without her?

"We'll get through this." I squeezed her hand. She squeezed mine back, weakly.

How could I not have seen what was happening to her? Answer: I'd been too busy kissing Bryson.

I vowed to take my calling as a witch more seriously, from now on. I'd have to. There'd be no one to pick up my slack.

"Or, really, *I'll* get through it," I corrected myself. "While you drink tea and catch up on your shows. You've been running the store for sixty years. You deserve a little relaxation."

"You know us Green Witches aren't good with retirement." She smiled ruefully. "When our work's done, it's time to go."

I wanted to argue, but it was hard to picture busy, practical Gran lounging around playing shuffleboard. As hard as it was to picture me running this place alone.

Inspiration struck me.

"What if your work *isn't* over?" I said. "Forget retiring. Why not stay on part-time, as an advisor to me?"

"That's not a terrible idea." She gave me a shrewd look. "But are you ready to be the one in charge?"

Her blunt question caught me off guard. I sure didn't feel ready, but what choice did I have? I answered as honestly as I could. "Gran, I love this bakery with all my heart. I've memorized your spells. Year by year, I'll add my own into the family recipe book. And one day, I'll pass it on to my own granddaughter."

Assuming, of course, that I haven't driven the place into bankruptcy.

"I have great faith in you, Hazel dear," Grandma Sage said as if reading my mind, which she swears is not something our line of witches can do. She patted my hand, but her gaze still looked troubled. "I only wish I weren't bequeathing it to you at such an awkward time. Java Kitty Café is, well …"

"Gonna get hairballs from eating our dust." It was only tough talk, but it made Grandma Sage smile. That's all I cared about at this moment. She deserved some peace of mind, after pouring her magical energies into this job for sixty years. "Why don't you work the register while I tackle this wedding cake—including the proper blessing."

Soloing the spell would zonk me out, but it would be worth it. Humming to myself, I tied on an apron.

I was measuring dry ingredients into prep bowls when a green vintage Mustang eased into our parking lot, its driver's tangled red hair raging in the wind.

A familiar twinge of frustration lit my chest as Maxine de Klaw sprinted through the lot in shredded jeans and Docs, her baggy sweatshirt printed with some math equation joke I'd never get.

When she first started coming to the bakery, I thought it was because she missed our friendship. Ten thousand orders later, I'd accepted she just saw us as a chill coworking spot to work on her news blog, *Blue Moon Roundup*, which had eclipsed the Gazette as our town's official paper.

"Least we still have our best customer," Gran said with a chuckle. Max's ability to devour pastries while she worked at her laptop was legendary. "I'll let you get your friend's order."

"Okay." I rolled my eyes. No matter what I said, Gran persisted in the delusion that Max and I were still besties. I set down my prep bowl of baking soda to head to the register.

Through the front window, Max looked lost in thought, but that was just her normal expression. She burst through the door, glasses foggy from the cold, her goofy half smile reminding me of all the times in high school when she'd thought up some crazy scheme guaranteed to get us both in trouble.

Now? Who knew what that smile meant.

When a romantic relationship ended, at least you got a breakup. But friendship, even one as close as ours, could simply end. With no explanation.

"Morning, Miss Sage. Hazel." My childhood friend nodded at Gran but didn't meet her eyes. Or mine. Hmm, that was odd … even for Max. "I'll take a large mocha to go, and three fudge brownies." She paused. "And a Blue Moon Mornin' Roll with cheddar."

"Will that be all?" I asked, not sarcastically. Two thousand calories was a light breakfast to Max and her genetic lottery-winning metabolism.

"Actually … make it an extra-large mocha. With chocolate whip."

"Coming right up." I grabbed a fresh wax paper liner and a plate, reached into the cold case for brownies. And blinked as two very un-Maxlike words registered. "Sorry, did you say *to go?*"

She fiddled with her key fob, again not meeting my eyes. "Yup."

"Cool. Great."

Confused, I tilted my gaze at our stack of compostable to-go cups and trays, as if I'd suddenly forgotten how to use them. Because none of this made sense: Max was our bakery's equivalent of a bar fly. For years now, she was our corner booth's laptop-camper, clack-clacking and racking up an impressive tab over the day with her mocha addiction.

"You didn't bring your laptop today," I realized, then gasped. "Is she broken?"

"Nah… I just can't stay, Hazel," Her green eyes darted to the right. "Something came up. A family thing." Man, she sounded squirrelly, like someone making up an excuse.

But an excuse for what? I wondered, in the awkward silence while I arranged her brownies onto a flimsy compostable tray that looked like a glare would melt it.

"I hope your parents are doing all right, Maxine?" Gran prompted. "And Kade, too?"

"Huh? Oh yeah … they're all fine." She glanced up from punching in her ATM code to frown at the counter. "Dude, it's just me. You don't need to get all fancy."

She swiped a brownie, stuffed it in her mouth, and pocketed the other two like a preschooler. Latte cup in one paw, roll in the other, Max nodded a solemn goodbye and backed out of the room, humming under her breath with perfect pitch.

It was either Beethoven or heavy metal.

As I watched her bump into the door and yelp at her coffee-splashed arm, then lick it, I was knocked down by a powerful wave of missing her.

It's not like I was without friends these days. Rose Verdant and the other girls from Magic Sprouts garden store shared my love of herbs. I met up with them for brunch or a show now and then. There was a Green witch spell book club that convened every other full moon to gossip over glasses of chardonnay. I wouldn't say I had a posse, but I had peeps.

Problem was, none of them were crazy weirdos like Max. And so, I never once found myself screaming with laughter at three a.m. in a tidepool with them. Or swerving off on a spontaneous road trip. Or fighting about something stupid, then making up, and arguing all over again during the recap. None of my other friends defended me by spraying Predator Pee through the locker slats of my enemies.

Max had set the bar too high.

I hefted the ten-pound baking soda package back onto its shelf in the pantry, and headed glumly to the walk-in fridge to retrieve the three dozen eggs our recipe demanded.

Max had appeared in my life just in time. Eleven years ago, the autumn I turned seventeen, my mother officially banished me from the daily Beige Magic lessons she taught my sisters and me. A ritual of failure that had made my stomach hurt every morning since I could recall. "I'm sorry to say it, but Hazel doesn't have our gift." Those were her exact words, and they made me start bawling. My big sister Bea's gaze filled with pity while I begged Mother to please reconsider. My younger sister Cindra averted her eyes from the gory train wreck.

After pronouncing me hopeless, Mother shipped me off to Gran's kitchen to learn to bake pies and cakes, which was, she said with a sigh, probably more my speed. She was right, but not in the way she imagined.

The Green Magic I was born with turned out to be ten times more potent than Beige. But more importantly, I loved every minute of working with Gran. On the fateful day when I helped her bake a mess of Thanksgiving pies for charity, she outfitted us both in silly three-cornered hats that made our customers smile. Holding up the first pecan pie I'd ever baked, I posed shyly for a *Blue Moon Gazette* reporter writing a feel-good story.

Unfortunately, that photo inspired Blue Moon High's resident mean girls—Ashlee Stone, Jenna Jeffries, and Britt Salazar—to start taunting me with the nickname "Goody Two-shoes." It was dumb, but it stuck to me thanks to their immense popularity … plus, my stack of citizenship awards wasn't helping. Where I used to feel invisible at school, now constant bullying drove me to tears daily. It soon felt as miserable as home did—and with no bedroom door for me to hide behind. Gran and the bakery were my solace, but I couldn't take them with me to school. What saved me was the tall, smart, red-headed girl in my class who was just as odd as me. Who fought the bullies back and looked out for me too. I'd even come out to her as a witch—and Max thought that was the coolest thing she'd heard in her life.

I cracked the first egg, separating its yolk with one expert gloved hand. The white part oozed into a bowl below. None of that old drama mattered anymore, I told myself firmly. Not the mean girl trio. Not the banishment. Not even Max, who I'd loved like a sister but who ghosted me. For reasons I'd probably never learn.

Only one person in the world had consistently been there for me: Gran. She'd seen the spark of magic in me when literally no one else did. Now Gran needed me, and I wasn't about to let her down. So what if I wasn't ready to take over the bakery? I'd make myself ready. It was the only way I could honor the witch who'd turned my life around.

Turning my attention back to the recipe, I turned on the electric mixer and cranked it to the highest setting. As I beat the eggs into froth, I told myself these things over and over. So firmly that I almost believed them.

CHAPTER TWO

THE NEXT FOUR hours zipped by. While Gran served coffee and pushed fresh rosemary scones on our (sadly too few) customers, I whipped up a cloud of buttercream in our industrial stand mixer, poured cake batter into molds, and painstakingly unrolled thick, satiny fondant.

As I stood at the counter chopping up magical herbs for the spell, Granny Sage watched me from behind the pastry case. The pride in her eyes warmed me despite my chilly wet clothing. As soon as this spell was in the bag, I vowed, I'd finally bite the bullet and tell her about me and Bryson.

At 11:03 a.m., I inspected the final product. Wedding cakes always brought out my inner perfectionist. I tended to work extra slow, meticulously obsessing on tiny flaws no guest would notice. But today's cake was by necessity a rush job, and, to my surprise, I was pleased with my work. Fresh cream-colored roses and strung silver beads made of sugar trimmed the smooth expanses of each tier. Raspberry and vanilla flavor would explode from every bite.

Now for the final ingredient …

"I, Hazel Greenwood, humble Green Witch, reach out to the universe with both hands open." Spreading my fingers wide, I rested my right hand over my heart. Then I plunged my left hand in the small bowl of herbs and charged water that I'd prepped while the cake was baking. Instantly my vision blurred. A familiar low rumbling vibrated in my ears, as if an earthquake was in progress. Then the bakery kitchen's colors grew bold. Vibrant. Boundaries and edges ran like paint, as if real life had slipped on a Van Gogh photo filter. Suspended in midair, bright green astral trees and plants bloomed between the physical objects in my line of sight. One hand in each realm. Me the living bridge between them.

Softly, I began to recite the incantation:

"Together shall your hearts endure,
Through all of life's trials unsure,
In times of laughter, times of tears,
When hair grows from his nose and ears.
Or when vacations feel like work,
because your toddler's gone berserk.
Like an acorn planted deep,
With roots of patience love will keep.
Growing stronger by and by—"

"Drat!" Grandma Sage cried out, rousing me from my magical trance. "Hazel dear, I see the bride, she's walking up now," she said in disbelief. "She's half an hour early."

Horrified, I glanced outside. Marching toward the front door was a model type with a platinum chignon. Her high heels tapped a staccato beat, growing louder as they approached.

"This can't be happening. I'm not that close to finishing the spell. I won't have time!"

"Welp." Grandma Sage sounded as crushed as I felt. "A dud marriage could build character, I s'pose."

Our welcome chimes dinged. Never had they sounded such a mourning tone.

I patted Gran's shoulder. "I'll handle talking to her. Can you box up the cake and put it on a dolly?"

This time, she didn't hesitate but vanished into the back room. Leaving me face to face with the woman whose marriage I'd inadvertently wronged.

Guilt scuttled like a roach through my guts as the gorgeous young bride strode up to the counter. Wowzer, that diamond of hers was bigger than a chocolate kiss. I shoehorned on my best "customer service" smile and chirped, "Good morning, miss. Congratulations on your wed—"

"I don't have time for chitchat." She waved me away with her sparkly hand. "You can go on and fetch my cake now."

I gritted my teeth. I was *not* used to rude customers. In a town as small as Blue Moon Bay, most locals knew better. Heck, even tourists knew better. "Miss, you are quite early. I don't suppose you'd be willing to come back in half an hour?"

She stared at me as if waiting for the punchline.

I sighed. "Hang tight, miss. We're boxing up the cake for you now."

"Cool, I love waiting around for stuff I've already paid for." She pouted with full, juicy, raspberry-hued lips. "I shouldn't even be here, you know. This is all my personal assistant's fault, for quitting the day before my actual wedding—can you imagine?"

"No," I said flatly, because I couldn't imagine having an assistant in the first place. Was rude lady a celebrity? She did look gorgeous, not to mention weirdly familiar.

Especially those eyes. Mean, green, hungry eyes. They looked me up and down appraisingly. "I don't suppose *you'd* want a job?"

"I have one." I paused for effect. "Here."

"Oh, you're so sweet. I meant a career job. Not a hairnet job." The blinged goddess wrinkled her perfect nose and smiled down at me. And the smile was in the neighborhood of a sneer and looked *tantalizingly* familiar.

"I cannot function without an assistant," she confessed. "My life's too complicated. I need a team member on hand twenty-four seven. What do they pay you here? I'll double it."

"You want to poach me from Sage's Bakery?" I laughed, even though something about this imperious woman made my palms sweat like nothing had in years. Since high school, if I'm being honest. "Thanks, but it's a family business."

The mean bride gasped. "You're old lady Sage's granddaughter, aren't you? Knew you looked familiar ..." A leer twisted her Angelina Jolie lips. That leer haunted my dreams. "How's it going, *Goody Two-shoes*?"

It was Ashlee Stone. Popular, mean Ashlee Stone, my old bully. She'd colored her mousy hair a pale blonde and added high-volume lips. She'd slimmed down her nose, too, and puffed up her boobs. But though she was now more silicone than woman, one thing hadn't changed. Her meanness.

I swallowed. "My name is Hazel, Ashlee."

"That's right, sweet little *Hazel.*" Ashlee slipped on a fake smile. Apparently, I was worth one, now that I'd been upgraded from clerk to classmate. "So. What's new and exciting in your world? Anything?"

She sounded doubtful, but I decided to treat it like a sincere question.

"I'm in a good place, thanks. I love my job."

She let out a squeal. "That's so cute! Someone 'loves' working in a bakery. You're as adorable as ever." She glanced at my bare finger. "And single as ever, too. Your life must be so ... uncluttered."

Helpless anger welled up in me. It was disappointing sometimes, how little people changed. Rumors had flown after high school that Ashlee had moved to Los Angeles, failed at modeling, and drifted into couch surfing, pot, and chubbiness. At the time, I'd imagined a little failure might humanize her. But everything about the woman in front of me screamed success, screamed it right in my face. From her designer bandage dress to her three-ton diamond set in platinum.

And the way she was eyeing my coffee-stained sweater made it clear she still relished the huge gulf between us. Like always.

But Ashlee wasn't just my bully now. She was my customer. I forced myself to keep it professional.

"Yep, that's me. Uncluttered. I'm even my own personal assistant, haha. But back to you, you're getting married tomorrow! Sooo great."

"I know, right?" At her queenly smile, I congratulated myself on not letting her jerkiness get to me. Much. Then Ashlee added with a coy look, "So what it's like, working for that batty old crone?"

My stomach fluttered. *Oh, she did not.* "Excuse me?"

Ashlee's smile was as sweet as one of those new diet sodas that you just know will turn out to cause cancer. "You heard me, Goody Two-shoes."

A painful truth I'd learned growing up was that Ordinals didn't always see Gran the way we witches did, as a wise leader. Some looked at my powerful mentor and saw only a slightly scatterbrained, batty old lady. My own mother, Gran's daughter-in-law, was forever encouraging her to replace her homespun dresses with jewel-toned jogging suits and clip her long white hair into a respectable Karen cut.

Gran was too big of a person to mind it all. But I wasn't.

I leaned forward so my face and Ashlee's faces were inches apart. Her floral perfume made me dizzy, but I forced myself to meet her dazzling wolfish eyes, the way I never could in high school. "It's my privilege to learn from one of our town's living legends," I said, as calmly as I could, and added under my breath, "They say that marriage changes a person, so congrats in advance to your fiancé."

Ashlee's eyes darted from side to side as she tried to figure out exactly how I'd insulted her.

Before she could huff out a rejoinder, a refined alto voice called out from behind her, "Why, look at you girls having such a lovely chat. I had no idea you two were old friends!"

A jovial middle-aged woman stood in the doorway, towering nearly a foot over me in her sturdy high-heeled riding boots. From her smooth grey pageboy, to her taupe suede car coat, to her Louis Vuitton handbag that contained a small, fluffy white dog, Estelle Kensington looked every inch the affluent matron whose family milestones were documented by local media. Seeing her in person always made me feel starstruck. Maybe it was because I'd grown up seeing her portrait on display at the town library, which she and her husband, Frederick, built in honor of their son.

The most eligible bachelor in town, dark-haired, broad-shouldered Drew Kensington was the closest thing we had to a prince. When his private school football team whipped Blue Moon High's, the girls on our side quietly cheered for Drew. One of our cheerleaders, Jenna Jeffries, went further and dated him. Even I, mousy Goody Two-shoes, had indulged the odd secret fantasy of being swept off my feet by our town's own heartthrob ... oh my Gods.

Ashlee was marrying Drew?

That alone was proof life wasn't fair.

"Mother Kensington!" Ashlee's voice honeyed as she rushed over to exchange air-kisses with Estelle. "Such a lovely surprise. I'm honored that you came. Hiya, Sammy Boy, you sweet puppy." The lapdog yipped indignantly as she stroked its ears with her ice-pink shellac manicure.

If Ashlee was faking her deference, she was at least putting in the effort. Or, was it possible even she felt cowed by the level of wealth and power she was marrying into? The Kensingtons dominated the elite Blue Moon Heights Country Club set. Now Ashlee would, too. *As the future queen of Blue Moon Bay's high society*, I thought darkly, *she'll probably outlaw libraries and museums from town.*

Leaving only lash-extension salons and Botox clinics. Maybe the odd Sephora.

Granny Sage took that moment to emerge pushing a dolly stacked with three neat, white bakery boxes. Mrs. Kensington and Ashlee crowded around it to peek inside at the cake.

"Such a timeless work of art." Mrs. Kensington gushed, as if it were a Renoir. To Ashlee she added, "In this vulgar age, it's hard to find a classic design like this anywhere but at Sage's Bakery."

"Yeah, um, super classic, right?" Ashlee echoed, sounding like a moron.

No doubt she was just shamelessly sucking up to her future mother-in-law, but the rain of compliments from them both made me squirm with guilt. I knew the truth about that cake, even if they never would.

It was unblessed.

Unmagical.

A failure.

I was relieved when a stylish mid-thirties woman with an ebony fauxhawk burst in, panting. "So sorry, ma'am, Kent couldn't find a parking space big enough for the hummer, so we're circling."

"Don't apologize, Leeza. I'm having such a nice chat with Sage's granddaughter."

"Ah, right, you must be Hazel." The stylish assistant nodded at me.

"You know my name?" I blurted out.

"Sorry, that may have sounded creepy." Leeza laughed, and it was that rusty bark of a laugh you hear from people who are wound too tight. "See, it's my job to keep tabs on all the up-and-coming artisans in Blue Moon Bay." She stole a glance around the shop and narrowed her eyes. Was she taking in the silence, the empty tables? Her inspection made me feel uneasy. "I keep an up-to-date spreadsheet listing every chef, baker, stylist, and what have you. We're always hiring for events and so on."

That was interesting, I thought, wondering what they might pay for a catering gig. The green cushion on the bakery's corner booth had the stuffing coming out of it, and too many of our mugs were chipped …

"Any friend of Ashlee's gets priority, of course." Mrs. K smiled and gestured to the space between me and Ashlee, as if there was something good happening there. "I never did get the story on how you two know each other. Horseback riding pals? Tennis camp?"

Ashlee snorted softly under her breath. For once I didn't blame her. The thought of us as BFFs enjoying rich-kid hobbies together was too much.

Ashlee had grown up on an ordinary street with modest ramblers and overgrown backyards. My street.

She'd moved in when we were eighth graders for the most unglamorous of reasons: her mom was online dating a townie, and they'd decided to shack up. By graduation, that romance was donezo, so Ashlee and her mom headed back to California. Forever, I'd hoped.

"We were classmates, ma'am," I said. Hoping that word made it plain we weren't close.

It didn't. Estelle Kensington was just too unflappably positive to glean that my friendship with Ashlee wasn't a thing.

"In that case. Here." Mrs. K reached into her Louis Vuitton bag, after giving Sammy Boy a scratch behind his white ears, and presented an engraved card on plush, cream-colored paper. "Hopefully, you can make it to our little reception tomorrow?"

I gulped. "Um, wow. I really couldn't—"

"Mother Kensington, you are too kind. Too, too kind. But I'm sure Hazel must be so very *busy.*" Ashlee shot me a murderous look. I almost chuckled at her desperate need to keep losers like me away from her exclusive party. As if she had anything to worry about. I had zero desire to buy my ex-bully a wok, waffle iron, or fondue set. She'd proved herself to be the same shallow mean girl as ever. All those nasty barbs.

Especially about Gran, who at this very moment was fixing me with a pointed look. Eyes wide. Grey head nodding. Eager for me to say yes, to pick up the engraved card Estelle Kensington was holding out to me.

Why?

The blessing spell. If I went to the wedding, I'd have one final opportunity to stand over the cake for a few solid minutes (without anyone noticing, somehow) and complete the spell.

To prove I was ready to take over the bakery.

Ashlee Stone, soon to be Kensington, was glaring daggers at my head.

I took a deep breath. Hex my life. "Ashlee, I'd be honored to attend your wedding tomorrow."

CHAPTER THREE

IT WAS ONLY a six-minute commute from downtown Ocean Street to my cozy house on Filbert Road. As I made my way homeward at dusk, blasting my favorite tunes couldn't stop my vague dread of Ashlee's wedding from blooming into a full-on freak-out.

What had I gotten myself into?

I belonged in my baker's apron. Rolling pie crusts. Whispering my little spells that made the world a little sweeter. I did not belong at the Blue Moon Heights Country Club party, mingling with the beautiful people.

I was still panicking when a red light again trapped me outside Java Kitty Café's glass window.

As usual, the place was buzzing. A fake fireplace in the corner glowed with a bold indigo flame. Laptop workers were arranged around it, lounging in white minimalist armchairs. I shook my head in frustrated admiration. How did these people do it?

Like any coastal village, Blue Moon Bay had its seasonal rhythms. Our tourist season blazed in summer and shut down once the autumn leaves had fallen. Sage's Bakery had switched to our reduced winter hours three weeks ago. Yet here it was, after six p.m. in November, and Java Kitty was packed.

Did people love clean, modern design that much?

If so, we were screwed.

While I was spying and stewing and fearing for my bakery's future, I spied a familiar form slumped over a laptop. In stinging disbelief, I stared at Max's tangled red hair.

"A family thing" indeed.

So much for our best customer. But why was I even surprised? *Loyalty never was your strong suit, was it, Max?*

People had the right to drink soulless coffee if they wanted to, I reminded myself, though I was literally seeing red as I pulled Trixie into the lot to get a closer look. It's not like she was cheating on Sage's Bakery to hurt me. Max was too logical to think in such terms, for one thing. For another, she was utterly clueless when it came to people's feelings. Hadn't I learned that the hard way, so many years ago?

I was itching to jump out of my car and confront her, but it was myself I was annoyed with. I thought I'd finally learned not to take Max's weird aloofness—her inscrutable Maxness—personally. None of it was personal. Not our coffeeshop chitchat that I kidded myself bordered on a hangout. Not her moving on from my bakery.

The way everyone seemed to be doing, nowadays.

Out of the corner of my eye, the traffic light changed to red again. Glaring at Max's traitorous hair had cost me an entire traffic cycle.

That's when the smell hit my nostrils.

The reek of something burning … and it wasn't coffee. More like grass. A crisp pungent scent, like freshly barbecued lawn.

My magical senses awoke as if to a blaring alarm. *Go, go, go!* Instinct screamed at me.

Trixie peeled out of the lot like a deranged bat, running the red light.

"Sorry, did I jump the gun?" Trixie asked in her purring voice.

"Hex no! We were on the same page that time."

It made two red lights run in one day, but I didn't care.

My breathing didn't slow to normal till I'd rolled onto my own street. Filbert Road was named for the sprawling hazelnut orchard that was cut down to make way for the neighborhood around ten years ago. But filbert trees are awfully hard to kill. Cut one to the ground and two new suckers sprout up next to it in spring.

The young zombie grove invading my planting strip never failed to make me grin with amusement as I passed by. But my head was still spinning as I tried to make sense of what I'd just smelled.

Unlike other supernaturals, we witches weren't born with a full set of super-senses. But we alone could sense magic. Human magic.

When I was a child, Gran once pointed out a noisy flock of crows in the dusky sky and told me that was Blue Moon Bay's biggest family of shifters. I remember feeling intrigued and asking if I knew any of them in real life. She'd only smiled, saying it'd be up to me to earn their trust someday, as she had. They sure seemed to be having fun together, flapping and cawing through the air, more fun than my family ever had. I must have made some wistful comment because that's when Gran told me we witches got to make our own families. And to help us find each other, we'd developed a special gift: if someone was casting a spell nearby, we could smell it.

Green Magic had a sweet, bright scent like mown grass. Like spring. When Blue Moon Bay's small community of practitioners met for a monthly pancake breakfast, our table smelled like a freshly cut lawn. But only to us.

Beige Magic smelled like perfume.

Red Magic smelled like berries or blood, supposedly. Since it was strictly outlawed, I'd never smelled it.

Then there was Grey Magic.

Considered experimental and not exactly safe, its use was first limited to academic settings. But lately, big corporations were starting to hire Grey Magic practitioners as consultants, on the theory that it gave their businesses an edge. I had no idea how that worked, but I did know what Grey Magic was supposed to smell like.

Burning grass.

Was that Java Kitty's real secret all along? That whoever ran this place was using an unstable form of magic to make their café wildly popular? And if it were true, what could I do to stop their stinky, over-roasted magic before they put us out of business?

Yesterday, I would have run to Gran for help. She always knew what to do … but Gran, much as I hated to admit it to myself, wasn't as strong as she used to be. Taxing her with this could harm her health.

No, if I was worthy of becoming a master witch and running the bakery, then I'd need to neuter Java Kitty myself.

Yikes, that sounded *way* more graphic than I intended.

But I resolved to do it.

Metaphorically.

As I pulled into the driveway, there was a slim blue carbon road bike parked on my English thyme and alpine-strawberry lawn. Despite the several impossible tasks that were on my plate, the sight of that bike made me smile. Because there was Bryson, leaning casually against my cranberry-wreathed front door. Looking serenely sexy like a catalog model in jeans and a brown bomber jacket, unzipped over a blue button-down that matched his sea-blue eyes.

I turned off the engine and ran straight into his waiting arms. His clean skin and leather jacket scent was pure aromatherapy, even better than my giant herb garden which hugged us on all sides. Bryson's sandy hair had that slightly messy look going on, probably thanks to the bike helmet that now rested at his feet. Next to it was a bottle of white wine, and a fragrant bag of Thai takeout.

"Thanks for bringing food—and wine." I murmured into his spicy neck. His big, leather-gloved hands smoothed my hair, then tilted my chin up so he could kiss me. His touch made me purr. If only I could escape into Bryson's arms forever, and never have to face the outside world again. "Work was a bit rough." I admitted. "I know there's no way you could have known, but a quiet evening at home sounds perfect."

"Oh, I totally got that you were having a bad day," he said calmly, the way he said everything. Zen was his default state. "The tone of your texts gave it away."

"Texts have a tone?" I pulled back in surprise and racked my brain to see if I'd said anything whiny or off-putting.

"Only your texts, Haze. And only to me." His sexy smile and wink put me at ease again. "Maybe I just know you well enough to read between the lines."

"You mean ..." I felt a pun coming on, unstoppable as a sneeze. "The *sub*text, if you will?"

Instead of groaning, he high-fived me. As if I needed more proof we were meant to be. We were both total dorks at heart.

He leaned down to pick up the Thai carryout bag while I grabbed the wine bottle and ran my finger over its cute, artsy label. Willamette River Valley Cellars. "Ooh, isn't this one of the little wineries we visited over the summer?"

He gave an offhand shrug. "Yeah, I might have noted all your favorites and had them secretly delivered to my place—figured we could open them when the weather got bad. You did say winters in the Bay can be grey with a lot of stay-in nights."

I batted my eyes at him. "For the record, you're a prince among boyfriends."

"Duh," he deadpanned. "I'm modest, too."

I laughed. "I would playfully shove you, but I don't want you to spill innocent Thai food."

"Should I be hurt that I rank below Pad Thai?" His dark blue eyes twinkled with amusement as he considered it. "Nah, Arpa's Bangkok Bar makes the best noodles. Your priorities check out."

It was truly amazing, I thought as I fumbled for my key ring at the front door, how much better I felt after just a few minutes with Bryson. More relaxed. More content. It made sense that a guy like him would become a professional therapist and life coach. In his calming presence, I felt I could deal with anything, even Ashlee's wedding.

That was it! I had to convince Bry to be my date for tomorrow.

The whole time we were peeling off our jackets and hanging them on hooks, I was mentally rehearsing how I'd make my big ask. Be my date for the Blue Moon Heights society wedding of the year? Hobnob with snobs, scarf canapés? Rescue me from loneliness and mortification? *Please don't leave me alone with this, not if you love me* ... nope, that was right out. We'd never said the L-word. Not yet. I wasn't going to wade into those piranha waters first, not when everything was going so well.

Almost too well, given my history of big romance fails.

My heart was pounding as I got out plates and silverware and walked them five feet over to the coffee table. My mini house wasn't much more than one big room, with a single-burner "kitchen" in one corner, a high loft bed in an alcove, one closet, and a subcompact bathroom that felt spacious, magically (that spell was Gran's housewarming gift). Built for one, my place was comfy and cozy—and it freed most of my property to be an herb garden. But now that Bryson and I were spending so much time together I couldn't help but wonder if I . . .. we? ... needed a larger space.

He'd peeled off his jacket and was pouring pinot gris into two long-stemmed glasses. As he handed me my wine, his blue eyes met mine in a loving gaze and a familiar warmth sparked through me. "So," he said. "How'd it go with that fancy wedding cake you were stressing about this morning?"

Talk about the last thing on earth I wanted to discuss. "Um … it ended up looking really good." On the outside, I thought.

On the inside it was a useless dud. Like the bride.

He beamed. "I knew you could do it, Haze. You were born to bake."

"Yeah, well, I'm just glad this long day is over." I settled onto the couch, unlaced my tall black granny boots, and kicked my socked feet onto the coffee table, on top of a stack of baking and gardening mags. I made room for him to scoot in next to me before I spread the fuzzy sofa blanket over us both.

I know. I'm a scorching hot date.

Bryson threw his arm around me, and I curled my body toward his warmth. Instead of kissing me, though, he just rubbed my back, then grabbed the remote and queued up our Netflix favorites. Did he sense I wasn't up for a make out session but just craved some quiet closeness? Darn it, the man was almost *too* good at guessing how I was feeling.

From the day we met, Bryson was tuned into me in a way no other guy ever had been. I'd even wondered if he might be a witch himself, since male witches tend to be very empathic. But my subtle questioning along those lines, on our early dates, had revealed that he was an Ordinal's Ordinal. The guy didn't even believe in magic.

Which meant I had to be very careful about how I brought up Ashlee's wedding and my reasons for attending.

"Bry? There's this big wedding thing ... but you probably don't want to go." I sighed. "To be honest, even I don't—"

"Babe, I'm in. What's the dress code?"

"Suit and tie." I sighed with a relief so deep that my dread of the wedding vanished like magic. "It's at the Heights Country Club."

He pulled out his cell phone and hit the calendar app. "Cool, what month?"

"Uh ... it's tomorrow."

His brows shot up. "*Tomorrow* tomorrow?"

"I just got the invite." I shrugged helplessly. "These are the rich customers whose wedding cake I made. Grandma Sage really wants me to go because ... ah ... they invited me."

Sure, it would have been easier if I could have told him about the cake spell I was charged with completing, but that was the thing about dating a nonmagical person. Telling him about that part of me would change his life forever. I figured we needed to be dating for at least a year before I rocked his worldview.

"Okay, where exactly is this country club?" He sounded wary at this point, and I didn't blame him.

"High in the hills, where the air is thin but perfumed with diamond dust. Here." I reached for my purse, which was on the floor, and pulled out Estelle's invite.

"Holy ..." He stared at the card as if it were a newspaper announcing war had broken out. "So engraving's still a thing."

"You don't want to go, do you?" I hated the insecure sound of my own voice. "You'd rather do something more fun, without a suit. You know what? Let's forgot the whole thing. More green curry?" I gestured to the takeout boxes on the coffee table, eager to change the subject. "I think there's some coconut rice left."

"Haze, look at me." He grabbed my hand and squeezed it. "The only thing I want to do tomorrow is put on my one suit and go to some rando's fancy wedding. With the woman I'm falling in love with."

Love.

The word left me so flabbergasted I didn't see the kiss coming until his soft lips were on mine. My mouth responded to his touch, and I unconsciously leaned toward him, wanting more. His fingers gripped my hair, sending warm tingles through my scalp and down my spine. At last, he pulled back from the kiss and looked into my eyes, his own no longer laughing but sincere and serious.

"Phew. I've been wanting to say it for weeks."

"I …" I was still too stunned by his words—that L-word—to manage any of my own. "I …"

"It's okay." He lightly kissed my cheek and murmured in my ear, "Just wanted you to know how I feel. I'm not one of those insecure types who needs to hear it back right away."

"Uh …? Um." I wanted to tell him I loved him too, but his admission had made me so emotional that proper words wouldn't come out.

"Here, let me distract you from the awkwardness of this moment with a dramatic reading." He grabbed the invite off the coffee table and read it in a silly pretentious accent: "Ms. Ashlee Marie Stone and Mr. Frederick Andrew Kensington the IV request the pleasure of your company at their marriage, Saturday the Eighth of November at six o'clock p.m. in the evening … like, who didn't know that was the evening?"

I giggled. Then I looked up and saw that Bryson's face was twisted with conflict. "What's up?"

"Crud, I just remembered. I'm signed up to be at a continuing ed workshop for therapists all weekend. In Portland."

Portland, the only big city I'd ever been to, was a couple of hours drive to the north. No way he'd make it back in time. It stood to reason, I told myself. His saying the L-word *and* escorting me to the wedding would have been too much goodness. Something had to be subtracted to balance the universe.

I'd have to cowgirl up and face this hexed wedding alone.

Bryson kissed the top of my head gently. "Sorry I can't be there for you while you upstage some poor bride."

I'm pretty sure Ashlee would have laughed her butt off at the idea of being upstaged by me, but Ashlee wasn't here. Luckily.

I'm not even sure what I said in response, because the clean, spicy scent of his skin was starting to turn my brains to mush.

Maybe it was just as well I was dateless tomorrow. I'd need my wits about me if I had any hope of completing this spell. And letting Gran know that her magical legacy was in good hands.

As Bryson tilted my head back to kiss me again, my phone buzzed on the side table. *Max Max Max* flashed on the screen.

I stared in disbelief, the sight of her name like a psychic IV that dripped nostalgia straight into my bloodstream. My old friend was finally calling, for the first time since Grad Night. Yet it all felt strangely bittersweet.

Now I had closure, but … too much closure. It was suddenly less than clear to me why I'd been so fixated all this time on having fallen out with an old gal pal from high school.

I was a full-grown witch, for crying out loud. Currently reclining in a blissed-out state with a gorgeous man who—it turned out—loved me. *Loved* me.

I turned my phone over and went right back to spooning.

Too bad I can't just stay here with him all weekend, watching Netflix and eating caramel corn.

Whoa, *that* was an odd thought.

I sat up, pulling away from Bryson to catch my breath. I was a homebody, but not normally a couch potato. Yet at this moment, I longed to melt into my velvet sofa cushions and hermit away from the scary outside world. Even as Bryson snuggled closer to me, I couldn't help but fear that the stress of everything—Java Kitty, Gran's magical health, the incomplete spell, my bully's wedding—was quickly spiraling out of control.

And I wouldn't be able to hide from it tomorrow.

CHAPTER FOUR

AT FIVE P.M. the next afternoon, Trixie and I were huffing and puffing up the twisty mountain highway that led to Blue Moon Bay Heights. Pine and eucalyptus trees scented the cool autumn air through my open moon roof. Panic dreams about Ashlee's wedding had haunted me into the wee hours, but after I gulped down some coffee, sleepwalked through my shift at the bakery, and wiggled into a fancy dress, my terror had faded, mostly, to resignation.

The curvy road forked again. As we chugged up the final hill to Country Club Crest, the forest to my right vanished, replaced by a wall of evenly spaced, bare aspens. To my left, a steep cliffside offered a heart-stopping view of the sun poised to set over the Pacific. Whitecaps crashed into the jagged rocks below.

At the top of the hill loomed a sprawling compound. Tennis courts, already lit for evening. In the distance, the green of a golf course.

Trixie whistled. *"Fan-cee. Gosh, doll, sure you're dressed right for this shindig?"*

Blink. Did I just get fashion-shamed by my own car?

And a clunker, at that?

"I'm not trying to pass myself off as one of the elite," I said grouchily. "As long as I don't get bounced out, I figure I'm okay."

"Not getting kicked out is a good goal. There's a decent chance you'll achieve it ... was that more positive?"

I rolled my eyes. "Thanks for the support."

"See what you miss by turning down my chat levels?" Copying the Porche and Tesla ahead of her, Trixie pulled up to a roundabout lushly planted with climbing jasmine over a garden fountain. Trixie muttered something that sounded like, "Hope *I* don't get bounced."

Aw. My stony heart melted a little. "Trix, are you feeling insecure, too?"

"Uh, noooo, doll, why would you say that? I'm just worried some young hunk of a valet is going to be tempted to take me for a joyride. You know, because I'm so ... red ." She whispered the word as if it was a scandal.

"You're frankly more of a maroon shade." One that was popular circa 1991. I hid my smirk.

A lanky youth in scarlet livery opened my door and waited politely while I climbed out, feeling shaky on my gold stiletto heels. A gift from Cindra, who was known in our family for her bold taste in fashion, three Christmases ago, but I'd never had occasion to wear them before.

What with my hairnet lifestyle.

Well-dressed guests were drifting from the roundabout toward the country club. I hobbled along after them, trying not to stumble in my heels.

I'd ended up wearing a semi-metallic wrap dress that I'd fished out of a bag my older sister dropped off months earlier. Though Beatrix was perfectly capable of conjuring her outfits with Beige Magic the way Mother taught us, she treated shopping like a sport. Smuggling shopping bags past her husband's TV chair into her overflowing closet equaled "goal." When she grew bored with her trophies, I was her Goodwill drop-off. The latest discard was copper colored, with a plunging V-neck that required a torture device of a bra. Though I'd done my best with the iron, the dress had been festering in a plastic bag since July.

I had no illusions I was pulling off a look.

"Stunning, my dear. All you girls look stunning."

I glanced up in surprise. A woman Gran's age, in a terrifying mink coat, fixed me with a knowing look and lifted her champagne flute. Who was she toasting … me? Or all women younger than her, who she apparently thought of as girls?

I stammered, "Thank you."

Weirdly, several other strangers in the crowd were shooting conspiratorial grins my way.

Before I knew it, I was I grinning back, grateful for the unexpected niceness of the other guests. Here I'd been so worried I'd be snubbed. But, no, these nice rich people loved me. Accepted me. Welcomed me with open—

"Miss, what on earth do you think you're doing here?" A striking man in an elegant suit yelled from across the lush lawn. Perhaps he wasn't talking to me? "Yes you, girl with the long dark hair that should be in an updo but isn't." Eek, was he calling out my fashion don'ts, too? The man himself looked photo-perfect in his grey tailored suit. He looked mid-thirties, with dirty-blond hair, a muscular build, and craggy, striking features. "Come on, you know you shouldn't be running loose out here." He made stern eye contact and waggled his finger. "No more raspberry cosmos for you at the open bar, do you hear?"

Cosmos, what cosmos? My heart thumped while two preteen girls in scratchy-looking party dresses rubbernecked my humiliation. Who the hex was this guy anyway? Undercover wedding security? The fashion police?

"All right, missy, don't move a muscle." As if I could. To my horror, he sprinted across the lawn to accost me. My face was threatening to crumple into tears. I'd never been kicked out … of anything. Of course, I'd also never tried to get into anything that a person was likely to get kicked out of. "Now let's get you back to the photography area," the man went on. Wait, what? "Yes, yes, I know you're thirsty for more vodka, but you need to stay in your proper place with the other bridesmaids."

"*Bridesmaids?*" I spat out the word. "So, you're just … the wedding photographer?" Not security. Not bouncing me. I could have squawked with relief. "There's been a huge misunderstanding," I explained breathlessly. "Ashlee would never ask me to be a bridesmaid. I'm the cake baker, barely a D List guest. I'm E List, possibly F or G."

"You don't have to say the whole alphabet, I get it." A look of horrified realization had taken over his handsome features. "So that dress thing's just an awkward coincidence?"

He gestured across the lawn, and I suddenly spotted the gazebo a couple hundred feet away where eight or nine women milled about. All in copper-colored dresses, each one clearly custom designed to accentuate the wearer's shape. Some were V-neck. Some halter-neck. Some were knee length. Some maxis with slits.

My dress fit right in … even if I didn't.

"If you borrow your date's jacket, it'll be okay." The photographer had dropped his condescending tone. He sounded concerned for me. Sympathetic. If I didn't know better, I'd say he respected cake bakers more than he did Ashlee's friends. Which gave me hope for the world. "Button it up, to be safe," he added. "Don't take it off for the entire reception. Now where's your date?"

"Oh, um, I don't have one."

I was about to add, "Because my boyfriend's got a work thing today," but that seemed like overkill. Why should I bog him down with some long, boring story, about a guy he didn't even know?

Great, now I was overjustifying to myself why I didn't immediately mention Bryson when talking to a hot stranger.

A stranger whose intelligent blue-green eyes were locked on mine, in sympathy. "It's a damn shame, kid," he said. "I'd loan you my jacket, but I don't know you from Eve. You could be a kleptomaniac. Or a heavy armpit sweater." My face flushed, and I felt ready to die of mortification … till with a wink he shucked off his jacket and presented it to me. "Kidding. I'm David, by the way."

Gratefully I slipped on the jacket. It smelled like his citrusy cologne, delicious. "Hazel. Greenwood. Nice to meet you, even if it started out weird."

"Sorry about barking at you like that," he said, grimacing. "My nerves are shot. I've never worked with bridesmaids like these."

"Oh, you mean drunk, entitled, or insane?" Oops, my ramble mode had crossed the line into catty mode. My cheeks turned hot. "Sorry, I—"

"Don't be." He smiled, and I couldn't help but notice his smile was dazzling. "That was validating. I'm here as a skilled professional, like you, but at the moment, I feel like a babysitter."

I laughed. "Bet the pay scale's better."

"That helps," he conceded.

A waiter in black and white approached us, balancing a tray of champagne flutes.

"This stuff helps, too." David took two and handed one to me. "Veuve Clicquot," he murmured. "It's always Veuve at these things. It's an unwritten law."

"You do a lot of fancy weddings?"

"I photograph all the Kensington events, and a lot of others in the Heights, too. Keeps the lights on in my studio."

He said it almost defensively, but I hadn't been about to judge him for "selling out." On the contrary, I was suddenly thinking of what tricks and gimmicks I could possibly try to keep our bakery lights on in the face of Java Kitty's magical mayhem. "Amen to paying the bills," I said.

"Spoken like a true adult."

We clinked our flutes as the sun disappeared below the horizon, and I savored the sensation of outrageously expensive bubbles sliding down my throat. Feeling like an extra in a movie about rich people, I stole another glance at the bona fide bridesmaids. They were eight different flavors of gorgeous. It made no sense that anyone would mistake me for one of them.

I kept trying to think up a way to mention Bryson. One that didn't feel forced, like "Oh by the way, I have a boyfriend." Stop overthinking it, I told myself. David was good looking, charming, and talented. No doubt he was taken.

Probably married.

To a woman, or man, much hotter than me.

"Well, well, look who got himself to the church on time," David murmured, and I glanced up along with everyone else sipping champagne on the lawn as Drew Kensington ambled past us, dazzlingly Greek godlike in his bespoke black-tie ensemble. White teeth, haughty nose, long legs. Big-boss shoulders like those billionaires on the covers of romance novels.

"Was there any doubt the groom would show up to his own wedding?" I asked, perplexed by David's comment. "I always got the feeling he was an upstanding guy."

Though, truth be told, this was the first time I'd seen Drew in person since his high school football team trounced ours a decade ago. He wasn't like Estelle, who treated talking to downtown shop owners as part of her job. Drew must have his assistant do all his shopping for him. Was he too busy? Too shy? Or a snob.

David leaned over conspiratorially. "Drew's a good kid at heart, but he's immature. Still goes out partying every night till dawn. Even last night."

"He and Ashlee stayed out late the night before their wedding?" So much for shy.

"Sure, yes … it was with Ashlee," David said in a smoothing tone, as if he finally realized he'd said too much to an outsider. "Well, anyway, all's well that ends well," he added vaguely.

"Huh." Marrying Drew was my number one childhood dream. I'd been convinced he was The One—me and every other pigtailed tweenager in Blue Moon Bay. But David wasn't making him sound like such a prince. Now that I thought about it, Drew could have picked nearly any woman to be with, and he picked someone as small and mean as Ashlee. What did that say about him?

Sometimes childhood dreams are pretty stupid.

"'Scuse me, I better get back to the bridal beasts-in-waiting." David gestured back to the gazebo at the pretty bridesmaids. Several now appeared to be throwing grass at a bespectacled young man with a camera. "They're about to tear apart my assistant."

"Good luck!" I couldn't help but feel a touch abandoned, irrational as that was. David had been easy to talk to. Easy to look at, too. But more importantly, without him, I was liable to spend the rest of the wedding standing awkwardly alone. I was grateful for the jacket loan, though. "When should I give you back your—"

"Don't worry about that right now." He flashed one more gorgeous smile. "But come find me later, and I'll introduce you to the right people. That is, the other party professionals and staff members. Or as we call ourselves, The Help."

"Sounds great." Maybe I'd get to talk to Estelle's right-hand gal, Leeza, and learn more about these mythical catering gigs. Then I'd *really* have no reason to feel guilty for sharing a drink with David. I wasn't flirting, I was networking. Doing a whatdoyoucallit—a side hustle. Saving the bakery.

So why was it still bothering me that I was drawn to David?

Speaking hypothetically, if Bryson were stuck dateless at a wedding, would I rather he be chatted up by a sexy, witty, vivacious woman—or that he be forced to stand there, alone and miserable? Hmm … I'd expected the answer in my head to be clear and resounding, but it was murkier.

Oh well, I couldn't focus on hypotheticals right now. A waiter with a catering cart was wheeling my three-tiered raspberry cake up the garden path.

Boom, the magic moment had arrived.

My cake zoomed past us, and I followed it down the path. Past a fountained courtyard, whose cobblestones almost tripped my stiletto-strapped feet, and into a large banquet hall. The waiter pulled his cart over, next to an enormous white stone fireplace where a beige and grey display table had been set up. Perfect. This was my opportunity. I'd never attempted a complex spell with a dozen waitstaff milling about, but I had no choice.

"Excuse me, sir." I approached the waiter as he was carefully transferring the crystal stands that contained each cake tier onto the table. "I'm Hazel Greenwood. From Sage's Bakery."

The waiter looked me up and down. Was he trying to gauge my worthiness?

"This cake is one of ours," I stammered, "and, if you don't mind, I was hoping to snap a few photos for our web gallery? It'll just take a minute … or thirty. Max."

He'd already stepped away and was busy arranging cream-colored rose petals on the tables, apparently not giving a rat's ass about me or my intentions toward the five-thousand-dollar cake.

Access unlocked; that was way easier than I thought.

I pulled my cell phone from my clutch purse and swiped up to access the camera app. Of course, I wasn't really planning to take any photos. But holding the screen in front of my face conveniently helped cover that I was mouthing the words of the spell.

Fifteen minutes later, the murmur of the banquet hall filling jarred me out of my concentration trance. Without interruptions, I'd zoomed through the core of the ritual, and the addendum for extra Kindness and Patience (which I figured Ashlee's husband would sorely need.) Doing Green Magic raised a witch's core temperature, and I was starting to sweat, so I shucked off David's grey suit jacket as I dived into the final incantation, the Soulmate Biorhythm Syncing script:

"Nothing makes a night owl surly,
Like a spouse who rises early.
Let your spirits grow together,
Let love's rhythm flow forever.
With the starlight synchronize.
No need for coffee and compromise—"

"Hey, spy chick. Yeah, you in the shiny dress." At the woman's belligerent taunt, I forced myself to look up. My head felt as heavy as a sandbag. Being interrupted when you're deep in the middle of a spell is excruciating, similar to being shaken awake at 3 a.m.

"How dare you try to dress like us bridesmaids?" the angry voice continued, slurring just a touch. "You're not one of us. You should *pay* for trying to imperson—impersonalize—you know ... pretend!"

I turned to face the very dull yet menacing brown eyes of a lean, caramel brunette beauty. It was Jenna Jeffries, former co-captain of the cheer squad and Ashlee's BFF.

Hexed rats. I'd been mere words away from finishing the spell.

Now I was about to get my butt kicked by an angry bridesmaid.

CHAPTER FIVE

UNLESS I COULD magic my way out of it.

"You're right, Jenna, I'm not part of the cool kids' inner circle, like you," I said, hoping my voice sounded placating. "My wearing the same color dress is just a coincidence. So, if you don't mind giving me a minute here to, ah, meditate with this cake—"

"Please," she scoffed. "Like I don't know what you're really up to over there."

I froze. "Whoa, you do?"

"Duh. You're spying on me."

I chuckled in surprise. "Please, you're not that important." Then I remembered I was supposed to be placating. "No one's spying on anyone, sweet Jenna. All is hunky-dory." Surreptitiously, I reached out to touch my locket with its enchanted lavender and valerian sachet. It was the pacifist Green Magic version of a taser, and I never left home without it.

Jenna blinked and murmured drowsily, "If you're not a spy, how do you know my name?"

"Seriously?" My head snapped back in annoyance. "I was in your class at BMH. It's not like it's a big school."

"Oh yeah, then why don't I remember you?" she shot back, clearly proud of her logical smackdown.

Too bad that high school was anything but logical.

Jenna Jeffries had floated through it in a charmed pink champagne bubble. It was as if the only people she could see were other beautiful people. Athletes, preps, fashionistas. Kids whose parents' frequent trips to Cabo and Bora Bora let them host ragers at their mansions in the hills. More vapid than sadistic, she was probably just aping Ashlee when she taunted me with the Goody Two-shoes nickname. For four years we'd occupied the same small campus, but we might as well have lived in separate dimensions.

Was I really going to have to explain this to her?

"People remember the VIPs," I said, gritting my teeth as I glanced around for other bridesmaids to come save me. "I guess not everyone remembers us cake bakers in life, but that's okay because we—"

"Ha! You're not a VIP, you just admitted it." Jenna slurringly decreed from behind me. "This dress is for bridesmaids only. You don't get to wear it." Her clammy hands were on my neck, suddenly tugging at the zipper. Where oh where were her handlers? In a blink she'd yanked the zipper down to my waist.

I gasped as the cold air hit my back. "Jenna, no!" I felt instantly naked, but darn that rule three of being a Green Witch! I wasn't allowed to Augment Mine Appearance. I tried to push her away, but she was strong as heck. It was going to take stronger magic to keep her from finishing the job.

I whispered:

"Since we can't avoid a rumble

One of us must take a tumble,

My apology is humble,

But I'm going to make you stumble NOW!"

Jenna tripped over her own stiletto heel and landed on her sculpted butt, crying out in surprise.

"Jenna!" Another copper-colored blur was approaching fast.

The petite, black-haired bridesmaid running to Jenna's side was Britt Salazar, Jenna's old buddy and my third high school tormentor. What a reunion, ugh. She must be back in town for the wedding since, according to various town gossips, she'd been living the party girl lifestyle in downtown Portland for the last decade. Though her tawny skin looked as smooth as ever, her once-rosy cheeks lacked their former glow. Her mischievous eyes and dark thick brows, however, were just as quick to express impatience as ever.

"Get up, idiot," she barked at Jenna, surprising me as I'd thought she was fixing to tell me off. "Your drunk-chick thing's not cute anymore, it's tired. You're almost thirty." While Britt was berating Jenna, I did my best to zip up my dress, then threw the jacket back on. "We all need to get in our places for the ceremony," Britt went on. "You have five seconds to get your crap together."

"Is everything okay here?" At the sound of a refined male voice, I turned to see Drew Kensington himself was at my side. I was so dazed I hadn't seen him approach with his long, strong legs, flashing his filet-mignon-chomping white teeth.

Every molecule of him was a visual argument for upping one's protein consumption.

Reaching out with both hands, Drew gently helped an embarrassed Jenna to her feet. Guided her to a nearby chair. Poured her a glass of ice water from a crystal pitcher on the table. Watching him, it struck me that perhaps he didn't need the infinite patience addendum. If this was how lovingly he picked up his fiancée's drunk best friend off the floor … oh.

That's when I remembered. High school. Jenna and Drew were a thing. Only for a few months, and I seem to recall it ended badly with him dumping her, but they were a smoking hot couple.

Weird how you could still kind of tell that.

And even weirder that he was marrying Jenna's best friend.

I flashed back to David's comment about Drew's being out late last night. If Ashlee wasn't with him, was it possible he was with Jenna? Normally, I wasn't one to rush to judgment, but those two seemed awfully comfortable with each other.

"Hazel Greenwood?" Britt narrowed her eyes at me. "I can't believe *you're* here!"

I just about jumped out of my skin. "You remember my name?"

"Why wouldn't I? We went to school together, and it's not that big a place." Her brown eyes flashed with amusement. "Plus, you were best friends with Max de Klaw." She chuckled. "Who could forget that weirdo?"

"Don't call her that." Despite the way Max had let me down when we were teenagers and kept me at arm's length as an adult, I couldn't help but feel protective of her against a member of the bully trio. "Look, she may have done certain gross things to your locker in revenge for that one time when you said we were—"

"Relax, I meant weirdo as a compliment." She smiled, a mysterious smile that crinkled her eyes. "In fact, I bet the three of us have lots in common these days."

I blinked. That … didn't sound like the Britt I remembered.

Before I could ask what she meant, she snapped her fingers in Jenna's direction. "Try to pass for semi-sober, idiot, it's go time." Okay, so *that* was the Britt I remembered. She turned back to me, her brown eyes dancing with mischief again. "Say hi to Max for me."

"You'll have to tell her yourself," I said, feeling bitterness rise. "She doesn't reliably speak to me. I may never see her again, now that she's ditched the bakery. Stupid, stupid Java Kitty."

Ok, so I was rambling, but I don't think Britt was listening at any point. She'd already wrapped her arm around Jenna, who was back on her feet but shaky, and was frog-marching her out of the dining room .

Drew lingered, his dark eyes settling on me. "I don't believe we've met yet."

My tween self would have swooned on the spot, but I told myself to stay calm and professional. I had a business to run. Drew was a paying customer.

"Hazel Greenwood, cake baker." I smiled politely and stuck out my hand. "At your service."

To my surprise, his square-jawed face lit up. "Wow. I'm honored to meet the talent behind such a work of art." He pumped my hand, his gaze utterly confident, yet somehow naïve, like a newly hatched T-Rex. His 1000 watt-charisma made it hard to look away. "At Kensington Industries, one of our core values is valuing those who add value," he said eagerly. "That's how we leverage power."

"Erm … Thank you …?" My inner tweenager still longed to think well of Drew, but I had no idea what he'd just said. And Kensington Industries? What did they do exactly? 'Leverage power?' I'd heard the family inherited its wealth from a robber baron ancestor. Was he talking over my head, or was he spouting BS? And I still was having a hard time tearing myself from his gaze.

Huh. Now that was suspicious. Discreetly, I sniffed the air for spells and came up with nothing but his leathery cologne. I racked my brain, trying to remember something Gran had once told me about the 'magical gaze' of … something or other.

Oh yeah: the magical gaze of vampires. Specifically, she'd said, *"Don't ever look one in the eyes."*

And yet Drew seemed harmless, compelling but not threatening. Odds were he wasn't a vampire but just a charming guy, and I wasn't used to being face to face with star power. Either way, though, I decided it would be hypocritical for me, a witch, to prejudge.

"Come with me, Hazel." With a dazzling smile, Drew finally broke eye contact and took my elbow—a gesture I would not have expected from a man of my own generation, but it felt nice if a bit stilted. Like he was trying to act more mature and overshooting by about fifty years. "I'd like to invite you to sit with the other talented artists and our honored staff at the ceremony."

"Oh … really? Now?" I stole one final glance at my cake, my poor unblessed cake. If I walked away now, the ritual was incomplete.

Drew laughed. "Like definitely now. My mom would never forgive me if I'm late to this."

Your mom? I nearly blurted out. *What about Ashlee?*

I tried to think of a graceful way to stall, but he was already in motion, practically dragging me along by the crook of my elbow.

"Come on, don't be shy." We were through the doors, back out into the beautiful courtyard where waiters hovered with copper plates of hors d'oeuvre. "These are the best people I know. They're like family, only better—because you can fire them. I'm so kidding!" He laughed at what must have been my shocked expression. "No, our family's never fired a staff member."

"Not even once?" That was crazy. Even I'd had to fire someone, once, a college girl we'd hired as a holiday bakery helper. She'd been too stoned to do much of anything but sneak fudge brownies from the kitchen.

"No, not once in a hundred years, Hazel." He tapped his chest with his palm and glanced down briefly, as if moved by the Downton-Abbey-ness of it all. "Of course, it helps that our extreme vetting process defines the state of the art. And look, here they are. The results of our patented process."

He led me toward a circle of people standing on the grass, and I felt a little thrill at the sight of David among them. I was starting to get used to Drew's over-the-top way of speaking, like he was pitching a tech startup at all times. But it was still a little creepy how he'd talked about the staff as "results" of a "process."

Drew dropped me off with one final glowing word salad—at one point, I believe he called me a "pastry pioneer."

At last, he made his regal way toward the shiny copper aisle where his attendants were already lined up, waiting to perform their ritual walks toward an altar laid with copper cloth and strewn with hundreds of beige roses.

As Drew ambled off to go marry the meanest bully in the world, a thickset, red-bearded guy about my age reached out his hand. "Nice to meet you, Hazel. I'm Landon, the 'culinary artist.'" He made finger quotes and snickered. "You know, like, I cook stuff for the Kensingtons. I'm a cook."

Everyone laughed good-naturedly. I noticed Landon, like most of the others, was wearing black dress pants and a matching turtleneck. They looked like a theatre crew. "Nice to see you again, Hazel." Estelle's assistant Leeza waved at me. She wore a simple black sweater dress and leggings. Her angled lob haircut and makeup was on point.

Only David was dressed fancy, maybe because he was interfacing with the public?

"So how goes the great Ashlee assistant search?" David asked Leeza.

She gave an exaggerated sigh. "It goes. Have you seen her latest requirement … 'must have a higher BMI than me, while not being overweight?' Seriously, are we supposed to weigh candidates now?"

David guffawed. "Just buy her a magic mirror already, that tells her she's the fairest of them all."

"I'd rather die than be that woman's assistant," I muttered under my breath, but Leeza must have heard it because she giggled and put a friendly hand on my shoulder.

"Don't take this the wrong way, Hazel, but you're not assistant material. I can tell. What you are is a creative, talented baker, which is far more rare. In fact …" She tapped her lower lip with her finger as if considering me. "I don't suppose you might be interested in catering dessert for one of our parties sometime?"

Oh, yay! The networking. It was really happening.

"Sure, I'd be open to that," I said with a smile.

"And so it begins," Landon said gleefully. "Welcome to the lucrative world of the Hill. Baby, these people cater everything, from breakfast in bed to tea with the governor. You could work every weekend if you want to."

"It's true, if you can get on their party list, they'll use you for everything," David confirmed with a smile. "They're loyal customers, Fred and Estelle."

"By the way, they're also excellent employers—and the pay's *fantastic*." Landon arched his eyebrows in a way he probably didn't know made him look like an owl on an acid trip. "We're talking brand new car money here. House down payment." Or bakery remodeling money? I thought. "Or you could buy yourself a boat if that's your thing."

"Small boat, darling," qualified a slip of a dark-haired girl, in a Russian accent. "Rowboat, leaky type. Or toy boat." She stuck out a slim, cool hand for me to shake. "Marina, Drew's personal assistant—and I sew. I helped with bridesmaids' dresses. Now Drew says I am 'emerging fashion designer,'" she added, and laughed raucously along with everyone else. "But seriously, he wants to help me develop my talent," she added. "He is very supportive boss. Dream boss."

I nodded and tried to square "supportive boss" with David's indulgent view of Drew as an overgrown party boy, his marrying the pretty but shallow Ashlee, and his over-the-top style of speech. Maybe Drew was maturing in layers?

Well, shoot, I could relate.

From the outdoor stage, the dulcet tones of a trio of harps indicated it was time for the guests to shuffle toward our seats for the ceremony. David took his leave to go shoot some photos, and I knew it was my last chance to slip out and attend to the cake.

I waved to The Help. "See you in a bit, gang."

"Hazel, no." Leeza's hand on my arm held me back. "There's no need for you to walk alone now," she said, with what I think was meant to be warmth. "You're one of us."

"Maybe she has to use bathroom," Marina said.

"Actually, I ... need a few more cake photos for the Sage's Bakery website." I was proud of myself for recycling that excuse, as it would account for why I was headed for the pavilion .

But Leeza's violent volley of eyeblinks didn't bode well. "I'm sorry, what? Surely, you're *not* suggesting getting in the way of the waitstaff while they prep dinner service?"

Dinner service. I stood silently processing the horror of what she was saying. She was right, the area would be swarming with servers. There was no way I could sneak back in.

"I guess not," I murmured.

I was too late to bless the cake.

Feeling numb, I trudged along with the group listening with half an ear to their chatter which was surprisingly frank and even catty at times.

"Check out the grins on Ma and Pa Kensington," Landon observed. "Has anyone ever seen them so happy? I mean, she's pretty much always chipper, but Fred..." Landon glanced at Leeza. "Let's just say he can be more on the moody side."

Leeza cleared her throat. "Fred may not be a jovial or carefree man by nature, but I'm sure he's bursting with pride for Drew, his only child." Her measured speech had the vibe of a PR rep's statement. Whatever Landon had been implying about Fred (that he was a jerk?), Leeza seemed to be trying to correct course. "This is a special day for our special family, isn't it, gang?"

"Aww ... sniff ..." Landon pretended to wipe away a tear.

The others laughed. This crew was obviously tight. And collectively, their attitude toward the powerful family they served was between amused and fond. For all their blustering humor about them, The Help did seem to care about the Kensingtons.

And Estelle and Fred did indeed look content. Arm in arm, grey haired but unbent, and dressed to the nines, they were the ultimate golden years power couple. They had it all: capital, class, effortless confidence, a loving son. It was jarring to see Estelle, for once, without Sammy Boy in her arms. Even her library portrait showed her cuddling a small dog—perhaps Sammy's dad or grandad. But maybe the venue didn't allow pets or some guest was allergic.

When Ashlee Stone, accompanied by harp music, stalked down the aisle with her brassy-haired, spray-tanned mother—the one person who seemed to fit in less at this wedding than I did—I wondered if this would be the first wedding I ever attended where I didn't cry.

But as Drew leaned in to tenderly kiss his bride, my bully's face seemed to soften before my eyes. She tilted her head, glanced down, and let out the lightest sigh. I stared, riveted as if by a wild plot twist on some TV drama. Was it possible a husband's love could humanize Ashlee Stone? What if these two were soulmates who shared a destiny? In which case, perhaps my little spell would have made no real difference either way? Watching them kiss, anything seemed possible.

As the rest of the wedding unfolded, I remained in a trance of sheer denial. While the cocktails flowed from the open bar during the photography hour, and at the elegant, grey-laid tables decorated with cream-colored roses where the waiters served Beef Wellington, and while the best man gave a rambling, self-focused speech during the champagne toast, I let myself daydream about my own wedding, someday in the future. Before Bryson, that kind of thinking was strictly off-limits for me. But finally, I had a man in my life that I could contemplate settling down with.

I glanced up from my reverie just in time to see a harried-looking waiter place in front of me a perfect triangle slice of raspberry crémeux, with silky vanilla fondant. My cake, my beautiful failure of a cake. All around me, guests were demolishing it with gusto. Fred Kensington wore a frosting mustache that his wife daintily wiped off, to the amusement of everyone.

Cake slices were disappearing fast as guests stuffed themselves with seconds and demanded thirds. No one had a clue what was wrong with my cake, only I knew its awful secret. Rarely had I felt so lonely. The friendly conversation going on all around me at the vendors' table blurred into noise. I was only dimly aware of applause when the groom gave a shout out to me as a "visionary in the cake space."

Plates were carried away empty. Guests began to mingle from table to table, sliding into each other's seats, though our crew of vendors remained steadfast, a working-class island amid the sea of plutocrats.

On stage, a rock band began warming up—an impossibly tasteful, avant-garde rock band, with a cellist (female) and designated tap dancer (gender unclear). Dancing looked imminent.

Time to make my escape.

As I stood from the table, my heart felt heavy, but it might just have been the Beef Wellington and all that Veuve.

"Hey, cake artist, I saw you using your phone to snap pictures earlier." A strong male hand was on my shoulder. David the hot photographer was standing right behind me. "For your website, right?"

I nodded, pleased I'd come up with such a plausible excuse for why I was, well, gawking at a cake. Of course we didn't have a gallery on our website, nor did we exactly have a website. But we should get right on that. Now that I was, gulp, in charge.

He smiled. "You know, I'd be happy to let you use some of the footage I got earlier."

"Really?" David was offering to contribute free photography for our website? I was touched. Perhaps there were multiple silver linings to my coming to this wedding? "That's awfully nice of you."

"No, it's not. I want them to be good pictures, not phone camera garbage." His wink and teasing look made me laugh, and before I knew it I'd reached out and playfully punched his arm.

"Hey, you're a ton of fun, cake artist." David clapped a friendly hand on my shoulder. "You really should join us for drinks sometime. We're always at the Drunken Barrel on Thursday nights. Rain or shine. We drink beer, we snark about the people whose money pays for our beer. Nipping at the hand that feeds us, as it were."

"Sounds like a good time." I pulled off the tux jacket that still smelled like David's bright, citrus cologne. "Thanks for saving my life with this."

"My pleasure."

I practically ran out the door and past the roundabout into the vast parking lot.

There was no way to rationalize it to myself this time. I was flirting. With another man. While my boyfriend worked on a Saturday.

I was a bad girlfriend today.

A bad witch, too. The thought of reporting my big fail back to Grandma Sage filled my stomach with dread—and since my stomach was already full of wedding dinner, it felt pretty crowded in there.

I was contemplating how to break it to Gran when I nearly crashed into a woman who was wandering the parking lot, hunched over her phone.

She was tall and thin, wearing skinny jeans and an oversized grey sweatshirt, furiously thumbing out a text, so she didn't even see me. Her hood was up, covering half her face. But I'd recognize that proud plastic chin anywhere.

What was Ashlee doing out of her wedding gown, wandering the parking lot incognito? If she and Drew were buying party drugs for their wedding night, you'd think they could afford a smoother hookup.

Or was this the type of thing a personal assistant handled, hehehe?

Curious, but not so curious as to risk her spotting me, I hurried on to my car.

Poor Trixie was sandwiched between a gleaming Porsche convertible and a blue BMW five series, near the outer reaches of the parking lot. The instant I hit the clicker to unlock her, she called to me through our psychic bond, sounding really down.

"Thank goodness you're back, doll. It's been so lonely. All these other cars out here are soulless hunks of metal."

"Sorry you had a bad time, Trix." Only a witch's car could have a soul, and I wasn't surprised if the Kensingtons didn't associate with too many of us. "Trust me, this bash wasn't exactly my speed either." I wedged the door open and squeezed inside. "Let's roll."

"About that. Did you have a plan for how we're getting out of here? What with all these cold, unfeeling chrome-piles blocking us in?"

Oh geez. The cars were packed in with tight efficiency. I'd forgotten it was valet parking. From across the lot, I could see the twelve-year-old kid in red livery striding toward me, an annoyed expression twitching beneath his three-hair mustache.

All right, so he was more like eighteen, but still.

Mentally preparing myself to be scolded by a teenage boy, I hopped outside to wait for him. That's when I noticed a bottle-green Mustang parked only two rows away from Trixie.

Was that Max's car?

Max hated Ashlee, even more than I did. No way had she been invited to the wedding, so what was she doing here?

Now would be a very good time to ask her in person, seeing as how Max was sitting right there in the car.

Or someone was.

The top was down, but I could see a long-haired silhouette moving inside. I stalked over to the driver's side window, weighing my options. Should I say hi? Confront her? About what, exactly? The wedding? Cheating on the bakery? Ditching me on grad night?

Funny how it never felt like the right time to bring up that night. But if I couldn't muster the guts to do it now, when would I? Sixty years from now at some nursing home, when orderlies gently poured us into side-by-side rockers, it would still feel too raw. Too soon.

While I was gathering courage to speak, a plastic coffee cup sailed out the back window, landing with a wet splat inches from my shoe. I stared at the cat logo on the cup's side with unbridled loathing. A large, iced coffee to-go cup from Java Kitty Café.

It was, no pun intended, the last straw.

Fuming, I banged on the driver's side window, ready to have it out with Max once and for all.

Only there was no Max.

The silhouette I thought I'd seen was gone. Incredulous, I peeked into the back window. A thick legal folder sat on the passenger seat, open and overflowing with papers.

But there was no one inside that car.

A gust of wind must have blown the cup outside.

Now that I thought about it, I couldn't even be 100 percent sure it was Max's car in the first place. I hadn't memorized her license plate. Other people had green Mustangs too. Still, it wasn't like me to imagine things. Maybe I missed her more than I wanted to admit, but this was weird.

"Ma'am?" The valet infant in scarlet caught up with me, his voice aggressively upbeat. "Do you understand how valet parking works, ma'am? You stand by the roundabout, and I bring your car right to you like you're a princess."

I nodded numbly and dug into my purse for a fiver.

One hour later, I was in flannel PJs, winding down in front of the TV when my phone bleeped. The screen lit up with Grandma Sage's photo. And for the first time in my life, I toyed with the idea of not answering her call.

I sighed. Who was I kidding? This was my ailing, aging grandmother, not just my boss. She was family. "Hi Gran. What's up? The wedding was—"

"Did you complete the spell or did you not?"

Right to business then. "Don't you want to know about how the wedding was? And how much people *loved* our yummy cake?"

"So the magic didn't go too well." I could hear the pain in her voice. It was clear she'd been anxiously awaiting this news.

"No. It didn't."

"Oh, Hazel." Her voice cracked on the line. "You must be devasta—"

"Because it went *amazingly* well!" Yep. I lied. Oh well. It was just like Gran had said about Ashlee and Drew. Spell or not, they'd never know the difference.

Well, neither would she. Even if Ashlee and Drew had a crappy marriage, it wouldn't implode overnight. Probably.

"Oh, Hazel dear, you've made my day!" Gran gave a huge sigh. "Lowered my blood pressure, too. Maybe I'm going to live to enjoy retirement after all."

"Semiretirement, Gran. And of course you will." As long as those bozos Ashlee and Drew can keep it together for a few years with couples therapy and maybe a dose of infidelity here and there, I thought guiltily.

Lying wasn't one of the three laws of being a Green Witch, so that meant it must be okay *sometimes*, right? When I became Gran's apprentice, I took a solemn vow that I would try to make things better, if I could. Well, there was nothing I could do now to bless that stupid cake of Ashlee's—every slice had been devoured. It was history.

The one thing I could do was make Gran feel better … that, and promise myself I'd be a better witch from here on out. Show up on time for work, for a start. Pick up some weekend catering gigs and sink the extra cash into investments in the bakery's future. Updating our kitchen equipment. Buying a shiny new espresso machine and hiring a dedicated barista.

Take that, Java Kitty.

And, as much as I feared the outcome, there was one final thing I needed to do.

"Gran? I have a boyfriend." There, I *could* say those four words. Just not to David. "His name is Bryson, he has piercing dark-blue eyes, and I want you to meet him as soon as possible. I want the whole world to know we're together."

CHAPTER SIX

"HAZEL DEAR, WHAT'D you say this young man of yours does for a job?"

It was the following Tuesday at 4:35 p.m.—almost half an hour before our early winter close time, but we hadn't had a customer in hours, so I'd already done most of the cleanup.

Grandma Sage was stirring honey into her chamomile tea at the cozy corner booth, while I discreetly repacked trays of our unsold rosemary cherry muffins into plastic bags for the homeless shelter three towns over. The treats were topped with brown sugar crumble and imbued with our Best Rest spell. At least the homeless would be sleeping well tonight, even if our bakery was doomed.

Remembering Gran's question, I said, "Bryson's, um, a life coach." I mentally high-fived myself for avoiding the word therapist. She tended to call them "head-shrinkers", and it wasn't a compliment.

"Life coach? What a peculiar-sounding job." Gran dropped her zig-zagged honey spoon onto a checked cloth napkin and leaned toward me with suspicion in her eye. "Almost sounds like a headshrinker."

I sighed. "Okay, fine, he is a headshrinker. But… what do you think of these centerpieces I just made?"

She fell for my distraction, turning her sharp gaze to the mason jar of cut sunflowers resting on the table. It was tied with a rough sisal bow for a country touch. "Never saw the point of a centerpiece." She shrugged. "But it's pretty."

"That is the whole entire point, Gran."

Plus, the flowers were from my garden, and we needed to go all-in on our homegrown branding if we had any hope of regaining market share from Java Kitty. It was key that we niche down from generic bakery café to a market space we could dominate ... yeah, I might have been reading a few biz books over the last couple of days. With Bryson busy with that continuing ed thing in Portland, I'd found myself with time on my hands for the first time in months and hit the library. And then the craft store. It had been, I had to admit, kind of nice to throw myself whole-hog into my work for the first time in so long.

"Great bats, are my old eyes deceiving me?" Gran squinted at the solitary pop of blue amid the otherwise deep orange blossoms. "Deadly belladonna has no place in a house of Green Magic."

I steeled myself for another minor battle. "You're being old-fashioned, Gran. Customers don't know anything about botany. Besides, if you're passing the bakery on to me, you need to start letting me make my own choices."

She pursed her lips. "Need is a strong word. I'm still your advisor, and I strongly advise against those death flowers."

Bryson took that moment to show up, carrying a bouquet of lavender which he handed Gran with a respectful bow.

He glanced at the jar on the table. "Hey, aren't those poisonous?"

"Indeed they are, young man." Granny gave me a pointed look. She brought the bouquet of lavender to her nose, then breathed out a sigh of satisfaction. "Ah, lavender. Safe, edible, classic."

It was all I could do not to roll my eyes. Here I'd been worried about Bryson not making a good impression. The man was making a better impression on Gran than I was lately.

As I watched them make small talk about Main Street's bad drivers—ok, so maybe I'd prepped him a tiny bit—the clench of my jaw began to loosen.

You have to understand that Gran's approval meant everything to me. Growing up, both my parents favored my sisters. Everyone did, and even I couldn't blame them. Mother proudly doted on my older sister Beatrix, who'd followed in her Beige footsteps, growing up to be Blue Moon Bay's number one Pinterest Mom—the alpha mom who toted the correct organic snacks. Meanwhile, Dad lived vicariously through Cindra, the baby of the family, who, having inherited Dad's perfect hands and feet—and Mom's Beige Magic,—earned a glam living jetting between London and Los Angeles as a glove and shoe model. Then there was me, the middle sister. What made me special?

Only that I was Granny's sole magical heir.

Her blessing was all I had, and all I ever needed.

I don't know what I'd been so afraid of, though. The conversation between Gran and Bryson went swimmingly. Even when she asked, with barely concealed bewilderment, what had possessed "a tourist" to pick up and move to Blue Moon Bay, Bryson met her eyes and answered with disarming warmth and sincerity.

"Miss Sage, I'm aware that it may sound crazy to you." He slid his hand across the table and I instinctively placed mine in it. "But I believe there's something special about this town. I had a feeling something wonderful was waiting for me here. You could call it destiny."

Awwwww! Nailed it.

Gran glanced thoughtfully from me to him and gave an almost imperceptible nod. "I can't think of a more perfect response."

Needless to say I was beaming from ear to ear.

After Bryson headed out and hopped on his bike, she turned to me and sighed. "Better luck next time, Hazel dear."

I gaped at her, bewildered. "You're joking, right?"

"He is *not* the one," she said in a very non-joking tone.

"But, but, but!" I sputtered. "You two got along like a house on fire."

"Well, that's neither here nor there," she snapped. "I can't help it if he's charming, but..." She hesitated, as if there was something she was debating sharing with me. "But don't you notice anything odd about him? He's too..."

"Too what? Perfect?"

Again the hesitation. "Yes, Bryson is too perfect."

I stared at her. "Whoa, you're not seriously suggesting I dump the man for a reason as dumb as that?" I couldn't believe her nerve. As if the choice were hers. But hadn't I been acting as if it were? Time to assert myself. "Look, it's one thing for you to micromanage my flower arranging—"

"Which reminds me." She snapped her fingers and murmured, "*Don't beguile us with your charm, when in truth you mean us harm.*" In a flash, my six blue delphiniums disappeared from their jars.

"Hey!" Anger was coursing through me like electricity. I never got mad at Gran. Then again, she'd never told me to dump Bryson. "What's gotten into you? You just said it was time I made my own choices and now you're trying to control everything exactly like before—and you're even trying to tell me who to date. Well, I have news for you. I'm not a kid anymore. And I am taking over this bakery."

"I know you're no child, Hazel." She sounded oddly weary. "Believe me, I've watched you grow through the years from a timid little mouse into a strong witch. I respect your talent. But if you really believe that … that *head-shrinker* is your soul mate, then you're not as ready as I'd hoped."

"Not ready, what's that supposed to mean?" This was spiraling out of control. Just because she didn't love Bryson, she was making judgments about my abilities?

"It means I don't feel comfortable passing the deed of the bakery on to you. Not yet."

"Why the sudden change?"

She paused. "I supposed it's hitting me all of a sudden how much you have yet to learn. Auras for example."

"Yes, yes, I know, and teleportation," I huffed. "Fine, geez, I was already planning to study that stuff in my spare time." If I ever got any spare time.

"See that you do," Gran said sternly. "Until I'm satisfied you're ready, I won't be going into any advisory role. I may not do as much magic as before, but you can expect to find me here, supervising you, a hundred percent of the time."

"That's way more than you supervise me now!" I cried. "Am I being demoted or something?"

She hesitated. "No, but maybe it's time we got a little more formal about our roles at work. Oh, and as your boss I formally request that you confine your flower arranging to nonpoisonous species."

"Great, anything else you want to change about how I live my life?" I said sarcastically.

How could a day go from bad to worse so fast?

"You think I'm overstepping my bounds, controlling your life?" She shook her head sadly. "This bakery is our family's legacy, Hazel. I hope one day you're as eager to protect it as I am now. *Miles may I roam, but there's no place like home.*" She snapped her fingers again and dematerialized as the flowers had done, leaving behind her rumpled black coat on the chair's back. Three seconds later, the coat vanished, too, like an afterthought.

Show-off. Magical commuting wasn't as easy as she made it look. Hopefully I mastered it before the old hunk of metal that currently housed Trixie's spirit wore out.

As I angrily bleached and scrubbed the counter, it hit me that magical commuting wasn't the only spell I still couldn't do as well as Gran. I was also terrible at reading auras. And organization spells—you know, the Mary Poppins stuff. And so much more. It wasn't unusual for a witch still in her twenties to have gaps in her education; I was about average. The problem was, Gran wasn't. Almost no witch my age had such big shoes to fill. I'd expected to be able to coast and keep learning for several more years.

What if she was right, albeit for the wrong reasons, that I wasn't ready to take over? And if she was right, what on Earth would become of our family bakery?

I was still wiping the counter when the bell rang to announce a new customer.

"Sorry, we're closed," I said in my super-sweet customer service voice, without looking up.

I didn't see the tall redhead approaching until her horn-rimmed glasses were inches from my face.

"We need to talk," said Max de Klaw. "It's urgent."

"Kind of busy here," I shot back, hating the part of me that was glad to see my old friend. Urgent. God, she was so arrogant. When I wanted to talk, I had to wait ten years. Now suddenly, time *mattered?*

I'd caved the other night and listened to her rambling voicemail, asking if we'd be hiring holiday helpers at the bakery this year. That was a puzzler. Max made a pretty good living with *Blue*

Moon Roundup. Local businesses all bought ads, including us. Why would she want a part time job?

Hey, not my friend, not my problem.

I sighed. "There's nothing left to say, Max. Unless you're here to drink our honest coffee instead of Java Kitty's high-tech swill?"

"Swill? Their white mochas slay." Her cool green eyes met mine without shame. "But that's not what I'm here to—"

"White mochas?" I should have let it go, but bickering with her felt as natural as slipping into a warm bubble bath. "That's the price of your loyalty, sugar that dreams of being chocolate?"

"Hazel, will you please stop interrupting me?" Max grabbed the rag out of my hands and tossed it into the sink. "I'm trying to tell you that Ashlee Stone's gone missing."

A chill snaked down my spine. "Missing?"

"She disappeared just over twenty-four hours ago," Max went on. "The police are involved, so we have to act fast. They're going to be calling you any minute. I had to warn you."

"The cops are calling me?" My head swam with awful questions. Was my failed blessing already having its effects? Was Ashlee's disappearance my own fault, somehow? But, no, that made no sense. Even if it was all my fault, there's no way the Sheriff's Department would know that. "Why would the police come after me?" I whimpered.

Nothing could have prepared me for Max's next words.

"According to Ashlee's diary, the last person to see her alive was that hot new guy in town—the guy I saw you kissing on the pier the other night. Bryson Goodman."

CHAPTER SEVEN

FEELING DIZZY AND more than a little nauseous, I followed Max out to the back parking lot. It was already nearly dark. "That's impossible. There's no way he could know Ashlee."

"You know I'm philosophically opposed to telling lies."

"Right, you're more into radio silence."

Max threw her hands up impatiently. "Whatever, you don't have to take my word for it. Sheriff Gantry will be calling you soon to interview you as the girlfriend of a 'person of interest.'"

I raised my eyebrow. "Since when does Gantry loop you in on his plans?"

"He didn't." She hesitated. "Elliot pulled me aside when I was down at the station earlier. Told me everything."

That at least made sense. Elliot James had been nursing a crush on Max since our high school days. He was far from the only attractive, desirable man to go for her, too. Guys liked Max. It was other women who looked down on her, for having the social graces of a feral cat. Or, well, a man.

I frowned, realizing she'd left something out of her story. "What were you doing down at the police station anyway?"

"Getting grilled by Gantry, what else?"

My eyes must have bugged out of my head because she said, "Relax. They don't suspect me of offing Ashlee. They just wanted to ask me some questions about Kade."

Well, that made sense. Like his twin sister, Kade de Klaw was sharp witted and scruffily good looking, with a muscular build, auburn hair, and freckles. They'd both been wild teenagers, too, but where Max had grown out of her screwup phase, Kade had spent too many years bouncing in and out of juvie, then jail, for stupid offenses. He was still struggling to transition to adulthood.

"Well, thanks for the heads-up," I said stiffly. "This all has to be a mistake. I'll go find him at work and clear everything up."

"Good luck." Max turned to go. Her Mustang wasn't in the lot, which meant she'd jogged over. Max was a fast runner and could have broken our school record if she'd stuck with track. But the running crowd was "too perky", and given a choice, she'd rather run alone, anyway, in the woods behind her house. The coach nearly cried.

I pressed the button to unlock Trixie, but nothing happened. I tried again, over and over. Couldn't even hear her voice. "Crud! The remote battery must be dead."

Max jogged back over, looking curious. "Maybe you could just fly to him, or something?"

Oh, right, she knew I was a witch. I rolled my eyes at her. "Witches don't fly, that's a myth."

"Not even with a broomstick?"

"Also a myth."

"Can you stop time?"

"I'm a kitchen witch, not freakin' Dr. Who."

"Teleportation spell? I seem to remember you talking about those."

"That is a real thing," I admitted grudgingly. "I'm just not very good at those spells yet. Or Mary Poppins cleanup spells. Or reading auras. Or—"

"Right then." Max sighed, closed her eyes, and grimaced.

"Wow, sorry my witch skills aren't up to your exacting standards," I muttered, miffed.

Max's eyes opened in surprise. "You think I'm judging you?"

"That's not your judging face?"

"No, it's my shifting face. I'm getting ready to sprint back home and get my car for you."

I stared at her. "Wait, what?"

"Yeah, I thought I'd leave it at home today, it was nice and sunny..."

"Not the car. You didn't by any chance just say you were shifting?"

"Guess I did." Max shrugged and made a lackadaisical "oops" face. "Welp, now you know."

"And you didn't think to share *that* with me when I told you I was a witch?" I wasn't even angry, just perplexed. Max barely had a filter. How could she have kept such a mega secret under wraps?

"It's complicated." Max looked guilty. "It took me years to admit to myself what I am, let alone accept it. Kind of a lot for a kid to process, you know? Sorry if this freaks you out. We can talk about it later, when I'm not a bobcat. First, I have to go get your ride."

"Um, okay." Did she say bobcat?

And why was she suddenly all about helping me?

I didn't so much see Max shift as I saw her clothes fall to the floor in a soft heap. A graceful, brown-spotted wildcat with black-tufted ears bounded past me. Picking up her still-warm shirt, I caught a whiff of the pleasant, woodsy essential oil blend she liked to mix up and use as perfume. Made sense. A bobcat liked the smell of the woods. Liked running in the woods, too.

There wasn't really much to process. Except what an idiot I'd been not to have guessed it all ten years ago.

This explained so much.

"Wait a minute." I finally connected the dots ten minutes later in her Mustang as we were speeding to Bryson's office. "When you said you were answering questions about Kade at the police station ... Does that mean he's a suspect in this case?"

"Person of interest," she growled. Post-bobcat, Max had changed into black shorts and flip-flops that she must have had in her car. I felt cold just looking at her legs. "Just like your boyfriend is a person of interest, Hazel."

That shut me up. Almost. "Did you know your shirt's inside out?"

"I know and don't care."

"Suit yourself."

"Ha." She smiled, presumably at my accidental pun. Then her face twisted up with worry again. "Kade is innocent, obviously. All they have on him is that he was seen talking to Ashlee shortly before her disappearance."

"Gosh, I can't believe Ashlee let herself be seen with a member of the criminal element." A snicker fell from my lips before I could stop it. "That came out wrong. I meant because Ashlee's such a snob..." I trailed off. I was the one who'd sounded snobby. "Sorry."

"It's okay," she said stiffly. "I'm pretty sure Ashlee only talked to him because he was making her a cappuccino. He just landed a barista job at Java Kitty."

"Of course, they're hiring." Would that place never stop haunting me?

"He's trying so hard. It's like he can't catch a break." Max seemed to be too busy talking to herself to notice my lack of a response. "The only reason they're flagging their conversation as suspicious is because Kade's got a record."

I shrugged. "People who break laws *are* more likely to break them again."

She scoffed. "Kade's crimes were all pretty trifling, though."

"Um, stealing?" As long as I was pissing her off, why quit now? "Stealing's kind of big."

"He took minor stuff. Souvenirs."

"Wasn't he also caught making fake IDs for every kid at Blue Moon High?"

"There was some minor identity theft. A long time ago."

"You keep saying the word minor like it makes everything okay."

Max blew out a sigh. "Hazel, I know everything's not okay with Kade. I'm not stupid. Why do you think I started spending all day in Java Kitty Cafe the moment he got a job there?"

"I assumed it was because you're a bad person and disloyal bakery customer."

"What?" Max's eyes darted to the left like she wasn't sure how to process what I'd just said. "No, it's because my brother needs someone to be his conscience." Her voice was sharp with desperation. "But only when it comes to the piddly stuff," she added quickly. "He'd never kidnap anyone."

"Yeah, but I can see why the sheriff ... never mind." The pain in her eyes stopped me. "Hopefully, Ashlee's okay and she comes back soon."

Max gave a weak smile. "Bet you never thought you'd pray for Ashlee's safety."

Her Mustang pulled up at a two-story office park at the edge of town, where Google assured me Bryson's office was located. Reassuringly, his blue road bike was locked up outside.

Max waited in the car while I stormed into the grey-paneled office building. I located his name on the marquee in the empty waiting room— Suite 200—and jogged upstairs.

The "Do Not Disturb Therapy Session in Progress" sign was on his door.

I hesitated for one moment. I'd never pried into this side of his life before, having been accused of not giving past boyfriends the "space" they needed. But this was different. I had to do something.

I banged on the door. When no one answered, I barged in.

Bryson whirled to face the door, looking a little annoyed—a look I'd never seen on him. Till he saw it was me.

"Haze?" His eyebrows pulled downward in concern. "What's wrong, babe?"

"Something terrible's happened." I felt slightly hysterical suddenly. I was here to warn him, about a mistake made by the police, yet it was easy to see how my words could all tumble out wrong and make it sound as if I was confronting him. Accusing him. I wanted him to know I was on his side. But what was the right way to phrase it? I decided to blame Max. "A former classmate—someone I used to know—said you were … oh ."

A dowdy, middle-aged couple were perched stonily on opposite ends of the sofa. As stonily as they could be given their soft middles.

"Sorry to interrupt your session."

"Don't be sorry." The man hitched up his Dockers and stood. "All this therapy nonsense is bunk anyway." He turned to his wife. "Want to just get a divorce already?"

"Finally, you said something that doesn't make me want to slap you upside the head." She rose and slung her purse over her shoulder.

"Honestly, I'm glad to have facilitated a peaceful goodbye for you two," Bryson said in a voice even calmer and smoother than his usual tone. "Sometimes there's no way forward, even with the best of intentions. I'm happy to follow up with each of you individually to plan your next steps."

I threw him a look of dismay. Was this a therapist mind trick? Surely, he was going to intervene to save their union.

He waved as the pair shuffled out. Nope.

"Trust me," he whispered. "Those two should have split up long ago. They've hated each other's guts for decades. It's almost like their marriage was cursed."

Guiltily, I looked away, thinking of Ashlee and the failed cake blessing. "Bryson, remember that woman whose wedding I had to go to?"

He looked uncomfortable. "The country club thing, where I'd have had to wear a suit?"

"The bride is missing," I explained, "and there's been some crazy error at the police station where they think—mistakenly, of course—that the last person to see her was—"

"Ashlee's missing? Oh no."

I gasped. "You're on a first name basis?" Why would he keep that from me? "Bryson, what on earth is going on?"

He sighed. "She's one of my clients. I really wanted to tell you, Haze, but I couldn't because of therapist-client confidentiality."

"Hang on, Ashlee Stone is in therapy?" I couldn't help but shake my head trying to picture that. Ashlee was the least vulnerable, least open-to-change person I could think of. "I guess she shares a lot of personal stuff with you, then?" It bothered me to think of lanky, gorgeous Ashlee lounging on this couch, sharing her deepest secrets with my boyfriend. "Does she have a diagnosis? Oh, right. You can't tell me."

"I was worried this kind of thing might happen, working in a small town." He cringed. "Was it wrong that I made an excuse to avoid going to the wedding?"

My mouth fell open. "So the continuing ed program in Portland was made up?" He'd lied to me. So easily. "I begged you to be my date that night. I was lonely." Well, not really, because of David, but details didn't matter right now. "You lied to me and left me to face it alone."

Bryson hung his head. "Haze, I'm sorry, okay? I knew the wedding was important to you. But if she'd encountered me in a social situation, it could have hampered her progress."

Progress in what? I thought. Filling out her personality disorder bingo card? "I still can't believe you lied."

"And I can't believe she's missing." He took a deep breath as if to steady himself. "If a client is in danger, it means I have a duty to share the records of our sessions with police. As much as Ashlee's going to hate that."

"Who cares what Ashlee hates, what about *me?*" I couldn't seem to stop picturing Ashlee parked on this couch, her snake eyes locked on Bryson's warm blue ones, seductively reaching for the tissue he offered. Ew. "You lied to *me,*" I repeated, feeling petulant.

"Haze, oh my gosh!" He laughed out loud, then leaned down to kiss me on the forehead. His touch felt as great as always, to my annoyance. "Do you see what's happening? We're having our first fight."

"Is that what this is?" It didn't feel good at all. But fighting wasn't supposed to feel good, I reminded myself. At least Bryson and I had made it a full six months before we got here. "I guess I can sort of see why you had to lie," I admitted grudgingly. "Protecting your clients' anonymity is part of your job." And when I really thought about it, he wasn't the only one keeping job-related secrets. I had a much bigger one I'd been holding on to. Like, hello, I was a *witch.*

Wasn't it irrational for me to be angry at him for a small lie when I lied every day by not mentioning this core part of who I was?

Our cell phones bleated at the same time, interrupting what could have been the start of making up from our first fight.

Both callers were from the Blue Moon Bay Police Station, each requesting our presence as soon as possible for an interview.

"I'll ride with Max, you take your bike," I told Bryson, feeling suddenly terrified again. "We should go separately. We don't want them to think we're in cahoots."

"Whatever you say, Bonnie. Get it? We're Bonnie and Clyde." He grinned at me. It was clear he didn't feel threatened or intimidated by the prospect of a police interview, and maybe he was right. After all, he had a perfectly valid reason for being the last person to talk to Ashlee. "More importantly, though," he added, "tonight we should celebrate having our first fight."

I looked at him like he was crazy.

"Oh, did I never tell you about my family's bizarre and hilarious tradition?" he asked.

I folded my arms. "A fighting tradition?"

"More of a making up tradition. It involves ice cream."

"I'm listening, I guess."

"Really rich ice cream, with gooey caramel. And I have to feed it to you, as penance for upsetting you. Crazy, but it works for my parents—happily married thirty-two years."

Despite myself, I laughed. "Twist my arm, why don't you?" How could I stay mad at Bryson for long when he was this adorable? "Your family traditions beat the pants off mine," I admitted, grudgingly. "My parents don't exactly fight, but they don't make up either. When there's a problem between them, Mother goes to her workout room and climbs the Stairmaster extra aggressively until my dad buys her earrings." I plopped down on the couch and sighed, maybe because thinking of my parents' marriage was such a downer. Before I knew it, he'd scooted in beside me and wrapped his arms around me. "Mmm, that feels so good," I admitted.

"Feels good to me, too," he said softly, reaching out to hold my hand. "Feels *right*."

Hearing him say that made me feel butterflies. "I know what you mean."

"Haze, I have an idea," Bryson said, calmly as ever. "Why don't you become part of my family? Then all of our ridiculous traditions will be yours, too."

I was so stunned I dropped his hand. "What are you saying?"

He smiled mysteriously. "I was gonna wait till the holidays ... but screw it. This feels right." He jumped up off the couch we were sitting on and quickly grabbed something from his desk drawer. A small black velvet box.

Oh my God. "Is this really happening?"

"This was my grandmother's." He opened the box to reveal a delicately filigreed gold ring.

"Bryson ... oh my gosh I'm going to hyperventilate!"

"But in a good way, right?"

"The best!" I gasped.

He dropped to one knee, the ring in his steady hand. "Will you marry me, Hazel Greenwood?"

"So how'd that go?" Max demanded when I returned to the car, dazed, ten minutes later. "Did you give him the third degree, or did you Hazel-out and give him a big old hug?"

"I did not 'Hazel-out.'" Blushing, I covered my newly shining ring finger with my sleeve. After I'd said yes, there'd been some kissing. He may have dipped me over the therapy couch, which, being a touch transgressive, gave me a major thrill. "I'll have you know I grilled him, like a … like a very comforting cheese sandwich. And you know what? He had a great alibi. I'm convinced he would never hurt Ashlee or anyone else."

"Oh? Care to share your good news with me?"

"Good news?" I stammered. How'd she know about the proposal?

"His alibi. Man, you're acting squirrelly."

"Am not." I shrank away from her narrowed gaze.

"I assume I'm driving you to the police station for your interview?"

"Yes, please." I straightened my posture. "You were right about them being about to call, thanks for the heads-up."

"Mm-hmm. You're welcome."

Two miles of silence.

"All right, fine." I had to drop her a bone. "I shouldn't tell you this but, Bryson is Ashlee's … therapist."

Max snorted. "Ashlee and her friends are the reason *other* people get therapists."

"I know, right? But apparently, she's got issues, too."

"Who cares about her pain?" Suddenly, Max sounded enraged. A vein had popped out of her neck. I didn't realize she still hated Ashlee quite that much.

For a split second, I was transported back to senior year. The way we used to stick together, a fortress of a friendship that Ashlee and her mean-girl gang could never breach. We walked to class together, the grey stone school buildings blurring and lost to our vivid conversations. Ate lunch together under the same giant live oak, our tree. Laughed together, sometimes so hard we had to wipe our eyes with the backs of our hands.

I was seconds away from blurting out everything to Max: my ring, the sudden proposal, Java Kitty, my problems with Gran … when she pulled into the police station lot.

"Welp, I'll wait here," she said brusquely. "Good luck."

This day was moving way too fast.

CHAPTER EIGHT

SHERIFF GANTRY WAS a hawk-nosed man with white, wispy hair, a perfectly ironed uniform, and a suspicious gaze. Before his defection from Sage's Bakery, his usual order was a double latte to wash down his sausage and bacon breakfast sandwich. (Yes, a double meat sandwich. No, it wasn't on our menu. We made it just for him.)

But even back when I saw him every single morning, I'd never felt comfortable around the guy.

He had a habit of not quite finishing his sentences that always made me feel tense. Like it was my responsibility to guess what he was driving at.

Or die waiting for him to get there on his own.

"Thank you for coming in at your earliest convenience, Miss Greenwood. I'm sure you understand the utmost seriousness..."

"Of the situation?" I finished for him, leaning forward.

"I'm going to ask you a lot of questions, and I want you to think carefully before..."

"You answer? I mean, I answer?"

"First question." Sheriff Gantry steepled his hands and looked at me appraisingly. "Have you ever thought about chopping your hair into a pixie cut, with a purple side-hawk?"

I blinked. "No!"

"Not even just now when I brought it up?"

"Well, sure. But I wasn't seriously consider—"

"I'll correct your earlier response." With a smug nod, he made a mark on his notebook.

"Okay, whatever, this is dumb," I muttered.

"How long have you been dating Mr. Goodman?"

I sat up. A real question. "Six months. Since the summer."

"And how did you two meet?"

"He walked in for a latte on a Sunday morning, extra foam." I couldn't help but smile at the memory. "Snagged the last chocolate almond croissant, and then asked me for a date. He was the best-looking guy who'd walked in all week," I added. "Though the competition's not steep. Our branding can be overly feminine, which I've recently read is off-putting to some male customers."

Gantry's pen hovered over his notebook, like he didn't know what to do with all that. Ramble mode. It was back, with a vengeance. I'd never been interviewed by law enforcement before, and there was something hypnotic about the recorder on the table between us, the bitter smell of black coffee in paper cups.

"You don't have to write all that," I said, wincing. "Anyway, he'd just moved to town from Minnesota—"

"From where, exactly?" His pen hovered over the page.

I frowned, realizing I wasn't certain. Bryson often said he was from "back east" just like everyone else who was new to town did. It was standard phrasing that acknowledged what the Bay's newcomers all learned quickly enough; no one cared all that much where they were from. As I got to know him better, he'd revealed that he grew up in the Midwest.

"What part of the Midwest?" Gantry snapped.

My mind flashed back to an old family photo I'd seen on Bryson's living room wall, of two cute kids sledding who I assumed were him and his brother. "Uh, the snowy part."

Gantry gave me an odd look, and I suddenly realized why. I was coming off like a moron. "So you never asked him."

I sighed. "Correct." Why had I been content to know so little about my boyfriend's past? Make that fiancé.

"And? What was his connection to the Blue Moon Bay area?" Gantry prompted me.

I smiled, thinking back on Bryson's inspired speech to Gran about destiny. "He knew something wonderful was waiting for him here."

"Something wonderful?" Gantry looked like he'd swallowed a lemon. "You mean like a job?"

I felt my face flush. Bryson's words had sounded tinny and lame coming out of my mouth, maybe because I was so nervous. "Yes, of course. A work-related opportunity, is what I was referring to, what else?"

Had he had the job lined up beforehand, or not? I didn't know, though Bryson and I talked all the time. Was it weird that we didn't talk that much about our pasts, the time before we met? A romantic would say nah. A detective would say yeah. I was sitting across from a detective, and he definitely thought I was a moron.

"Why's this relevant?" I asked.

"Never know what might turn out to be relevant. He's not a True Mooner so what drove him to come to our town, hang up his shrink shingle, and suddenly get involved with a local … well, you know … a local…" He coughed.

"What? Old maid? Spinster?" I held up my beautiful gold ring like a talisman against all the old-fashioned, sexist labels that might be floating through his grizzled head. "What were you going to call me? Oh. A local baker, duh." That was embarrassing.

Worse, Gantry's weaselly gaze had lit on my ring. "My, my. Six months is a wee bit early for a proposal. When's the baby due?"

"Excuse me? I am *not* pregnant."

"You sure?" He gave me a look.

"Oh, for gosh sakes, we've been doing a lot of takeout dinners lately," I sputtered, sliding into ramble mode. "And we split desserts sometimes. A lot. I probably eat the lion's share, if it's one with chocolate. I've only gained three pounds. Maybe seven."

With a frightened look, the sheriff retreated to his notebook. "Let's go back to Goodman's reasons for moving to town. Does he have family in the Oregon…"

"Coastal area? Not that I know of."

"How about…"

"Friends? No. But that's not weird," I hastened to add. "Who even has friends nowadays? Everyone's so busy with work, their kids, their side hustle. I don't even take it personally when people flake on plans. Or make excuses. Or don't call me back for ten years because—"

"Thank you, that'll do, Miss Greenwood." He cleared his throat. "Let's refocus on Mr. Goodman and his odd scheme to pick up stakes and move to a random small town, on a…"

"Whim? It wasn't a whim. It was a work-related—"

He talked louder over me. "Where he ends up being the last person to see a beautiful, wealthy young bride before she…"

"Disappears without a trace." My fists felt hot suddenly. It was one thing for Gantry to take condescending potshots at me, it was another for him to target Bryson. "I wasn't aware that moving to Blue Moon Bay was against the law. You might want to inform the dozens of newcomers who show up on impulse every year."

What I didn't add—didn't want to think about—was that few of those people stayed. Blue Moon Bay was a phase for divorcees, widowers, and those recovering from the rat race. They always said the same sorts of things, like that the pounding waves on the rocks improved their yoga high. The gentle cloudy skies rejuvenated their souls. Frankly they sounded like cult members. Or drug addicts. But this town was small and cliquish, and when tourist season died down, the winters—while mild—were grey with little respite from November to March. Inevitably, after a year or two of "soul rehab," most of those converts got married or rejoined the rat race, leaving Blue Moon Bay in their dust without so much as a postcard. Locals knew better than to befriend anyone who hadn't been through one winter. Preferably two.

Normally I knew better, too. But I'd made an exception for Bryson. He wasn't like the typical tourist. He didn't *gush* over Blue Moon Bay. He gushed over me.

"There's nothing crazy about the idea of someone falling in love with me," I asserted, feeling the tiniest bit defensive of my own appeal. "Or the idea of moving to a picturesque little town for a fresh start." Immediately I wished I hadn't picked those words.

Sheriff Gantry seized on them. "A fresh start? From what? Was Mr. Goodman running from a checkered past? A history of drugs, crime?"

I swallowed. "Of course not!" No way was Bryson covering up a record or an addiction. He was almost boringly clean cut. Sure, he'd lied about Ashlee's wedding. But I understood why he'd had to.

If grudgingly.

"So let me get this straight." Gantry's smile was more of a triumphant sneer. "Guy moves out here without knowing a soul, just to get a fresh start, and within three months he's engaged to a local..."

"Baker," I filled in. "An adorable local baker, with pretty hair and a sparkling personality. That's what you were going to say, right? And he's not just some guy," I plowed ahead before he could respond. "He's a top-notch, skilled therapist."

"Is he? Looks like he got his degree online. Just last year."

"What?" That was news to me, but I rallied quickly. "I mean … so what? Are we really going to engage in a debate about computers versus classrooms?" I tried not to think about the couple he'd happily waved away toward divorce court. Maybe their marriage *was* cursed. "He's an asset to our town."

"Yes, he seems to have been quite therapeutic for Ashlee Kensington."

My hands felt clammy suddenly. I didn't like his tone, or what he was implying. "Bryson wouldn't hurt a fly. He's all about helping people."

"Our investigation will reveal the truth." Gantry closed his notebook. "I pray that Ashlee is still alive to tell us exactly what she thought of Mr. Goodman's therapy techniques."

I stared at him. Even if Bryson did turn out to be a merely average therapist—much like I was turning out to be an average witch—that was no crime. So why was Gantry trying to use it to build a case against him? What was his motive?

I dug through my purse for one of Grandma Sage's homemade toffee chews. I kept a few on hand just for emergencies like this. They contained a drop of—well, you couldn't call it truth serum. It was more like … ramble juice. A filter remover. If someone was determined to lie, they'd lie. But if they were simply caught off guard, they'd likely give something away before the effect wore off. "Toffee chew?"

Too late, I wondered if I shouldn't have provided one of these in bacon form. But luckily, Sheriff Gantry had no qualms about carbs. He gobbled the treat almost before I could frame the question in my mind.

"Mmm, that's good. May not be pretty but you sure can bake."

So, the effects had already begun. "Sheriff, why are you trying to build a case against my guy, when you've got nothing on him?"

He smiled dreamily. "Oh, well, it's because we just don't have any idea what really happened to that girl."

Seriously? I leaned in. "Why not do some police work and find out?"

"That's too hard. Takes too long. And her family's rich, so they're going to want swift…"

"Justice?" *Unbelievable.* Had the sheriff always been corrupt and incompetent, and I'd only now noticed?

"Er…?" Gantry shook his head and looked confused for a moment, as if he wasn't sure if he'd really just said all that. As if to steady himself, he reached for his coffee cup. "That'll be all, Miss Greenwood. I have other interviews to conduct."

"Conduct! Oh, you already said that." I rose and stormed out, angry tears stinging my eyes.

"Hazel?" The low, gravelly voice made me turn to see that Elliot had caught up with me in the hallway. "You look upset. Let me walk you out."

Numbly, I walked at his side down the echoey hall. I hadn't been this close to him for this long since high school, close enough to smell his woodsy skin scent. What the hell was wrong with Max? She got along great with Elliot, and he'd do anything for her. Why weren't those two together?

Elliot pushed through a side exit and held the door open for me. I stepped out into the drizzling rain.

"I wouldn't worry too much about the sheriff," Elliot said.

"Really, why not?" Elliot's intelligent, brown gaze was so steady that looking into it actually made me feel better. A tiny bit better. "Are you saying you trust Sheriff Gantry to do the right thing in the end?"

"Oh, no. Gantry's as crooked as a barrel of snakes."

His admission stunned me, even if the facts of the matter didn't. "But … then …" I stammered. "You think Ashlee will come home soon?"

She'd have some 'splaining to do, but at this point I'd be willing to bake a Welcome Home cake for the b—

"Nah, she's probably dead," Elliot said, and my heart skipped over that word. Dead. Murdered. "It's just that when it comes to possible suspects, your boyfriend is at least fourth down on the list."

I tried to digest all that. It was heavy stuff. "All right." I gulped. "Who's first on the list?"

He gave me a mock stern look. "You know that's classified."

"Her husband, Drew Kensington," I answered for myself. On TV shows, the husband was always prime suspect. "What about numbers two and three?"

Elliot's square-jawed face remained blank. "Now surely you don't think I'm about to share that information with you?"

"Bet you'd tell Max de Klaw," I muttered.

"You're right, I would." Elliot didn't hesitate. "That's different."

"Right." Was he going to carry a torch for Max forever?

It'd be a real waste, I thought, waving goodbye to Elliot at the door. Other than milking him for free police intel, she seemed to have no interest, in him and perhaps in the concept of dating, full stop. She was the same socially clueless, frequently aloof weirdo she'd been in high school.

Yet, in some ways, there was very little to connect the handsome officer in front of me with the quiet loner of a teenage boy Elliot once was. A beanpole in a black leather jacket that matched his hair, with a sharp, skeptical, dark-eyed gaze that seemed to take in everything, even things you wanted to hide. Teachers treated him like they thought he was a gangster or some other type of criminal, but he'd never been in trouble with the law. Now that he had a respectable job—in law enforcement no less—and filled out his height with solid muscle, plenty of women wanted to date him. But he hadn't settled down.

I hurried into the parking lot, where the heartbreaking bobcat herself stood beside a dusty pickup truck. She was energetically lecturing a pale-skinned, muscular guy whose ripped chest and defiant, bad boy smirk had starred in many of my high school daydreams. A shock of auburn hair covered one of Kade's brooding hazel eyes, and he had the same slacker posture as all of the guys I'd crushed on who never even noticed me. Except as someone to borrow homework answers from.

Thank goodness I was a bit older now and understood the appeal of nice, normal guys. Stability. Commitment. Rings.

Kade was still hot as hades, though.

"*This* is what you bought with your savings?" Max was saying, hands on her hips. "You couldn't have held onto it to give to some lawyer? Besides, this piece of junk's on its last legs."

Kade threw up his hands impatiently. "What was I supposed to do? You won't loan me your car anymore, how am I supposed to get to work?"

Alarm bells went off in my head. Kade had been borrowing Max's car … what if he was the one who took it to Ashlee's wedding?

And if so, didn't that suggest his relationship with the missing bride went further than "guy who makes your coffee"?

If Max's brain was making the same connection as mine, she didn't show it. "Work, genius? How're you going to park that behemoth at work, when Java Kitty's lot is packed to the gills from dawn to dusk?"

Her devastating question left both Kade and me speechless. Though for different reasons.

Before Kade peeled away in his truck, he gave Max a sad look that nearly broke my heart. He was clearly upset to have disappointed his twin, just as I knew she was distraught from worrying that he might be in danger.

The irony was, even that painful interaction between the siblings still showed me how much they loved each other.

Which meant I really didn't want to ask this question.

"I can tell you're worried about your brother," I said gently, approaching her side. "But do you think…" How could I say this? "You don't think he had anything to do with Ashlee's disappearance?"

"Oh, God, Hazel, of course not." She sounded affronted, and I guess I didn't blame her. I'd be the same way if she insinuated Bryson might be guilty. "I talked to him. He knows nothing. All he ever did was take her order at the coffee shop. Witnesses thought it looked 'suspicious.' Gee, I wonder why."

"His rep?"

"Bingo. He can't catch a break."

Something about her casting Kade as a victim didn't sit right with me. He'd earned his bad reputation, unlike Elliot who'd been unfairly typecast when we were growing up. And I was pretty sure Kade wasn't telling the whole truth about how he knew Ashlee. I cleared my throat. "Well, it is sort of his fault that he's viewed as a criminal. Because of being a criminal."

"Phhhhhhhhhhhht." Max exhaled forcefully and fast, sounding like a dragon. "Must feel pretty sweet to be you, Hazel Greenwood. Citizenship awards coming out of your ears. Baking cupcakes for the homeless. Judging everyone else for falling short of perfect."

"Wait, now you're mad at *me?*" I was mystified. "I'm just pointing out how it must look to everyone in town." So far. I hadn't even gotten to the part about the Mustang at the wedding.

"Yeah well, everyone in town can kiss my furry spotted butt. Shifters have a very hard adolescence, Hazel Greenwood. Kade and I are just lucky we survived." That was the second time she'd said my full name. Yep, she was mad all right. Spitting mad. And was I hallucinating just now, or did her hazel eyes flash yellow, like a bobcat's? "Remember how unfocused and chaotic I was in high school?"

I nodded. She could stay up all night speed-reading and scarfing pizza, yet never seemed to show up at school with a matching pair of shoes on. Let alone finished homework. She'd always played it off with apathetic coolness, like she didn't care that her C- average was a poor reflection of her curious, quick mind.

Maybe she'd cared more than she let on?

Max's gaze seemed less angry suddenly and more frustrated. "I wish I could say my twenties have been a big improvement, but to be frank they haven't. I'm still trying to get my life together in some pretty key ways. As it is, I can't even afford to keep a houseplant."

"Okay, now you're exaggerating."

"Because I would eat it," she went on, as if I hadn't spoken. "And then I'd have to have my stomach pumped. Again. If you can't sympathize with those kinds of problems, great." The anger was back. "But don't rub your good fortune in my face."

"You don't get to blame everything on being a shifter, Max." I folded my arms. "Being a witch isn't always a piece of cake, but I still manage. I don't go around committing crimes. Or being a crappy friend."

"Wow, really?" Max tilted her head in consternation, then pursed her lips and looked down. The bad-friend accusation hung in the air like a fart. I hadn't exactly meant to take things there, but for once I was relishing the awkwardness I'd created. She deserved to stew in it.

"This isn't the right place to talk about … all that stuff," she said, finally, pushing a rebellious wave of red hair out of her face. "Right now, I'm too scared for my brother to think about anything else."

How convenient, I thought. But at least I'd said my piece. "So what? I'm scared for my boyfriend." Who doesn't deserve to be on the suspect list at all.

She shook her head. "You don't understand. Kade's record makes him the perfect scapegoat. Everybody else on the suspect list is way more respectable."

"So Elliot *did* tell you who else is on that list." Knew it.

"Nah, I looked over the receptionist's shoulder on the way in." She grinned sheepishly, then remembered to glower at me. "Now you probably think I'm a criminal too, but whatever. It's a small town, police security ain't exactly world class. Besides, I can't just sit here and do nothing. I don't trust Gantry more than I can throw him."

"I don't either," I admitted. "He asked too many questions about Bryson's connections to Blue Moon Bay. I'm afraid he's trying to pin Ashlee's disappearance on someone who isn't well connected here, someone not too many people would come to the defense of. Also he was gross to talk to. Was Sheriff Gantry always so … terrible?"

She gave me another *you don't get it* look. "Hazel, Elliot's the only reason this town's legal system functions at all. He's been gathering intel to expose Gantry's corruption, but it could be years before it all comes to light. Till then, we're on our own."

My stomach flip-flopped. "I don't like being on my own."

Her feline eyes narrowed at me. "Hey, are you thinking what I'm thinking?"

"Probably not?" I'd just been thinking that Max sure seemed to like and admire Elliot, so why hadn't she ever dated him? Instead, she was wasting her time with a succession of cute but scruffy-looking guys who turned out to be jackasses. The latest one had absconded with her ham radio gear. Meanwhile, Elliot was always there for her. What was their deal?

"If we want to protect our menfolk," Max said, leaning in, "we're going to need to work together to find out what happened to Ashlee."

So that's what it was. Now that her brother's freedom was at stake, she wanted someone else—me—on her team to help her solve the mystery.

"How about we meet tonight at the Drunken Barrel for our first strategy session?"

"Can't." I wasn't going to fall into line so easily. "I'm getting ice cream tonight with Bryson. We're kinda celebrating our enga—first fight." I surreptitiously cupped my right hand over my left, hiding the ring.

"You're what now?" She looked at me like I was as dumb as a box of hair. "Bryson is in danger, Hazel. If we don't intervene, you might not have any more dates with him outside of prison visiting hours. Come on, I'll even buy your drinks."

I gulped. "Fine, I'll text Bryson and let him know there's a change of plans. But you can't make fun of me for ordering rosé."

"Why would I make fun of you for drinking pink wine soda?"

"I don't know, given that you yourself eat live rabbits."

It was deeply annoying, also deeply comforting, how easy it felt to fall back into friendly trash talking and making plans.

All I had to do was keep it clear in my head that she was only doing this for Kade—her real family—and I was only doing it for Bryson, who would be mine.

Then I wouldn't mistake it for friendship and all would be well.

CHAPTER NINE

OF ALL THE wine bars and beachside beer gardens that dotted Ocean Street, the Drunken Barrel was by far the biggest dive.

Moments after I swung open the saloon-style wooden doors, my high-heeled granny boots crunched into the inch-thick layer of peanuts shells that littered the floor.

In the far corner, a willowy, college-aged woman in a peasant skirt made sweet love to her Irish fiddle. Tourists ate that stuff up, in the high season. But it was a damp Tuesday night in November, and only a toothless old drunk guy tapped his foot half-heartedly to the beat.

At the other end of the bar, a mannequin in a hot pink dress and thigh-high stockings had been strapped into a stool, a plastic beer can glued to each of her immobile, bone-white hands.

The Barrel sure seemed to revel in its reputation for classic, old-school tackiness.

I scooted past the bar to a table along the opposite wall, where Max sat chugging beer from a frosted tall boy glass. I'd stopped by the bakery to wait for AAA to tow Trixie to the shop, giving Max a head start.

Settling into my seat across from her, I instantly felt overdressed in my work clothes—a long jean skirt and a fuzzy grey knit cardigan worn open over my Sage's Bakery T-shirt. Max was still in her ridiculous beachy getup, complete with flip flops. How was she not freezing her butt off? Shifters must have insane metabolisms.

She waved a buffalo chicken wing by way of greeting. "Glad you didn't chicken out."

"Ha." I nodded to the skinny, hipster waiter, and he beelined for our table. He looked disturbingly young, but maybe I was just getting older. Looked familiar, too, but I couldn't place him. "I'll have a glass of your cheapest, sweetest rosé. Something out of a box would be ideal, if you have it."

"Boxed wine energy, gotcha." He stroked his sparse chin, thoughtfully. "The lady knows what she likes."

"You know it." It wasn't till he brought me the wine with a little bow that I realized, holy crud, it was the valet parking kid. I nearly spat out my first sip.

Sometimes the whole "small world" aspect of living in Blue Moon Bay could feel suffocating. The same old faces. Or in this case young faces.

Please let him be over eighteen.

"So?" Max's sparkling green eyes focused on me, and this time I was sure they flashed yellow-orange. Just for a split second. How had I never noticed that happened whenever she got excited? "Hit me with your best ideas."

"Er … ideas?" Why did it suddenly feel like I was at a job interview?

"I'm sure we both have tons of great ideas to share." Max's prompting voice poked at my silence. "On how to run our investigation and protect Kade and Bryson from being unfairly accused. Without getting ourselves in legal trouble."

"Right." Just hearing the words "legal trouble" sent butterflies fluttering through my stomach. "Okay … um … I guess we could talk to people in town, see if they have any information on Ashlee?"

"Well, yes, duh." Max looked impatient. "Of course we're going to talk to every person of interest, and their kin. Here, I made a list." She reached into her shorts pocket and fished out several napkins, each covered with ink scrawl. She frowned. "No … wait." She lifted the sleeve of her hoodie. A blueish list of names was scrawled on her arm. "Oh cool, there it is. But seriously, we need to think bigger."

"Can you give me an example of bigger?"

"Sure, sure." She rubbed her hands as if for inspiration. "Got one. I break into the suspects' homes as a bobcat and eat their pets. To see how they react."

I rolled my eyes. "Come on. Gimme a serious example."

"I was trolling you with the pets thing," she admitted. "But breaking in might be necessary to collect evidence."

I felt dizzy and gripped the stem of my wineglass for support. "That's so very illegal."

"If you don't like it, speak up with an alternative. I know you can do better than 'um, interviews.' Yes," she added. "I am talking about your powers of Green Magic."

I gasped and glanced around in case anyone at the bar had overheard. But, of course, no one had overheard, and no one cared besides.

And why should I have inhibitions about discussing magic when Max seemed to have no inhibitions, period?

The woman had shifted into a woodland animal before my very eyes—shedding a pile of clothes, including sassy purple boyshort panties, on the ground at my feet.

"That reminds me," I said suddenly, lifting a knotted plastic shopping bag out of my satchel and tossing it to her. "You're probably wondering what happened to your outfit."

Max laughed without a trace of self-consciousness. "Oh yeah, clothes. I lose so many in a month I don't bother to keep track. Thank goodness for Goodwill."

Wow. I'd never considered some of the practical problems of being a shifter. They *sucked.* "Sorry, I left your shoes stashed in my cubby at work." I cringed. "They were too bulky to carry in my bag."

"It's cool. If I forget to grab 'em by the end of the week, you can chuck 'em." She stood and fished her rumpled jeans from the sack. In full view of the other barflies, she shucked off her shorts and stepped into the jeans. It was a lightning-fast wardrobe change, especially considering she kept her flip-flops on throughout the procedure.

That did it. Maybe I'd never be as free and uninhibited as Max, but it was time I owned being a witch.

"Fine, we can use my ... my *magic* to help find out what happened to Ashlee."

Max rewarded me with one of her patented troublemaker grins, like a capital D tossed onto its side. "Aw yeah, now you're talking. Show me what you've got, witch!"

"Working on it." I shook out my purse. Various odds and ends popped out, including Kleenex, breath mints, and ... a magical toffee chew. "This candy is more than meets the eye," I said proudly. "You see, it's been imbued with a single drop of—"

"Magical truth serum, oh my God! This is awesome." She eagerly grabbed the tiny candy from my hand and pocketed it.

"Hey, wait—"

"Who should we try it on first?" Suddenly, she was talking fast, tapping her fingers on the table. As if there was coffee in her cup instead of beer. "Can it double as a weapon? Could we spike the town water supply with it?"

"What ... um ...no." I'd forgotten how Max could make me feel like a human sloth at times. Her mind and body were forever in motion, and they often raced to the most anxiety-producing places. Weaponized candy? Tainting the water supply? "Think one step down from truth serum," I said, realizing the thing I was most anxious about was disappointing her. "It's not nearly that powerful or consistent. But it's safe, with no known side effects. It opens people up to talk more freely. And it's yummy."

She frowned at the toffee and settled back down in her chair. "So it's less of a truth serum and more of a … ramble juice?"

"Yes!" I banged on the table, not really a me thing to do, but I was excited we were on the same page for once. "That's *exactly* how I think of it."

"What can I say, great minds think alike." She clinked her beer against my water glass. The ice trembled, and a warm, pleasant shiver ran down my back. I realized I couldn't easily recall the last time I'd gone out to a bar for any reason.

Or the last time I'd hung out with a friend.

I'd always been on the quieter side, but when did I become a recluse?

"Hey, Max, maybe you and me should do this kind of stuff more oft—whoa." While I was musing, Max had unwrapped the toffee chew and was gnawing on it.

"Qumick, ask muh a qumestion," she commanded stickily through the chew.

My heart raced. Was I really going to do this, right here right now? "Okay. Why did you ditch me at three a.m. on graduation night and then never call me back again?"

Max's eyes went wide, and she spoke in a robotic tone as if in a trance. "Because … you're … annoying … Hazel."

"Oh. Right. I see." I stood, feeling shaky on my feet. Shaky wasn't the right word exactly. Stricken fit better. Mortified. Crushed. Also, totally confused.

As a teenager I'd spent hours obsessing on the sudden, traumatic death of our friendship … was it possible she just never liked me all along? It was my greatest fear come to life: that people secretly find me annoying. But something didn't add up. Why would she spend so much—

"Hazel, I was messing with you!" Max grabbed my hand. Hers was burning up, thanks to her magical metabolism. "This stuff doesn't work on shifters. That's what I was testing for, to see if nonstandard humans would feel any magical compulsion to spill their guts. I felt nothing. See, this experiment taught us a lot."

"Yay science." I refused to look at her.

"Don't be like that. You're actually the third-least-annoying person I've ever met, if it helps. No, fourth least."

"Stop trying to make it better, please." I took a deep breath to steady myself. "That was a not a cool thing to joke about."

"I know," Max said quietly. "But that was not a cool thing to truth serum me about."

Anger poured out of my core, heating my hands. She wanted to be magical Nancy Drew twins with me, but still not give me closure? "Then why don't you just tell me, what the hell happened?"

"I … it's … " Max swallowed and stared into the middle distance, then she went silent. Her face looked super still.

"Hello?" I waved my hand in front of her, worried. "Max?"

"Sorry … " Slowly, Max unfroze, anguish coloring her features. "I'm okay."

"Yeah, you seem totally okay."

Wow. Was talking about this harder for Max than it was for me? Unsettled by *that* bizarre possiblity, I sat back down.

"So, um, the ramble juice." My awkward transition back to a safe topic. "Its effects only last a few seconds. But they can be extended a bit if the vic—er, the subject feels relaxed and comfortable." Out of nowhere an idea came to me. "Hey, what if we get people to come to the bakery and interview them there?"

"Riiiight, because the bakery's relaxing and comfortable," Max said, making a V sign with fingers pointing to her own eyes, then mine. "I see where you're going with this."

She didn't really, though. I had an ulterior motive: luring our old customers back to Sage's Bakery. To get them to remember how authentic and lovely it was, compared to Java Kitty Café. "We can present it as a special deal coupon. Offer them a free cinnamon peach scone. Only it's a special scone … one that gets them talking."

"Ooh, now that's genius." Max's look of admiration made me immediately suspicious. "So you'll interview them at the bakery," she went on, "and keep 'em comfortable. Meanwhile, I shift and sneak into their houses to search for evidence. Brilliant idea!"

My stomach felt sick. "Max, no. We can't commit crimes to solve a crime."

She tossed me a perplexed look. "Undercover cops do it all the time."

"We're not cops, we're just regular people … well, you're also a bobcat, I suppose. But they don't even have opposable th—"

"Hazel." Max hissed at me.

"Also when you're in bobcat mode, isn't your mind affected by it?"

"Hazel, shhhh!"

"Are you able to have complex thoughts or are you like, just thirsty for rabbit blood?"

"Would you like another glass of rosé, miss?"

I turned to see the young waiter standing inches away. Whoops! Maybe he hadn't heard me, somehow?

"I'm afraid we're fresh out of rabbit's blood." His pimply face twitched with a smirk. "Is that a local microbrew?"

A piece of paper sailed past me to the peanut-covered floor.

"Oh, look, I dropped my character sheet." Max announced in a loud, wooden voice. "I am a role-playing gamer, who plays a shifter. In a game that is not real."

"Yep, here you go, miss." The kid handed her the paper back, looking surprisingly bored by the whole subject. Apparently, he'd bought her ruse. "Want to hear the rotating IPA special?" he asked me.

"Please no, never." I cringed at the thought of all that bitterness. "But another rosé would be, uh, sweet."

At my pun, he stared stoically into the distance. The younger generation appreciated nothing. "Coming right up, miss."

"And another share plate of fries," Max put in. "With extra ranch sauce."

"Sorry, I'll be more careful not to be overheard," I said once he'd walked off with our order. "That was pretty creative, though, keeping a fake character sheet in your purse for such situations."

She gave me a look. "Who says it's fake? Who says I don't play *Werebear: The Forsaken* with a real nice group of guys and gals, down at Gunnar's Games on alternating Sundays?"

"Of course you do."

"And I'm not just 'thirsty for rabbit blood,' for your information. When I'm in that state, I'm still myself, sort of. Or half myself, half something else."

I asked the question I'd been wanting to ask since I first learned there were beings who could shift. "Can you control it?"

She seemed to take a moment to think about that one, finishing her beer and setting it down. "Control is too much to ask for," she said finally. "But sometimes I think I'm finally getting it together. And sometimes I still wake up naked in the woods with half a lizard in my mouth. Does that answer your question?"

"Yeah? But it also brings up a whole bunch of new ones." I closed my eyes, trying to imagine what Max's life experience might feel like. There was that one time, after my last breakup, when I'd tried in vain to go on a diet. I woke up from a three a.m. dream about gorging on devil's food cake ... only to find I had sleepwalked to the kitchen—well, kitchenette area—and was sleep-gnawing on squares of bittersweet baking chocolate. Chocolate fingerprints on the counter and everything. That memory still made me shudder, but it was still a far cry from the gruesome scene Max was describing. As for how much money she must have to spend on clothes... Her haphazard fashion game was starting to make sense.

Suddenly, I felt the deepest empathy for Max. No wonder if she seemed a little off sometimes. Being a shifter sounded like a nightmare that never ended.

"Hello, Hazel? Did you zone out thinking about Bryson's hot body or something?" Max tossed a french fry at me. "I ordered these for the table. Feel free to eat up to 50 percent of them. Anyway, let's table the burglar thing for now. I can smell that it's stressing you out."

"Er, thanks." I was honestly grateful. And really not wanting to delve into the smell thing.

"Why don't we plan our interview strategy? Who's up first? Who really strikes you as the most suspicious person?"

"Hmm," I said, trying not to think of the elephant in the room. I wasn't 100 percent certain Kade was innocent. But since he was a shifter, those toffee chews wouldn't work on him, so it was a moot point. I decided to steer clear of this delicate territory, for now. "Well, there's Drew. The husband."

"No offense to the bakery, but a dude that rich would never deign to come down from the Heights and mingle with rank-and-file Blue Mooners. Not even for one of your Gran's scones, which are to die for."

"His mom came in to pick up the cake," I said, remembering with some shame how gracious she'd been. "Her driver and assistant went with her, but Estelle was personally involved."

"Huh." That stumped her for a moment. "I guess you're right, I've always seen her around here and there. Sometimes with Fred too, though not in a while. But Drew's generation seems different. Have you noticed no one ever sees him walking around downtown? He must have assistants who shop for him. We're going to need a special strategy just to talk to the guy." She sounded doubtful. "Even talking to one of his assistants would be tough, I bet."

"Or maybe not." My mind flashed back to the wedding. "There's this group," I said. "They call themselves the Help." I told her about how long they'd been working for the Kensingtons and their peers in the Heights. "They meet Thursday nights for beer, here at the Barrel. And I've been invited to stop by."

"That's only two nights away. Definitely go to that and learn as much as you can. Great idea!"

I ducked my head at the praise. "So, what were the other names on the police list?"

"Oh, you're going to love it." Max chortled like she couldn't even get it out without laughing. "Jenna Jeffries ... and Britt Salazar."

"No." I gasped. "But they're Ashlee's best friends!"

"Almost too delicious, isn't it?"

I knew exactly what she meant. All those years when Max and I struggled to get by as lonely outsiders, the popular crowd seemed like one big happy family, their life an endless beer-soaked reunion, sisterly bonds tight as my neck muscles. I thought back to Britt barking orders to Jenna at the wedding. What if all along, our trio of tormenters couldn't stand each other, and their friendship was just BS? What if one of them had killed Ashlee?

"There's no way it could be Jenna," Max added.

"Why couldn't it? She's hardly a nice person." I shuddered at the memory of Jenna's cold, shaking hands yanking down the zipper of my dress. Come to think of it, why were her hands so shaky? Was she really *that* drunk? She'd also kept on saying I was a spy. "Do you think too much kale can make you paranoid?" I asked hopefully.

Max shrugged. "I find it hard to believe that a criminal mind lurks within Jenna. Or any mind."

"So Jenna's more likely innocent on the grounds of being dumb as a post." I seagulled a fry and settled back in my seat, feeling smug and like I might have it in me to be a real detective. "That leaves Britt Salazar. She doesn't strike me as stupid. I think she's pretty smart."

"More importantly, she's devious," Max said.

"The two of you could stand to be a little more devious."

At the sharply amused soprano voice, I looked up to see Britt herself standing in front of us, balancing two cobalt-blue plates of wings. I hadn't even noticed that the child-waiter's shift ended.

"That one's not my fault," I whispered to Max. "You didn't warn me."

"Because she wasn't anywhere near us," Max growled back.

"Nope," Britt concurred. "I could hear you two geniuses loudly gabbing about your 'investigation' *and* your magical powers clear from the other side of the bar."

Max clutched her character sheet tightly, like she was considering using it again to explain away our odd conversation. But it wouldn't help, of course. Once, ten years ago, Britt had seen magic—mine—up close and very personal. Her look of repulsed horror was even harder to take than the screaming and four-letter words she'd unleashed at the sight. Had to give her some credit, though, she seemed calmer about the whole idea now.

"So?" Max set the crumpled page on the table. "What business is it of yours, Brittany?"

Emboldened, I added, "And since when do you work at the Barrel, anyway?"

"Ladies, I can assure you that the answers to those questions are connected." Britt sighed a long-suffering sigh. "Out of boredom, I drove back to town last weekend to go be in an old friend's wedding, and got stuck in town indefinitely. For reasons you two apparently know about."

"Oh wow, the sheriff literally told you 'don't leave town'?" She wasn't even pretending she was worried about Ashlee, I noted. Flat out admitted she'd done the wedding 'out of boredom.' Who was this cynical, blasé woman, and what had she done with the image and clique-obsessed cheerleader I used to know? Suspicious though she was, I found myself spellbound by her new, world-weary cool factor. "Did he say it like you were a femme fatale in an old movie?" I pressed.

"Yes, Hazel. It was all highly glamorous." Britt looked at me as if I had all the brainpower of a lobster. "Anyway, my cousin Ula manages this place, and she's letting me work here temporarily. While I'm stuck in town. I already know the ins and outs because I waitressed here the summer I was eighteen."

And it was annoying how much she still could pass for an eighteen-year-old small-town waitress, I thought. Her shiny, dark hair was up in adorable, youthful pigtails and her petite form perfectly filled out the requisite white Drunken Barrel T-shirt with its picture of a winking cartoon wine barrel, its mouth an "O" that leered up at the full moon.

A blue moon with a butt cleft drawn in the middle.

Keep it classy, Drunken Barrel.

Britt bit her pouty lower lip. "I don't know exactly what you two ladies are up to ... and it sounds incredibly amateurish and risky ... but I want in."

Max and I looked at each other, shocked.

"What?"

"You want to hang with *us*?" I wasn't proud of the little squeal that escaped me, but this odd girl out's heart was skipping beats at the idea of a popular girl asking to join us. Thinking back, I'd never really hated Britt Salazar. Well, okay, I had. I totally had. But my hate-on for her was only wounded love. I'd always wanted Britt and her friends to treat me with kindness and respect, yet none of them ever had.

Till now.

Max's death glare told me great minds didn't always think alike. "I'll go deal with our tab." She already had her wallet out. "Come on, Hazel."

I hesitated. Max was my ride home. Trixie had been towed to a shop in the next town over, and she wouldn't be back for a day or two. "Maybe Britt has useful info." Wasn't Max being a little hasty? "A fresh perspective. And she's nice to us now, see?"

"She is working you, Hazel. The way people like her always do." Max's voice held more patience than usual, like she was talking to a child. It made me miss her usual blunt-as-a-spoon style. "Don't you find it suspicious that she's never given us the time of day before, and now she wants in on our party?"

"That's not suspicious," Britt protested. "That's called growing up."

"Yeah, well, your timing's pretty hinky." Max folded her arms. "Couldn't you have grown up *before* your buddy Ashlee disappeared into thin air?"

"Shoot!" I snapped my fingers. "Britt did want to talk to us before, at the wedding. I totally forgot to tell you. She specifically asked me to say hi to you."

"To me, why?" Max narrowed her eyes. "What's your game, Salazar?"

"To be honest, I assumed you'd mellowed a little." Britt shrugged. "Guess I was wrong."

While Max stormed off to throw cash at the bartender, Britt lingered by our table. "Isn't some part of you curious about what I could offer your team?" she said. "My powers of persuasion alone would put you two leaps and bounds ahead. I mean, take you. You're sweet, Hazel. This whole town trusts you not to poison their muffins. But you have about as much presence as a jar of apple butter. No offense."

"None taken. Apple butter is a palate pleaser with a unique flavor profile." Paired great with muffins, too.

"Of course you would think of it that way, honey, you're so *nice.*" Britt flashed a look of queenly amusement that reminded me eerily of high school. She'd been royalty back then, and apparently, in her mind, she still was. "Now, me, I can make people do things." Her voice grew soft and hypnotic. "People would follow me anywhere. It's crazy. Not to toot my own horn, but I just have that something. I've got *It.* I've got it going on. I'm an It Girl. Face it, you two *need* me."

It wasn't until she broke eye contact that I noticed the table of middle-aged moms across the room tossing her dirty looks. Britt may have still had that royal vibe, but she was no longer worshipped by the world at large. Trying to hide my amusement, I asked, "What about the hangry customers who *need* those hot wings?"

Britt rolled her eyes. "My freedom is at stake here, Hazel, not some Yelp review. Now what would it take for you to give me a chance?"

I shook my head. "Max has made it pretty clear she's not—"

"Stop hiding behind Max and answer me."

Man, Britt sounded eager. Bossy as ever, but also a little desperate. It struck me that for the first time, I had leverage over a popular girl.

"Well. At the bakery, we give away free samples of our new products." I could hardly believe I was saying this to Britt Salazar. "Give me a sample of what you'd have to offer our investigation."

Irritation flared Britt's perfect button nose. "Really, you're making me try out for your amateur detective club? Ugh, fine. Here's something." Britt leaned down and whispered in my ear. "Max was right about one thing: Jenna's too fluffy headed to carry out a murder. Turns out she can't even make out with a married man without doing her drunk cheerleader mating call shriek loud enough for me to hear. Oh yes, our dumb little Jenna's been having an affair with Drew Kensington. I heard them doing it in the dressing room at his wedding."

I swallowed, stunned that my guess had been right. "I thought I was just being petty to suspect them."

"You can be both right and petty. I'm an expert at it," Britt said cheerfully. "Jenna always kept in touch with Drew even while she was married to that other guy. What do you want to bet they've been each other's designated side dish since then?"

"Get away from my partner." Max was back, shoving Britt's shoulders from behind.

To my surprise, Britt didn't even drop her plates. The little pixie was a lot stronger than she looked.

Max glowered. "There's something different about you, Brittany. I don't like it."

Was Britt different, I wondered, or were Max and I the ones who had changed? Current me almost wanted to give Britt a chance, while Max was dead set against her.

Britt tossed me another queen-of-the-school grin. "Think about it, Hazel." And she jetted off with the rapidly cooling chicken wings.

Someone was getting a two-star Yelp review tonight.

CHAPTER TEN

ON THE SHORT car ride to Filbert Road, I caught up Max on everything Britt said to me.

"She really seems desperate to join forces with us," I said.

Max made a face like she'd smelled dog poop. "How do you know she's not trying to sabotage our efforts? She could be involved in Ashlee's disappearance or is covering up for the real culprit."

"Then why would she give me such a hot tip about Jenna and Drew?" I was really proud of how I'd finagled that.

Max scoffed. "You really believe her crazy story about Jenna having an affair with Ashlee's new husband?"

I remembered Drew gently helping Jenna to her feet at the wedding, the grateful way she looked up at him. "Actually, I do. I saw those two together. They looked . . . you know how people look when they know each other pretty well and there's an attraction?"

"Comfortable? But also, uncomfortable?"

"Bingo."

Max bit her lip. "All right. I trust your hunch. You think you can get Jenna to the bakery and give her a special scone?"

Jenna worked only six blocks away from the bakery. As a trainer at Swole Tim's Gym. "No chance she'd go near a scone. Not even if it was gluten-free."

"Then we'll have to tail her, old-school detective work. While she's at work tomorrow, I'll slap a spy cam with a GPS tracker on her car. It'll let us know where she goes when she goes out."

I squirmed in my bucket seat. That GPS tracker and camera business was exactly the type of nerdery Max got excited about. But it made me uncomfortable—not the least of which because it would make Jenna's paranoid ravings that I was a spy correct.

Then I realized Max was fairly itching to break into Jenna's house, probably in bobcat form. The car tracker was a compromise, for my sake. I sighed. "I'll cook up a few vials of truth serum, er, ramble juice, so we're stocked up for the scones."

"Great," Max said. "I'll design a coupon, advertising them as free on Friday."

"Has a nice ring to it," I said, thinking that if free didn't draw people in, nothing would.

Max pulled up to my house and put the car in park. "I'll post it to the blog tomorrow morning. Get ready. You'll have droves on Friday morning."

"Fingers crossed." I opened the door and stood, only to trip on something light but bulky on the floor mat. A legal folder, like the one I'd spotted on the night of Ashlee's wedding … but now it was empty.

A chill went up my back. I held up the folder. "Is this by any chance Kade's?"

Max groaned. "How'd you guess? He treats my car like it's an extension of his apartment. Oh, and Saturday night, he took it without even asking—rude. That's why I had to ban him from driving Mustang Sally."

Saturday. The wedding. It *was* Kade in the car … had to be. But where had he gone?

Kade was a shifter. Had he simply changed form to hide from me? Obviously, I hadn't checked the car floor, but you'd think a bobcat would be too big to fit in there, even crouched into a ball. I wanted to ask if the de Klaw siblings had the ability to shift into baby bobcats—bob kits?—but Max wasn't dumb. She'd sniff out the suspicion in my question.

Vowing to pin her down about Kade another time, I waved as the Mustang drove off.

Then I dug into my satchel for my key ring, looked up … and screamed.

A man, hulking and hunched over, was blocking my front door.

"Haze," the man croaked.

I screamed again, tumbling backward into a pile of maple leaves I'd raked over the weekend. Mid-tumble, my brain registered that the man—who was now rushing to my side—was Bryson.

"You weren't answering texts." He helped me to my feet. In the moonlight, I could see the concern in his blue eyes, as well as something else—hurt. "I brought over the caramel ice cream to feed you. But it melted." He held up a sad mini tub of Ben and Jerry's.

"Oh geez. I'm so sorry, Bry." How could I have forgotten to text him that our date was off? Worst girlfriend ever. "My phone ran out of juice while I was out with Max, and—"

"Who's this *Max* guy?" His mouth twisted with confusion. Or was it anger? I'd never seen Bryson angry so I wasn't sure.

"It's a woman," I corrected him quickly. "Maxine De Klaw."

He blinked, looking relieved but still confused. "Is she a friend of yours?"

"Honestly, I don't know anymore. I mean, we *were* friends but…" My mind flashed back to Max's thousand-yard stare at the bar. "But something happened."

"Wow. Okay..."

I realized Bryson was getting the wrong idea again. "Not like that! We had a falling out."

"It's just you never mentioned this person, Haze. You don't talk about your friends. I sort of wondered … never mind."

"You wondered if I have no friends?"

"No, not that..." His tone said, yes, that.

"Well, I *don't* have a lot of close friends right now. But I should have told you about Max, because we were best friends once."

Suddenly, it occurred to me that Bryson and I had never done that thing all couples eventually must do. Introduce each other to your people.

He was new in town. But what was my excuse? I had no doubt most folks in the Bay wished me well, but I lacked besties. Didn't help that there were no other Green Witches in town around my age. And friendships with Ordinals required too much lying.

But I hadn't just failed to introduce him to Max; I hadn't even told him about her. Maybe because in doing so, I would have to talk about the girl I was in high school: "Goody Two-shoes," a shy, eager-to-please middle sister and baker-in-training. That Max was the one friend who truly showed up for that girl … until the night she didn't.

I drifted to the front door, fingering my engagement ring nervously. Forget how well did I know Bryson … how well had I let Bryson know me ? All that time I'd spent crushing my lips against his was like medicine to me, but in retrospect, some of it would have been better spent getting to know each other.

I was marrying a near stranger.

The stark revelation overwhelmed me, and I focused my attention on turning the house key in the lock. Bryson followed close behind me and said nothing. Weird how small and silent my house felt after the cavernous buzz of the bar. It felt eerie, being alone in the dark with just him. What if the rest of our lives together felt this empty?

They would, unless I dared to let him in.

"Bryson, there's a lot you and I don't know about each other," I blurted out, just to kill the quiet. I flipped on the main light switch and set my satchel on its hook. "I don't even know exactly where you grew up. What your family's like. Or what you did before you became a therapist ... you know, this year."

It felt refreshing to be this assertive, even if it didn't feel quite like me.

I looked over to gauge Bryson's reaction. It was lukewarm. "Tell you what, Haze. On our next date, I'll break out the family photo album. Talk about my career woes. But you're the one who stood me up tonight. So, maybe we should talk about what *I* don't know about *you*?"

"All right." I swallowed. "Max and I, we were best buds in high school. Like sisters. Then ... something happened. We had a falling out." Call me insecure, but I didn't want to say she ghosted me. In case that made me seem more dumpable, in general. "Anyway, she's worried to death about her twin brother, Kade—"

"Yeah, well, *I* was worried about *you,*" he cut in sharply. "You were out awfully late without calling. And you're not the kind of woman who likes to go out at night to begin with. You're my little homebody."

I opened my mouth to argue that I'd had a pretty good time, considering. But that would not help matters. "You're right."

"And it's not like you to ignore texts, either. How did I know you hadn't disappeared like Ashlee?"

Wow, I hadn't even thought about that. "You're right." I touched his arm. "I'm sorry I missed your texts. I goofed, big-time."

"Yeah, you did . . . but it's okay." He let out a breath, then leaned over and planted a kiss in my hair. He no longer felt like a stranger. "To be honest, it's sort of a relief to know you're not perfect," he said. "Especially after my big screwup with the Ashlee thing. I should have trusted you with the truth, Haze. I'm sorry, with or without ice cream."

"It's okay," I said, relieved that things were feeling more normal already. "I promise not to worry you like that again."

Now that I thought about it, maybe it was for the best he'd cut me off before I revealed that Max and I were teaming up to do our own investigation. That would surely make him worry more.

He'd never seemed worried about anything before that I could remember. But then, I'd never done anything to stress him out before, like standing him up. Our relationship was like an unspoken pact against anxiety.

"Hey, want to go to the grocery store and buy more caramel ice cream?" I asked, realizing we'd just had our *second* fight.

"Nah, sounds like work. Let's stick this bad boy back in the freezer till it's half frozen and make milkshakes."

I whistled. "I like your style."

"Thought you'd approve." Bryson gave me a knowing smile. "And there's just enough time for two episodes of *Frankie and Grace* before you'll want to kick me out and draw yourself a nice hot bath. With fizzy bath bombs."

Maybe I was wrong.

Maybe Bryson knew me pretty darn well, after all.

At least in the ways that mattered.

That night, after my fizzy bath, I couldn't get to sleep.

I closed my eyes and breathed in the lavender scent of my eye pillow. But kept thinking about Kade's being at the country club during Ashlee's wedding. Was he the one she was searching for in the parking lot?

Even if he were secretly meeting up with Ashlee, and maybe handing her a stack of papers, it was probably for some dodgy yet fairly innocuous reason.

Still, it was awfully damn suspicious behavior.

I needed to know the truth about what he was doing there … but ramble juice didn't work on shifters. I was—grudgingly—appreciative of Max for having established that.

But there had to be another spell that *did* work on her kind.

I rose from bed, flipped on the light, and stalked to the built-in cookbook shelf above my kitchenette's work counter. Sweeping aside the bread-baking bible and a stack of King Arthur Flour catalogs, I dug out the row of magic books that were hidden behind it.

I spent the rest of the night combing through them.

Halfway through the last book, I found what I was looking for.

The spell was called "A Dreamland Visitor."

It was in a section of the book called "Spells that Require the Help of Demons."

Gran had never taught me how to summon a demon. Though there were a handful of Green Magic spells that used demon partners, it was way more of a Grey Magic phenomenon, and she clearly didn't approve of it. So of course I'd never tried it.

Well, I thought, *first time for everything.*

My hands were shaking as I chopped the herbs to make the calling potion:

"With this catnip and savory, I call you
Honor'd demon, who plays many roles
Sandman, King of Sleep, they call you

Make me an extra, on the sets of dreaming souls."

Poof.

Suddenly, there was a woman in my kitchen, or what looked like a woman. She had dark blue skin and even darker blue hair, and she wore a silver caftan-thing that looked awfully comfortable.

"Pleasant greetings." Her voice was rich, and extremely relaxing. "Who is the witch that summons me tonight?"

I opened my mouth to say my name but yawned instead.

"What are you looking at?" The demon covered her mouth. "Something in my teeth?"

"No, it's just that you're female." I was having to blink a lot to keep my eyes from closing. "I thought the Sandman would be … well, a man."

"The first one was." You could tell she was tired of getting this question from ignorant witches. "Our line has gone on for thousands of years. There are quite a few of us now, it's one big happy family. Sandman One, as we affectionately call our ancestor, still does a few gigs here and there. But mostly just for celebs at this point. If you want *him* to answer your call next time, you're going to need to bake something extraordinary."

"Wow, you know that I'm a baker?" I was suddenly reminded of Leeza and her spreadsheet. "Don't tell me, you have a database of all the Earth's active Green Witches."

"Nah, it was obvious you bake." She pointed to the stacks of baking magazines on the counter. "I mean we do keep note of prominent witches in our family book, but you wouldn't be in it yet. We spend so little time on Earth that usually by the time a witch gets listed, her power's on the wane. The best we can do is contact her successor."

"Well, I'm Hazel Greenwood. My grandmother's Sage Greenwood. Her grandmother was Marjoram Boyd, known to Ordinals as Marge."

Her eyebrows went up slightly. I wouldn't have noticed except that her face was so still otherwise. "Ah, I knew Marjoram. She once had me look into her husband's dreams to see if he was having an affair … and goodness boy howdy, was he ever."

I cringed. "Yikes, I really didn't need to know—"

"Lovely witch, Marjoram. Smelled like rosemary." She shrugged. "It's a shame that your lives are so short, I would have liked to chat with her again. She had great energy."

"I…" What was there to say to that? I was starting to get a sense of how demons were not quite like us. "Thanks? And what shall I call you?"

"You could try my name." She took a deep breath and said something that sounded like a sneeze mixed with a spit. "Or you may call me Sandman Three Hundred and Six. The Ancient Greeks called me Nyx, but I've never loved that nickname."

"Oh, don't worry, I'm not into nicknames either. Nix on the Nyx."

"Excellent." Her calm face did not break into a smile, and I realized she had no smile lines, which was part of what made her look unearthly. "Now, if you're here for a dream spell, you'll first need to bake a batch of dream cookies. I'll email you the recipe."

"Seriously?"

"Don't worry, it's super simple. But it's vital that you add this." She reached into her caftan pocket and pulled out what looked like a pickle jar. I stared because the jar was much bigger than the pocket. Suspended inside were what appeared to be tiny chocolate clouds. "They produce vanilla rain," she explained. "It creates an exquisite mouthfeel, this ingredient. You can't find this texture anywhere in your dimension. Split one cookie in half, and offer one to your subject, while eating the other yourself. Next pluck one hair from the head of your subject and place it in a boiling cauldron along with this list of herbs."

I winced. "Sorry, do I really need to pluck their hair?"

"No, no, that's just poetic language. Any way you can get it is fine. Oh, and the final step. To enter your dream-observer body, which I'll be custom crafting for you—"

"Nice."

"—you'll need to plunge your own hand into the boiling cauldron."

"More poetic language?" I asked hopefully.

"No, you really must experience that searing pain for the spell to work. But the cookie is awesome! And don't worry, the agony will pass in a second or two. I can already tell it will be a pleasure working together."

"Me too," I said, and wondered what the hex I'd gotten myself into. "Wait. Before you go, it doesn't say anything in the book about how I pay you?"

Sandman 306 again made that subtle eyebrow twitch that I thought might be a smile in a human. "This is a funny question, Hazel Greenwood. There is no need for money to exchange hands between two such as us."

Two such as us? "Really, is that because my family has a credit line or something? Or … is this a free sample?"

I blinked, and she was gone. I threw myself on my bed and immediately fell into a deep, still sleep.

CHAPTER ELEVEN

JENNA JEFFRIES WAS sitting sideways in her SUV's driver's seat, pretzeled into a pose that only a Booty Camp instructor could pull off. She tugged on a pair of ultra-high heels—the fourth pair I'd seen her try on here in the parking lot of the gym where she worked. A reject pile of sexy stilettos covered the upholstery of her passenger seat.

Thanks to the spy cam Max had hidden in Jenna's moon roof, I could observe the endurance sport that was Jenna getting ready to go out, all from the comfort of my couch.

It was nine p.m. on Wednesday night, and Jenna finally started the car, looking more date ready than I've ever looked in my life. She wore a little black dress with a low scoop neck. Her glossy caramel brown hair was styled half up, half down. Her cheekbones were as hard as glass.

Wrapped in my Snuggee blanket, watching the feed from my couch, I felt exhausted just from looking at her.

Then again, it had been a long day.

At lunch, Max dropped me off at the repair shop to pick up Trixie, whose engine was running again.

But Trixie wasn't herself.

Instead of, *Hey, doll*, or even grumbles about my choice of auto shop, she'd greeted me with, *Can I interest you in a complimentary bottle of seltzer? That comes with our VIP package.*

Her voice was upbeat and polite. Actually, she was less annoying, believe it or not. But it was like the brass had been scraped off of her.

I checked my purse for my invisibility mints, threw on a pair of comfy flats, and jogged to my car, where I dictated a text to Max: "It's go time. Jenna's driving somewhere, looking super dolled up."

"Get the juice, girl!" Trixie piped up, in her new perky tone. "*Have a fab time spying on Jenna.*"

I shook my head. "What exactly did they do to you at that shop?"

"Service was good to excellent. Four stars. Would get repaired there again."

I hesitated. "Honk once if you're okay?"

"I'm beyond okay, I'm achieving self-actualization."

"Well, all right then." I still had no idea what caused the electrical hiccup that shut her down in the first place, but the shop had assured me that with a car this old, it was just a matter of time. I was grateful they'd given her a new lease on life, even if getting serviced scrambled her personality.

Max texted back what we were thinking: Hot date with DK ?!

That was the tantalizing possibility on both our minds, of course. If Jenna was secretly seeing Drew Kensington, Ashlee's husband, the two of them would become our joint prime suspects.

Which means I would be following two possible murderers. Gulp.

Hey, want to join me, for backup? I wrote to Max.

Max: I would but to be honest... I've kinda been stalking Britt tonight.

Me: U Serious?

Max: Sorry not sorry. Something about her I don't trust. Can't put my finger on it.

Me: Maybe you just don't like her?

Max: No maybe. Oh! She's walking out the door now.

Me: You were spying inside her house?!

Did Max have no sense of privacy whatsoever—also, had she ever spied on *me?*

Max: It might interest you to know that Britt's wearing all black.

I typed furiously: I don't care what she's wearing. How is that any of our business???

Max: Because that's not how she rolls normally. She's dressed to commit a crime.

Oh. I swallowed. Britt, much as I wanted her to be new and improved, might have grown up to be a killer.

Me: Stay safe. :/

Max: Whatever, I could kick her skinny butt and would enjoy doing so.

She was just posturing. I hoped.

Me: Down, kitty.

To my disappointment, the GPS tracker suggested that Jenna was heading toward downtown Ocean Street. Well, she was unlikely to be having a tryst with Drew Kensington out in public like that.

But that didn't mean Britt had necessarily lied about Drew. A floozy like Jenna could easily be dating multiple peoples' husbands, including ordinary Joes who would deign to be seen downtown.

I ordered the new, sleek and personality-free Trixie to head to the waterfront after her.

"Sounds like you're looking to chillax after a hectic day!" she said smoothly and turned the radio to the 80s station. Trixie turning the

channel to something I liked without my having to beg her? Now that was a first.

Maybe I could deal with this new version?

Minutes of my singing along, offkey, to Madonna's "Like a Virgin" later, my camera app showed Jenna parking her car along the beach. The night was overcast, but just enough moonlight shone down that I could see the gentle waves breaking, through her driver's side window. It was low tide.

As Jenna grabbed her coat from the back of her SUV, an odd detail caught my eye. She had one of those bumper stickers that says, *My Kid is an Honor Student*. I almost laughed at the thought of wild, flighty Jenna being a mom, let alone of an honor student. It didn't fit my image of her.

But of course, she *was* a mom. Famously so.

How had I forgotten that Jenna had a kid, a kid who must be around ten by now? After crowning all high school clichés by getting pregnant on prom night, she and the girl's father got married and then, a few years later, divorced—an all-too-common story in Blue Moon Bay. The rare high school sweethearts who stayed together were envied and held up as examples. It was a jungle out there.

I sent a sigh of gratitude to Bryson for rescuing me from the jungle of singleness. Then, I parked a block away from Jenna and hid behind the Blue Moon Bay Rowing Club's boathouse to crunch my invisibility mints.

They worked disturbingly fast. I waved my hand in front of my face and saw … nothing. The spell could only be undone by the first word I spoke.

Jenna retrieved her purse from the trunk of her car and threw on a long black peacoat. But instead of turning toward the bars and restaurants on the waterfront, she hopped down the concrete steps that led to the beach. Was she meeting her date there? Romantic, if a little cold this time of year.

I hurried after Jenna, whose pointy heels sank into the sand, making her easy to follow from ten or twelve feet behind. The wind covered the wet crunch of my own footfalls on the sand. Luckily no one else was strolling the beach at this hour, to note the eerie sight of footprints that appeared not to be attached to anyone.

But if no one else was here, what was Jenna doing? Was it possible she was just taking the long way to the bars—bonus cardio?

She kept walking, swiftly, eagerly, toward a dimly lit cove. Oh my! She wasn't meeting someone at a bar after all. This really could be a tryst with Drew.

"Yoohoo, over here, babe!" called a high female voice.

Perched on a boulder in the little cove was … Britt. I groaned inwardly. Jenna had gotten this dressed up—just to impress an old friend?

At times like this, I didn't understand my gender.

"Hey, girl, what's happening?" Jenna simpered. "I was so happy when you texted. Let's do a shot at every bar, just like old t—"

"I am *very* hungry, Jenna." Britt didn't even bother to try to sound charming. "I need you to lean to the side and stretch your neck before I starve."

I froze. Holy goodness. Britt hadn't called up an old friend to hang out.

She really was a freakin' vampire and Jenna was about to be a liquid meal.

"Sure thing, girl…" Jenna sounded dreamy, and I remembered with a chill Britt's statement that people would follow her anywhere. Of course. She had the vampiric power of compulsion.

"Good job, J." Britt's fangs were out—damn it, they looked adorable on her. "Now move aside all that flat ironed hair and extensions. I don't want to choke on that mess."

"No problem, Britt!"

Oh God. Now what? All I had with me was my calming herbs necklace, but what if it didn't work on vampires? It barely worked on anyone.

Where was my backup? Where was Max?

I stood petrified, wondering how I could stop the murderer from striking again. Because now the pieces all fit together, and for the first time, I really understood that Ashlee was not coming back. She was dead. Britt must have lured her old buddy Ash out here too and feasted on her blood.

I had to save Jenna.

Eww. But I had to.

I reached for my necklace, but opening the locket wasn't a cinch while invisible. While I was messing around with the stupid thing, Britt lunged for Jenna's neck.

As she chomped daintily, a spotted feline leapt from the shadows.

It charged Britt, knocking her down.

"Oh, for gosh sake!" Sounding more annoyed than harmed, Britt sat up and threw the bobcat several feet. Whoa.

The cat snarled, sounding pretty annoyed itself.

"Do I hide in the woods, Max?" Britt continued to address the cat as you would a person. "Do I wait for you to sink your teeth into a rabbit so I can knock it out of your mouth? And I'm not even hurting her, see?

Jenna did not, in fact, appear hurt. Sighing with pleasure, she sank into the sand beside Britt, who touched her lips to the bitten spot on her neck. The mark vanished.

The bobcat hesitated.

"There, now she's healed." Was it my imagination, or did Britt sound relieved? As if she hadn't been 100 percent sure things would go well. "After five minutes or so, she'll remember nothing, so I usually shoo her along by then. This was the highlight of her week, bruh . In fact, that's a problem." Her fangs receded as her expression grew serious. "She's gotten a bit addicted to the high."

"Wowee, is that a bobcat?" Jenna said dreamily. Britt was right, she was high as a kite. "Omigosh, it's so cute. I want it to be my pet so I can love it forever. No … I want to turn it into a fur blanket. No … a coat. Area rug."

While she was deliberating, lying in the sand staring at the sky, the bobcat's fur began to shimmer. Max stood in front of us, naked.

"Uncalled for." Britt averted her gaze, as did I.

"You said she'd forget everything in five minutes." Max shrugged, clearly not embarrassed in the least. "Couldn't pass up a chance to freak out an Ordinal without consequences."

Jenna finally looked up—and shrieked. "Oh my God, it's … that weird girl from my chemistry class. Maxine de Klaw!"

I threw up my hands in disgust. "Seriously, you remember her and not me?"

Poof. Speaking turned me visible.

"Hazel?" Britt's eyes widened.

"What are you two losers doing here?" Jenna tittered. "Hey, wait." Suddenly she looked like a kid whose balloon got popped. "What happened to that bobcat? It was going to be my nice new coat."

"Yeah, well, not everyone deserves a coat." Max turned to Britt. "You know what to do, vampire."

"Gladly. Jenna, give Max here your coat. And then go away and forget all this."

Within thirty seconds of Britt's "suggestion," Max was clad in a red satin peacoat tied with a thick tulle ribbon belt. It was the fanciest thing I'd ever seen her wear, and with her tumbling red hair and impish grin, she looked like a rampaging fire spirit.

Wearing just her little black dress and a blissed-out expression, Jenna minced away. Shivering in the general direction of the bars.

"Uh, is she gonna be okay?" I asked.

"Sure." Britt shrugged. "Besides, I sealed the wound. So even if she keels over, no one's going to connect it to me."

"Wow, spoken like a true friend."

"What do you want from me, Hazel?" Britt snapped. "I outgrew Jenna when I got turned. I outgrew a lot of things. But a girl still needs to eat."

"Just ignore Hazel when she does that pinched-face look. She can't see past her human privilege." Max sounded surprisingly eager to have someone to complain to about me. "Hey, at least you don't have to kill to eat," she added generously. "In that sense, you're more evolved than I am in cat mode."

"Aw, that's sweet of you to say, Maxy." Britt smiled at the woman who'd once sprayed bobcat urine in her locker. "But I actually think you're the one who's most evolved, in that you're so adaptable and deeply connected to nature."

"Okay, what is going on here?" I was now officially creeped out by the love fest between the two of them. "How do we know you're not using compulsion right now, to make Max like you?"

"Oh, haha, no, I still don't like Brittany," Max said, surprising me again. "Can't stand her."

"Samesies," Britt said with a smile, and they high-fived.

"But we're both mature enough that we can work together, anyway. Now that I can see my suspicions about her were, well, animal instinct."

"Well said, for an animal."

"Thanks, bloodsucker." Max turned back to me. "Also, her undead mind games don't work on shifters."

"So true." Britt looked wistful about that. "If Max and I ever had a serious disagreement, it would be claws versus fangs. And I honestly don't know who'd win that fight."

"I'd win," Max said calmly. "Your strength surprised me tonight. But I've been at this longer than you, and I have allies."

"Allies?" That was news to me.

"All over the woods," Max said, pointing vaguely to the north where Corvid Woods Park was located. Whatever, I'd ask for details later. When Britt wasn't listening in.

"So ... ladies...?" Britt grabbed my hand and Max's. Her skin was ice cold, as one might expect from a vampire. Or a human, on this cold November evening. "Margaritas?"

"Wait, fire doesn't kill you, does it?"

I was mostly asking to be polite. Since the three of us were sitting at an outdoor table at Dark Blue, a chichi bar that faced the beach and featured firepit tables. But I was also suddenly feeling awkward in my own ignorance of Britt's kind.

She was the first vampire I'd ever met, and Gran, it turned out, had really not prepared me for the occasion. All the wisdom she'd passed on on that front was being quickly revealed as superstition that made both Britt and Max chuckle into their giant margarita glasses.

I was getting sick of that sound.

And Britt, evidently, was getting tired of my questions. "No, sweetie. Fire doesn't kill me. Crosses don't stop me. Even sunlight won't seriously hurt me till I'm over a hundred. Now it just gives me a migraine."

"And garlic—?"

"Is so yummy. So's this." She held up her pink margarita.

"Sorry, one more thing. Can booze still get you drunk?" I asked, trying not to stare. "Or ... do you have to puke it up or something?"

She sighed like she was tired of humoring me. "Blood's the only thing that nourishes me. But I can eat regular food, too. I don't get drunk because alcohol magically moves out of my system too fast. But I get a nice buzz."

Splendid. In other words, her life was even more perfect now than in high school.

"Hazel. Google 'vampires' sometime and stop wasting everyone's time with your basic witch questions." Max was back in control, and back in her own jeans and sweatshirt, having retrieved them from behind the boathouse. "Let's get on with business. Britt, catch us up on how you came to be a suspect. So I can officially scratch you off my list."

"Ugh, I was having one of those days." Britt sighed. "It was Sunday, the day after Ashlee's wedding. I was super hungry, even though I'd just fed on Jenna at the wedding. For some reason, she got extra high from it—so high she was acting crazy. Paranoid."

I sat up. "Yes, she was. I remember."

"So, I didn't take much from her then. Just to be safe."

Max shredded her napkin, looking thoughtful. "I wonder why she had a bad reaction to your bite that time, but not tonight?"

"It happens occasionally." Britt shrugged helplessly. "If my sire wasn't such a deadbeat and a jerk, I'd ask him. Anyhow, I was still hungry but I decided not to snack on Jenna again for a while. So, I called up Ash. Asked her to come to my hotel room ... well, the same thing happens with her. Gets totally wasted after one bite. Worse, she wanders off and jumps into her chauffeur's car in that paranoid state. They took her to the hospital thinking she'd been poisoned."

"Oh man, that's scary," Max said, and I knew she was empathizing with Britt, not Ashlee. She might not like her, but the two of them were definitely bonding over the challenges of being supernatural creatures. As a human with just a little magic running through me, how could I not feel left out?

"Took her seven hours to 'recover,'" Britt said, finishing her story. "Well, I guess she'd told staff members who she was going to visit and even though her memory wiped like it's supposed to, the hospital sent their full notes to Gantry's office when she disappeared. You can see where it doesn't look great for me."

"Okay, I'm satisfied with that explanation." Max licked the salt off her glass's rim and turned to me as if Britt wasn't even there. "I know she's everything we hate, but she clearly had nothing to do with Ashlee's disappearance. I'm sorry, but you're going to have to consider the possibility that it might have been your oh-so-perfect boyfriend."

"My boyfriend?" I nearly jumped out of my seat. "How about your jailbird brother? Because I have news for you. He definitely borrowed your car to go meet Ashlee for some nefarious reason—at her own wedding!"

"What?" Max looked jarred. "If that's true, why didn't you tell me before?"

Britt twirled her hair. "Wow, I see now why it was so important to the two of you to suspect *me*."

We both whipped our heads around.

"You needed me to be the bad guy because you secretly suspect her boyfriend, and you secretly suspect her brother."

"I don't like secrets." Max stood, still looking unsettled, and dropped a few bills on the table. "I'm going to go clear the air with Kade. If he has something to confess, I'd rather he confess it to me first."

"Fine, I'll go with you," I said. I had an ulterior motive, as usual these days. That "Dreamland Visitor" spell that was going to let me see into Kade's dreams required a hair from the subject's head.

"We'll all go," Britt said, pushing in her chair. "Team field trip!"

"Sure you want to come, Hazel?" Max looked pained. "Kade's at work. I know you don't like that place much."

I shook my head. "He can't still be there, it's almost ten p.m." No café would stay open that late.

Max's pained look deepened. "They're open till midnight as of this week. They're working towards being a twenty-four-hour coffee shop. I thought you knew."

"No," I moaned softly. That was it. The bakery was as good as dead.

The smell outside Java Kitty was getting worse. That, or my magical senses were growing more powerful. I stood outside by the front door, holding my nose. Taking deep breaths through my mouth.

Britt and Max looked at each other as if I were nuts.

Britt spoke up. "What's your damage now, Hazel?"

"Grey Magic," I explained, feeling a bit smug. "You two wouldn't know it if it bit you in the butt, only witches can sense it."

"Like I can sniff out vampires?" The geek in Max looked intrigued. "Is there something wrong with Grey Magic?"

"For starters, it's toxic, and it's taking over towns all over America. Grey Magic witches become corporate consultants. They help companies with their bottom line … but the community never seems to be better off."

"Interesting." Max frowned. "How's it work?"

"If I knew the secret sauce, I'd be a Grey Witch myself." I shuddered. "I'd probably have to wear a pantsuit."

Britt frowned. "But this place isn't corporate, it's an indie shop. The owner, Elton is passionate about 'community.' He's actually a real drag to listen to, and usually ends up so emotional he has to run for the Kleenex. I'll stand out here if y'all don't mind."

"Thanks for the warning," I said and steeled myself to walk inside.

It wasn't full, but it wasn't empty. Kade was the only barista on duty, but as far as I could tell the machines sort of made the coffee on their own … was that Grey Magic, too?

Max entered right behind me and marched toward Kade but was forced to get in line behind a woman who was waiting to order coffee.

Breathing through my mouth was no longer cutting it. That smell was getting through anyway, burning my throat.

"Can I help you find the perfect vibe for your wind down?" asked a soft male voice. He was a lanky young dude, very young, almost a teenager. With huge blue eyes and hair that looked permanently hardened from gel. "Now are you a cozy fireside girl, a comfy velvet couch girl, or a no-nonsense counter girl?"

I shook my head. "I don't need help. I was just looking for someone … and I found him, so. I'm good."

"Wow. You just described the human condition." Tears filled the man's eyes. "Aren't we all just searching for each other? Thank you. That was beautiful. I'm Elton, by the way."

"I figured. I mean, I'm Hazel." At the sound of a familiar bell-like laugh, I turned to see a striking young woman with white statement glasses, dyed-black hair, and an undercut. She was seated at a table with two hot young guys, both of whom were hanging on her every word. "Excuse me," I told Elton, and marched over to confront my little sister Cindra.

"Cin? Why didn't you tell me or Gran you were going to be in town?"

At the sight of me, her mouth turned into an "O" of surprise. Which she then covered with her one of her perfect, hand-model hands. "This is awkward … I just flew in for a few days and didn't have time to see *everyone*, so…"

"But you have time to see them?" Britt was suddenly at my side, gesturing to Cindra's two male companions. Was that a thing nowadays, going on a date with two dudes at once? My sister was always on the cutting edge. "Who even are these guys?" Britt demanded.

Cindra looked down, totally cowed by Britt's star power and now also vampire power. It was satisfying, to a petty part of me I didn't know existed. "I don't know," she stammered. "Just … some guys?"

Her two dates looked a bit anxious to hear that. Couldn't blame them.

"I'm so gonna kill Bea," Cindra said under her breath.

"Why?" I knew even as the question left my lips. "She promised you this was the one place in town you'd never run into me. Because they're Gran's competition."

Cin shrugged, not bothering to deny it. It's not like I hadn't always known I was the odd sister out. Still, getting confirmation that Bea and Cin talked behind my back about me was a lonely feeling.

Luckily, Max was returning from the coffee line clutching a white plate with a tiny, shriveled-looking brownie on it. From the spring in her step, I figured whatever Kade told her had been reassuring.

"Hey, if it isn't Hazel's baby sis looking all grown up." Max's tone was fond and sincere, but I cringed, knowing Cindra would take it as a diss. "Did I just hear you putting on a British accent, Cindy? Wow, you have like a million talents!"

"I'm not putting it on." Cindra sounded super defensive (and American) suddenly. "Change happens organically when you immerse yourself in a vibrant culture. Not that you bumpkins would understand."

Max tilted her head, then to my surprise, a chuckle escaped her. Britt was soon giggling too, and finally I joined them. Cindra's commanding presence meant I'd never dared to view her as silly. I laughed till I snorted. My sister and her boys turned away in disgust.

"So, Kade came clean," Max said softly, when the three of us were sitting side by side on the fireside couch. "He admitted that he and Ashlee did have some real conversations. Apparently, it started as her joking around with the barista and grew into a bit of a flirtation between them. He didn't want to tell me because, well, she was such a jerk to me in high school."

"Typical Ashlee to lead your brother on while marrying a millionaire," I said.

"Tell me about it." She rolled her eyes. "But she confided in him that she was having second thoughts about Drew and was already planning her exit."

"Exit?" Britt's voice was sharp. "I'm trapped in his town, begging sketchy neighbors to feed my cat, all because Ash disappeared on purpose?"

I blinked. "You mean she pulled a *Gone Girl*?"

"Not quite that organized," Max said. "More like she planned to fade out on the guy. Slip quietly away and start a new life … she'll resurface somewhere no doubt."

"At which point I can go back to Portland, back to my real life," Britt said. "Well, that's the best news ever."

"There's something you and I can agree on." With the earnest preciseness of an eight year old, Max split the dry-looking fudge brownie in three and we each stuffed a piece into our mouths.

"Oooh, now that's one mediocre dessert." Britt wrinkled her nose.

"Yeah, it's a garbage brownie," Max agreed and turned to me. "I feel like apologizing to your grandmother for defiling my tastebuds with this."

"It's meh, but it eats," I said, feeling I could be generous in this moment, sitting between my two friends.

It was a nice moment, a hopeful moment. But we were still inside Java Kitty Café. The smell was catching up to me, getting too powerful to withstand.

Gagging a little, I ran out the back door.

"Hazel! Honey, are you okay?" Britt with her supernatural speed was on my heels, with Max right behind her. We were standing by the parking lot, next to the dumpster.

"Whoa," Max said and we all three stared at the top of the dumpster.

At the pair of long, shapely legs that were hanging out from it. The feet were wearing sparkly champagne-colored hose and putty-colored pumps, the heels so high they made the foot look J-shaped. From the stillness and splayed angle, you could tell the person was not alive. Not in the slightest.

That, and the fact that their head would be covered in garbage.

"Looks like Ashlee just resurfaced," Max declared.

"Aw, Ash, no." Britt shook her head. "What an undignified exit. You deserved better. Well, no, not really. But still. This is just humiliating."

I was still in shock. "Are you two *sure* it's Ashlee?"

"Dude, I can see her butterfly ankle tattoo." Britt pulled down her sock. "See? I have the firefly that matches it. Jenna miscommunicated with the tattoo artist and ended up with an earwig." She turned to Max. "Sorry, Maxy, I just realized this looks pretty damning for Kade, her body being at his place of work."

"It does look like my brother's being framed, yes," Max said pointedly. "Not to mention we're all going to look suspicious for discovering the body."

"Good point. Ooh, are you suggesting we tamper with the evidence?" Britt was sounding way too intrigued by that idea.

"For goodness' sake." I'd had enough. "Am I the only sane, law-abiding citizen in this group?" Before I could get pushback from the shifter or the vampire, I—Goody Two-shoes—whipped out my phone and called the police.

CHAPTER TWELVE

I CHECKED MY LIPSTICK in Trixie's dusty mirror, then hopped out and locked her, more out of politeness than any real fear that someone in the Drunken Barrel's parking lot would steal her.

"Get that Me-Time, girl!" she called out to me as her engine cooled. *"You look amazing, but not in a try-hard way."*

"Thanks, Trixie."

Feeling a bit guilty for preferring the sleek, phony-sounding version of her, I fluffed my hair one last time and headed inside to meet The Help.

The last twenty-four hours had been intense, and then some.

When the police arrived on the scene outside Java Kitty, they didn't just wrap up Ashlee's body and bag up forensic evidence. They blocked off the building, turned it into a temporary police station, and spent hours individually questioning every single person inside, including us, Kade, Elton, and Cindra, *and* her two dates.

Predictably, a café full of people was one too many to keep a secret. Someone must have snuck out a tweet, because within a half-hour of my calling the cops, reporters from both small and major news outlets had swarmed the place. Ignoring Elton's heartfelt entreaties to "respect a community space," the pack of them began rolling film and shoving microphones in people's faces. I couldn't blame them, really. Dead, rich blonde found "trashed" in an idyllic beachside town? It was all too easy to see it—and us—as the juicy headline of tomorrow's papers.

Fortunately, Britt applied her powers of compulsion to ordering the press to leave and destroy their own footage. They'd still have a story, no doubt, but it'd be a lot more vague with the details, and that was a good thing for the three of us.

I had to admit vampire powers were handy to have at our disposal.

Though if I ever found myself unclear on what I'd been doing the last five minutes and feeling inexplicably giddy, I was gonna be mad.

The three of us were in the police station till two a.m. because Gantry kept us in separate rooms and kept going back to check our stories a million times before he reluctantly released us to go home. From the slant of the questions, it was clear they were trying to pin down the time of death and whether Ashlee had been murdered at Java Kitty, or if her body had just been dumped there.

So to speak.

Bryson had texted me this morning to say he, too, had been called in for further questioning, and I knew Gantry took an extra-long time grilling Kade as well. No arrests had been made, but Max was fearful that the axe would soon come down on her brother.

I was just as fearful about Bryson, though I had no doubt *he* was innocent.

Now that the pressure was on Gantry to find the killer, time was running out for our investigation to bear fruit.

After the craziest night of my life—vampires, naked shifters, the corpse of my bully, mediocre brownies—I'd expected to be too tired to make it in to work. But to my surprise, I bounded out of bed, straight from a pleasant dream about an orange tea cake with thick cream cheese icing (I jotted down the recipe in eyeliner pen on my steamy bathroom mirror).

Of course, when I did show up to work all Gran did was pester me about if I was okay after the "traumatic experience" of seeing Ashlee's dead legs.

It turned out Cindra had promptly jump on the gossip horn to inform the rest of the family that Ashlee had been killed, and I'd found the body. Between her and Java Kitty's other evening customers, who needed TV news?

I was nearly at the door when it struck me that I probably shouldn't have assumed The Help were still gathering tonight for beers. Given that the family they staffed for was in mourning, they were unlikely to be, collectively, in a fun, social mood. I'd been so focused on taming my social anxiety and getting my butt out to this event that it didn't occur to me the event might be off.

Well, I'd just have to walk in and hope they'd be there.

As soon as I swung open the door to the Drunken Barrel, fiddle notes rang out sharp and sweet over the warm buzz of conversation that enveloped me.

Right, it was Thursday night.

And Thursdays were busier than Tuesdays. I vaguely remembered that detail, from having once vaguely had a life. Tonight, the scrappy fiddler chick playing her reels in the corner had more of an audience, and some were spry enough to dance. Their nimble feet crushed peanut shells, while older folks sitting on barstools clapped to the beat. I stood mesmerized by the idyllic scene.

Gran could side-eye the tourists all she liked. Without their passion, Blue Moon Bay wouldn't be half as magical. Come to think of it, maybe I should come out more often on a Thursday night to appreciate the awesomeness of my hometown. Lately I'd been spending so much time lying inert on my living room couch that I was starting to see its paisley pattern when I closed my eyes.

A camera's flash made me blink. David knelt ten feet away, snapping photo after photo of the fiddler and her dancers.

"Cake baker?" he called to me. "I was hoping you'd come out tonight."

I headed over to say hi, kidding myself that the little flutter in my heart was from nerves about my recon assignment. Not a reaction to his tight navy polo shirt that showed off his muscular arms and set off his blond hair.

"So, are these photos art for art's sake?" I asked, genuinely curious after our conversation at Ashlee's wedding. "Or is someone paying you to take them?"

"Neither, I'm just having fun." He dropped to a lunge to take another flurry of shots of the fiddler and her thralls. "Can't resist a sight like this. Call it hometown pride."

"No way, you did not grow up here." My voice was coming out flirty, high and teasing. "I would remember you from high school."

"Got a couple of years on you, cake baker." He winked and showed off his greying temples, the only physical sign that made me guess his age at mid-thirties, instead of twenties like me. "But yep, born and bred in the Bay. My family's lived in the area nearly a century. Blue Moon, True Moon, vic-to-ree!"

I laughed at David's spontaneous, off-key chant of our school fight song. "How funny that both our families have been local for so long and we never knew each other!" Gran would probably want me to dump Bryson immediately and get with David.

"I find that the Kensingtons have a way of bringing people together," he said. "As a matter of fact, my great-grandmother Maude worked for the Kensingtons as a kitchen maid."

"For real? That's so ... *Downton Abbey*!"

"You'd be amazed how many people in our little crew have a similar family history."

"Hold on, you're saying you *all* had family members who worked for the Kensingtons, going back generations?" What were the odds?

He nodded gleefully. "Everyone but Marina. She's the only fresh blood. Things around here don't change as much as some people like to imagine."

"I sure hope not," I said. "I'm counting on Sage's Bakery sticking around for a few more generations."

David's look of sympathy made me wonder if I'd said too much, or if he was intuitive enough to have sensed my anxieties about the bakery. I felt drawn to him, there was no doubt about it, and I was probably being more open than usual.

More open than I should be with a guy who wasn't Bryson? Or was it okay for me to be friends with David, even if attraction was in the mix?

Before I could choose a direction, the fiddler wiped her brow and announced she was taking a break.

"That about does it for my spontaneous photo series," David said, smiling. "Come with me, cake baker. I'll escort you to our booth."

I beamed and headed toward the big table in the back where Landon the chef was presiding over what looked to be a rollicking good time. He was doing an impression of someone, chortling and wearing a baseball cap so it covered half his head. Marina the clothing designer was laughing herself silly, while Leeza, the senior member of the group, was trying valiantly not to crack a smile.

So much for Ashlee's gruesome death and the family crisis getting them down. It was party central over here.

Leeza saw me and waved, but as David guided me to a seat on the end—sadly not next to him—Britt sauntered over, a glass of rosé in her hand.

"On the house," she said, then more softly, "Good luck, Apple Butter."

What was it with her ilk and giving me horrible nicknames? I rolled my shoulders to shake it off, then pulled the Ziploc baggie in my purse that contained my secret weapon: triple-strength toffees.

"Everyone, I want you to help me test these new toffees we're going to be selling at the bakery. Please take as many as you want. I need feedback."

I was overjoyed when everyone at the table dug into them and praised them. Everyone but Leeza, who I couldn't help but notice had ordered a plain kale salad. Great, she would turn out to be a health nut.

Hopefully everyone else opening up would make her less guarded, too.

Should I ask them questions or just see where the conversation went naturally?

"Excuse me." Marina the emerging fashion designer tapped me on the shoulder. "You, never wear crewneck. Is bad neckline for you." She wrinkled her tiny nose.

I glanced down at my Sage's Bakery T-shirt. "Um, this is my work uniform."

"But a woman with your endowment in bosom must have neckline to show off girls, or else looking as if have no neck."

"Excuse me?" I placed my hand on my neck, partly just to make sure I still had one.

"Sorry if my point is not across, I am in America not long."

"No," I huffed, "your point is across."

She grabbed my hand and broke into a toothy smile. "I like you, Hazel. I want that you go shopping with me. I charge for my time as a personal shopper..." Ah, there we go. The pitch. "Very affordable, don't worry."

"Sorry, I don't think I can handle yet another makeover attempt." Mother and Bea had attempted to glamour me with Beige Magic many times, but the magical makeovers never held. My own Green Magic seemed to fight them off. "I can never seem to put together the looks like they do at the stores anyway."

Marina slid me a business card. "You change your mind, call or text." It was a really cute card, with a shiny, cartoon little black dress on it.

Landon put his arm around Marina. "You're making her feel pressured, baby. Blue Moon Bay is a casual town, normal people don't stress their neckline."

Marina pouted. "I am only trying to help Hazel go from small-town beauty to goddess."

"Well, geez, if you'd led with that line we'd be at the mall already," I said, inwardly awwing that the two youngest staff members appeared to be a couple. The sparring I'd noticed between them earlier was just banter.

Marina and Landon looked almost done with the hummus appetizer plate they were sharing and Leeza had heroically hacked through much of her kale when Britt bounced by with a pitcher of beer and a huge, bone-in ribeye steak. She set the plate at David's elbow and he dug right in. I had to admire a dude who didn't fear mixing sweet and savory.

I noticed Britt's hands were shaking a little as she poured. Was she hungry again? I wondered how often she had to eat but didn't want to ask more ignorant questions. Max had made it sound like researching vampires online would be easy, but so far my Google searches were all clogged up with Dracula movies and silly Halloween costumes.

"To closure," Leeza lifted her glass and everyone else followed suit, faces suddenly sobering. "To peace for the family."

"Here, here." David turned to me. "We joke around a lot, so it may not seem like we care. But we're all close to the family and feeling their pain right now."

"Of course," I said. "I'm sure I'm joining everywhere here in praying that Ashlee's killer is swiftly brought to justice."

The whole table burst into peals of laughter.

"You think that's what we wish for?" Marina said. "No, we all just want our beloved family to be out of the spotlight."

"Yeah, now that they've found that airhead's body, it's only a matter of time before the story goes national," Landon added, chewing several toffees at once. "It'll be a media frenzy, reporters kicking down the doors. One last f-you from that little gold digger."

Whoa. "You mean … none of you were fans of Ashlee?"

I knew I liked this crew for a reason.

Leeza put down her fork in her plate of untouched kale salad and tried to explain. "It's not that we didn't like her, exactly."

"Though, of course, we didn't," Marina cut in. "She was very terrible—"

"We're a bit concerned is all," Leeza clarified, fixing Marina with a "zip it" glare. "Concerned about negative press coverage. We were able to keep her disappearance quiet, but now with the body and especially the way it was found…" She trailed off and I did too, mentally, reliving the sight of Ashlee's splayed legs and feet sticking up inert from the top of that dumpster. The room spun a little, and I was glad Leeza didn't know I was one of the people present at the discovery. "Let's just say we're afraid the Kensington family cannot withstand too much media exposure."

"Really?" That surprised me since they were always in the papers, albeit normally in the lifestyle section. "Estelle always seems so gracious and composed."

"She is, but her husband isn't," David said, cheerfully unwrapping another toffee even as a platter of chicken wings was set at his elbow. In the next life, I want to be a six-foot-four guy so I can eat like a trash compacter. "If anyone interviewed Fred, they'd quickly see the guy's not in mourning. Personally, I think he's delighted that young woman is out of the picture."

"Mm-hmm!" Leeza shook her head and looked like she was grinding her teeth in addition to her kale salad, but my ears perked up. Who would be happier about Ashlee's demise than her murderer?

Hmm, was the wrong Kensington on the suspect list?

"I wouldn't say he's delighted," Leeza said as soon as her mouth wasn't full.

"You mean you wouldn't say it in public," David said, grabbing his fourth toffee. "But Hazel isn't public, really. She's one of us."

Leeza still looked a little panicked but at least she didn't attempt to shut him up again. Just sat there with her mouth in a flat line of disapproval while David went on, and I tried to ignore the warm fuzzy feeling I got from his saying I was one of him.

I mean one of them. Man, I needed to check this crush.

"Fred Kensington always believed in prenups," David continued. "I heard he even made Estelle sign one all those years ago. But Drew? He let Ashlee talk him out of it, meaning she could divorce him and take half his fortune. Fred must have been livid."

That stunned me. "But he seemed so happy at the wedding."

"And I'm sure he was happy," Leeza said smoothly.

No one backed her up. The table was silent.

With a shrug of abandon, she reached for a toffee, unwrapped it, and chewed aggressively. *Score!* "But also, when you're in the public eye like they are," she continued, mouth full of candy, "you learn to put on a game face. But they're a family like any other, with conflicts."

"Wow, I had no idea Drew had problems getting along with his parents." I'd never sniffed the slightest amount of drama around the Kensington family.

"Not his mother." David unwrapped yet another toffee. He was turning out to be a goldmine of information. "She's as warm and caring a soul as can be. The problem is always with Fred. Let's just say he's the kind of person who would kick a little dog," he added.

I blinked. "Fred Kensington kicked Sammy Boy?"

Leeza looked pained. "By accident. I think. I hope." She paused. "Actually, I don't remember if it was Sammy Boy or the one before, Snowball."

"Oh, yeah, Snowball." David laughed. "Almost forgot about him."

"How does a dog lover stay married to a man who kicked her dog?" I wondered.

"How?" Landon laughed. "They're rich, that's how. It's easy. In such a huge mansion they're able to lead separate lives. They don't drive each other crazy."

"But if they're already living separate lives," I began. "Then—"

"Why not get divorced?" Landon anticipated my question. "Pretty sure those two old farts would rather die than split up!"

"Because of their strong family values?"

The whole table laughed again.

"Good one, Hazel," Landon said, tapping me on the shoulder playfully. "Keeping the family's wealth and influence consolidated is their family value."

Interesting. If someone would rather be dead than divorced … wouldn't they *much* rather their estranged spouse be the one to die?

"So, uh, does Drew agree with his parents?" I asked, trying to sound conversational and light. "About divorce being the worst possible outcome?"

"No." Marina smiled, and I remembered how much she looked up to her boss. "He is modern man. If something is not working, he will be honest and move on. Even the way he grieves Ashlee now is modern. Using work and solitude as meditation. No outdated, phony rituals."

"He's been skipping all the family memorial events and hiding in his rooms," Landon translated. "Whatever his reasons are, it's a bad look."

Oof, I couldn't help but agree.

"I almost forgot." Leeza snapped her fingers. "Hazel, would you have any availability to cater pastries and desserts for a small family gathering next weekend? It's not Ashlee's official memorial, it's more of a somber event afterward where close friends will be showing support."

"Sure, I can do that." Perfect. I could put ramble juice serum in *all* the food.

"Excellent, hope you'll be bringing your A Game." Leeza smiled at me, but her expression looked subtly harder. "My suggestion is to serve your rosemary pie for dessert." Her tone was still friendly, but a shade more clipped and professional than before. "Landon does a killer cherry ice cream that would go fabulously. Your apple butter, pulled pork, and blue cheese sliders would be perfect as appetizers. Especially if you could please do a Hawaiian taro bread instead of your usual potato rolls? Fred's crazy about Hawaiian stuff."

Uh…ok. "I must say, you sure know a lot about our bakery's menu." Especially for someone who's never been a customer.

"Oh, Estelle loves Sage's Bakery. And it's my job to learn all about the things she loves." Leeza stabbed another forkful of kale, stared it down, then pushed away her plate of salad like she was tired of pretending it was food. "I'll email you the details, and we'll provide transportation."

Driving home, I reflected that we had absolutely no connection to Hawaii and I had no burning desire to master baking taro bread.

And the rosemary pie already had cherries in it, for Pete's sake. So cherry ice cream was overkill.

More to the point, there was a little piece of me that just didn't like someone else meddling with my own recipes, dictating to me how to change them.

Was that why the bakery was failing? I had a giant chip on my shoulder?

Geez, I hoped that wasn't it.

But maybe that stubborn little piece of me didn't care. Didn't think it was worth it to keep the bakery open if it meant changing everything about us and baking on someone else's terms.

Who knew what the future would bring? But I was glad that for the moment, I wasn't answering to anyone but Gran.

She may be a curmudgeonly old witch, but I was realizing anew how lucky I was to have her as my boss. Considering the other options.

CHAPTER THIRTEEN

FRIDAY MORNING, FOR the first time in months, I rose before my four a.m. alarm began to bleat. Instead of groaning and hitting snooze, I bounded out of bed in the dark and belted out 80s ballads in the shower along with the radio.

I was early to work.

Today was it. The big day: I was giving away free scones at the bakery all morning.

Special free scones.

It was, I thought, while I caramelized yet another batch of peach slices in cinnamon butter at dawn, the perfect illustration of how nothing in life was truly free. Of course, I was hoping to get something in return—information that could help Bryson.

And Kade.

I was still rooting for Kade to be innocent. But man, he sure did look fifty shades of suspicious. I'd been too tired last night after meeting with The Help to try that Dreamland Visitor spell, so I'd have to do it tonight. Luckily, Max had plucked a stray auburn hair off his jacket when she hugged him and delivered it to me in a baggie.

As for Gran, I'd told her I expected it to be a slow day and encouraged her to sleep in. Obviously, I didn't want her to know what I was up to in terms of magically truth seruming the population and asking questions about a dead woman. But also, I didn't want her to be crushed if it was a bust and no one showed up.

If that happened, my own disappointment would be bad enough.

I mixed the dry ingredients, then squirted a cup of simple syrup into a saucepan, measured out dried herbs from the labeled mason jars on the high shelf, and quietly stirred the serum as it heated.

"With this small treat, I bid thee speak,
Freely as long as the potion lasts.
All facts expose, all secrets leak.
How bittersweet, the spell truth casts."

At seven a.m., I turned over our sign to OPEN, and made myself a pot of green tea. We had nine dozen scones, all baked golden brown, crunchy sugar topped, with generous chunks of peach in every bite. They were bee-you-ti-ful, if I did say so myself.

Oddly, I wasn't nearly as tired as I'd expected to be. Maybe I was running on adrenaline lately.

The first people to walk in were a pair of white-haired ladies, trusty regulars, who'd scootered over from the old folks' home at the south end of Ocean Street.

"Did you two, uh, hear anything about Ashlee Kensington?" I asked once they'd started munching.

"What?" asked the first woman, her mouth full of scone.

"She's talking about the murdered gal," yelled the second.

"Oh that," said the first and tsked. "I say it's a scandal to have such a thing happen in our town. A girl getting murdered."

"I know, it's terrible." I leaned in. "Do you have idea who might have—"

"I only pray it doesn't hurt tourism," the same lady interrupted. "What, she couldn't have got herself murdered over in Cannon Beach? Florence? Astoria? Had to be here, of all places?"

"Now why do you gotta go blaming the victim?" The second woman shook her head. "You got internalized misogyny, Helen."

"Well, you're full of yourself, Margaret. And you put on airs and use big words nobody understands, including you."

There was a beat. I recognized it as that silent moment of transition, when the potion wore off.

"Weeeell…" Margaret looked around, as if trying to get her bearings. "These scones are delicious, Sage. Or no, that's not Sage." She chuckled at her mistake. "It's her kid."

"Grandkid!" Helen corrected her. "That's Hannah, you silly."

"Hazel." I smiled. They were kind of adorable.

"That's right, Hazel." Margaret rose with effort from her chair. "Mighty fine scones, miss, worth the trip."

"Bye, Helen and Margaret!" I called as they scooted out, happy to have finally learned their names.

The same scene repeated itself with minor variations through the morning.

All told, nearly a hundred people came in. Ate a free scone. Engaged in unfiltered, politically incorrect, and sometimes bawdy conversation. And each shrugged off the potion and shuffled off in turn, leaving me none the wiser about Ashlee's murder.

Maybe because, duh, none of the people likely to walk in today were among the suspects:

Jenna loathed sugar, and me (when she remembered me at all).

Kade was busy working for the competition. Plus, he was a shifter so the magic would be wasted on him.

Drew Kensington would never set foot in my bakery; he was probably waking up right now in his mansion, stretching, ringing the breakfast bell, and having Marina deliver a tray with six eggs cooked by Landon.

Then there was his father Fred, my personal pick for murderer as of last night's conversation. Fred sounded like such a nasty human being that it made perfect sense he'd be the killer. On the other hand, he had to be aware that a scandalous murder would lead to the media frenzy his family sought to avoid? Maybe, being so wealthy, he'd hired a hit man to do his dirty work … and the hit man hadn't done a proper job of disposing of the body?

Guilty or not, there was no chance Fred Kensington would be hauling his billionaire butt into my store, on the promise of a free scone (they were normally $3).

I really hadn't thought this through. No wonder it was a dismal failure.

But I'd still had a lot of fun talking to customers. For a while the place was hopping, and plenty of people did buy coffee drinks and other pastries. That was something, right?

Around lunchtime, we had a surprise visitor. Bryson. I ran around the counter to hug him.

He squeezed me tight. "How are you holding up, Haze?"

"I'm surprisingly okay," I said. "We had lots of people come in today, so maybe that cheered me up. And you?"

"Good, good overall…" His face went grim around the eyes. "Except that I've been officially told by Sheriff Gantry not to leave town."

My heart skipped a beat. "It's okay," I said, though it was terrifying, in fact. "Just a formality, I'm sure. We'll get through it, and anyway, they'll find the killer soon."

Or I will.

"I like your energy today, very positive." Bryson kissed my head. "How about I come by at seven with Indian food? We can search for a new comedy on Netflix."

"Can't, I'm meeting the girls tonight at the Barrel." It was an emergency meeting called by Max in a midmorning text.

He gave me an odd look. "You're having a girls' night out ... you?"

"Yes, I have friends, thank you very much." Did Max and Britt qualify as friends? It had been long enough since I had real friends that I wasn't sure. But it was starting to feel that way, in moments at least.

Bryson shook his head in wonder. "You're surprising me lately. I thought after the stress of these last few days, you'd be more likely to ditch me for a nice hot bath with a book." How well he understood me. "But it's cool, you're keeping me on my toes." He turned to leave, then spun back around. "Oh, before I go, I wanted to ask. What are you doing for Thanksgiving?"

"Uh, usually my sister Bea hosts or my parents do ... why?"

"What would you think about us hosting this year?"

Gulp. He wanted to meet my family? "I don't know." I reached for a handy excuse. "My place is so tiny."

"Yeah, means it wouldn't take long to clean. I'd even help," he added. "I really want to get to know everyone."

He left, after I promised to think about it.

Five minutes later, Gran finally poofed into work, well-rested and in a devil-may-care mood. "What a morning I had," she bragged. "Did the crossword puzzle, made myself an omelet, watched two soaps. What'd I miss here, the usual crickets?"

I hid my smile behind my teacup. "Nah, we had quite a few people come in. Some interesting conversations."

"That's my girl, positive attitude." She clinked cups with me.

"Hello?" A stocky tween girl with nervous doe eyes and long hair in a messy ponytail was standing mere inches from the counter. She'd tiptoed in without my noticing her. "I know it's after twelve."

She held up a printed version of the coupon Max had designed for the blog. "But are you still giving out free scones?"

"Free scones?" Gran narrowed her eyes at me. "Samples, surely. Not full-size!"

"You gotta go big to get people's attention nowadays, Gran." I tried to sound confident. "All the marketing books say so."

"Marketing schmarketing. Seems like a lot of money wasted." Shaking her head, she shuffled to the back to check on inventory.

I squinted at the girl, mentally clocking her age at about ten. I couldn't see myself questioning a child about a homicide. "Would you like a free chocolate cupcake instead?" I asked.

"No, thank you." She looked down shyly. "I've never had a scone before, and I want to know what they taste like."

Dang it, we didn't have any other scones today but the dosed ones.

I definitely wasn't going to bring up Ashlee, though. If she wanted to ramble about cute boys or horses, I'd listen.

"My mom's best friend got murdered," the kid blurted out moments after she wolfed down the pastry. "They found her body in a trash can. It's all I can think about. What if someone else gets killed, like me or my mom?"

"Oh, sweetheart, that's not going to happen," I said, wanting to give her a hug then and there. Wait, her mom's best friend? "What's your name?"

"Sophie. Sophie Jeffries."

Holy smokes. So this shy, polite kid was Jenna's daughter?

Now that I was looking at her closely, they had the same exact shade of brown hair.

I crossed the counter and sat with Sophie at her table. "Sophie, are you talking to anyone about your fears?"

Sophie shrugged. "Don't really have anyone to talk to. I'm not that popular, you'll be shocked to hear."

Her deadpan delivery was a thing to behold. Oh, this kid was going to melt my heart. "That's okay, I wasn't either at your age. What about talking to the school counselor?"

Sophie pushed away her empty plate. She'd gobbled the treat—sugar was probably outlawed at home. "Mom said not to."

"She did?" Was Jenna one of those tough-love parents who thought counseling was coddling?

"Yeah, but I think it's just because of Drew."

Those words gave me chills.

"Because he's Mom's friend," Sophie went on, "and he helps her with money, but Ashlee wanted him to stop. Mom wouldn't want me to tell a counselor about that stuff."

I hesitated. Sophie wasn't a regular here and she didn't look especially relaxed or comfortable. So, I knew I didn't have much more time before the scone's power gave out. I could ask her more questions, but it seemed awful to ask a child to incriminate her own parent.

"Sophie," I said instead, "I want you to talk to the counselor anyway, but don't talk about your mom, okay? Just talk about you and how you're feeling. You deserve to feel better, not scared and lonely."

Sofie blinked and looked around, disoriented. "That was yummy. And it was nice talking to you … I think."

"Come back and talk anytime. There might be even more free scones in it for you."

"...And it was like talking to my own younger self," I told Britt and Max that night at the Barrel, wiping away a tear. "Sorry, allergies." Not really.

"Can't you magic away your allergies?" Max asked innocently.

"Mine vanished when I got turned." Britt paused. "It's a good thing, since I cry blood tears now. The stains are a real witch to get out."

"You guys are missing the point of my story, and why is it okay for *you* to say 'witch' like that?"

We were lounging around the back booth, having a drink. Britt, just finished with her shift, was wearing her Drunken Barrel T-shirt with a blue miniskirt that probably scored her mad tips.

Britt's stomach growled. "All right, time for you to tell us why you called this meeting. I'm feeling a little peckish, gonna need to grab that waiter soon and shove him into the manager's office to bite his neck."

I cringed. "Not the super young waiter."

"Thomas isn't as young as he looks." Britt folded her arms defensively. "Domestic animal shifters tend to have youthful looks. He's some kind of terrier, and he's about twenty-five. Not fifteen like you're thinking."

I *was* thinking that.

Max looked stunned. "That kid is a dog?"

"You can't tell, Max-y?" Britt clearly found that amusing. "I can smell a shifter a mile away."

"Funny, I can smell a dead bloodsucking monster a mile away," Max said.

To my surprise Britt laughed. "You know what? I can't. Vampires have no radar for other vampires."

Max cracked a smile. "Guess we really do need each other, Brittany."

"Yeah, for now," Britt agreed. "But once this case is closed, we can go back to being mortal en—"

"So, why *did* you call the meeting?" I asked Max, anxious to speed the conversation in a less ominous direction.

Max fidgeted in her seat, looking nervous for once. "I need to tell you something. Both of you, but especially Hazel."

That cranked up my anxiety. "Why especially me?"

"Hold on, there's some backstory." She pushed her glasses higher on her nose and I sensed her professorial vibe coming on. "See, every shifter family has an animal totem, a spirit of that animal that's watching over their family. Most shifters can *only* turn into their family's animal. Kade and me, we're pretty sure we were born to parents with two different animal totems, which is taboo. It's probably the reason we got dropped off in the woods as babies."

"You were left in the woods?" My mouth dropped open.

I'd always known Max and her brother were adopted, but I'd never connected it to them being shifters. Her parents, the Dwecks, were normal people. A healthy, wholesome couple who grew cherries and plums on their organic farm and ran the local farmer's market. They always seemed bewildered as to how they'd ended up with kids as odd as Max and Kade. When Max turned eighteen and changed her name to de Klaw—she'd done some digging and discovered it was a family name—her mom was crushed.

I'd never paused to consider Max's side of the story. No one had fully been able to prepare her for what she was. The first time she shifted, it must have been the most frightening thing in the world.

No wonder she worried about Kade—she felt responsible for protecting him. They were all each other had.

"Okay, cool, what's your other animal?" Britt was clearly not as interested in the details of Max's emotional past as I was.

Max grinned. "Guess."

From her boastful tone, I figured whatever animal she could turn into was pretty powerful. "A grizzly bear? A great white shark? Dire wolf? Velociraptor? Phoenix?"

"Nope, way better than any of those. Common housefly."

"Ew." I recoiled as one of those tried to land on our plate of fries.

"Is that Kade?" Britt joked.

"Better not be," Max said. "He's not supposed to go flying—that's what we call it—without checking in with me first. We came up with that system together after the last time he got out of jail. He's too tempted by the stuff he sees when he goes exploring on the wing."

"Whoa." Finally, I got it. "That's how Kade became a thief. He never had to break into places, he'd just fly through open windows. And that's also how he got out of the car at Ashlee's wedding when I could have sworn someone was in there."

"It's nice to know," Britt said cheerfully, "that if I ever do need to kill you, I can just use a fly swatter."

Max rolled her eyes. "Better not miss, or I'll fly into your mouth and shift back inside your throat."

"Can you two please try and *act* human?"

Max turned to me. "So, here's the thing. Last night, I went flying. And … I ended up flying into Bryson's apartment."

"Because you got lost?" I leaned into my denial.

"No. To spy on him."

"*What?*" Confusion fought with betrayal inside me. Betrayal won. I turned to Britt. "Never mind, swat her to death."

"Sorry." Max didn't sound a bit sorry. "It was driving me crazy how suspicious he acts. Lying about knowing Ashlee. Acting like the perfect guy, but you always seem tired and depressed after you've been with him."

"What are you talking about? I'm content and … settled."

"More like settle-ing," Max muttered. "He's hot but he's boring. When you talk about your dates it sounds like all you do is binge TV shows."

"We also kiss. And eat takeout."

"Oh, girl." Britt looked me up and down. "Your life sounds *sad*."

"To each her own," I snapped. "Anyway, you had no right to do that, Max. Especially when Kade's the suspicious one," I added, looking away guiltily since I was about to do something similar if not worse. I'd already baked the dream cookies and was planning to spy on her brother's dreams, this very night.

"Listen, I know it was wrong. But you're lucky I did it, because I learned something crazy about good ol' boring Bryson."

Britt rubbed her hands together. "Oooh, I love me a good crazy boyfriend story."

"Do you two mind? You're talking about the person I'm in love with."

"But *is* he a person?" Max said. "Because Bryson—get ready for it—does not sleep. At least not in a normal, human way."

"Dun, dun, dun," Britt intoned.

"Oh please." I shrugged. "He probably got really involved in a video game."

"No, Hazel, he wasn't looking at screens. He was standing up, in the dark, in one corner of his studio apartment, all night. Sweet waterfront unit, by the way. Do you know what he pays for that? Is there an HOA fee?"

I gave her a look.

"Fine, I'll move on. The point is, he was like a robot powering down. He was breathing really slow, too. Yoga teacher slow."

"That is odd," I admitted, unsure how to the creepy picture she painted to my sweet Bryson. "Maybe he sleeps standing up?" I'd seen a documentary where monks trained themselves to do exactly that, to help with meditation. I could even see that being his thing. "Were his eyes closed?"

"I'll admit my fly vision never quite adjusted to the darkness, so I couldn't tell for sure."

"Not to be rude, but how can you be sure of anything you saw with a fly's eyes?" Sure, what she was describing sounded odd, but it was all highly speculative. I mean, she was talking about what she'd "seen" as a criminal housefly. "Maybe your fly brain recall isn't as reliable as you think?"

"Or your fiancé isn't as human as *you* think."

Britt spoke up. "That *is* weird sleep behavior. We need to investigate him further. And I'm sorry but you need to be on board with that, Hazel, or—or you're out of the group."

My mouth dropped open. "How dare you? I'm a founding member, going all the way back to last week."

Max looked contrite. "The bloodsucking cheerleader is right, though. I'm scared you might be dating someone who's capable of murder. Or at least really weird stuff. Bad-weird."

"Okay, ladies, here's an idea," Britt said, standing with a glance at her watch. "And then I really do need to go bite that waiter. You suspect Maxy's delinquent brother, you suspect Hazel's boring man—"

"Hey," I protested.

"So, investigate both of them, as a team. No more secrets. No more suspicion. Just get it all out in the open and hopefully they're both cleared and Bryson just has a weird sleep disorder." She looked from me to Max. "Deal?"

I sighed. Well, fair was fair. "But only if Max promises no more breaking and entering."

"Flying and entering," she corrected me. "And if I don't do it, how else are we going to gain information?"

I snapped my fingers like I'd just suddenly thought of something. "How about a dream spell? We want to know what's in their hearts, not their apartment. So why not go right into their dreams and take a look around their psyche?"

"Wow," Max said flatly.

"You can really do that?" Britt said.

This was more like it. Respect for my witch magic; I drank it in.

"Yeah, and remember I only just thought of this spell idea now, on the fly," I lied. "Get it? On the fly?"

Ok, but they *had* looked impressed with me there, for a moment.

"Hey, bro!" Max swung into the Java Kitty lot and yelled out the car window just as Kade was about to hop into his POS truck.

He turned, eyes flashing orange in the moonlight. "What's up?"

The parking lot reeked of Grey Magic, as always. At the sight of its dumpsters, I shuddered from recent bad memories. How this place was open after being the scene of a murder only a day earlier was beyond me. Guess Gantry had to have his usual double latte.

"My friend Hazel wants to talk to you for a minute."

A minute, I thought, would be about all I could stand.

"Talk about what?" Kade looked nervous, almost like he was about to bolt. He must have just gone off-shift.

I hopped out of the car and presented the dream cookie I'd baked that day. "Would you mind trying this cookie and letting me know what you think? It's a … new recipe."

"Oh, sure." He looked relieved. "I thought my sister sent you to talk to me about the Ashlee stuff." Kade took the half of the cookie I offered and bit into it. His pupils dilated, then his hazel eyes flashed orange. "Wow, it's amazing. Like a chocolate cloud with vanilla rain inside…"

"…that drums softly on your rooftop as you sleep," I finished, having taken a rapturous bite of my half.

Kade sighed happily. "Sage's Bakery makes the best cookies. The best everything." He stuffed the rest of the cookie in his mouth and nodded to himself. "Mmmm." Without the defiant perma-smirk, his face looked startlingly different. I wondered how much of his bad boy attitude was just self-protection. "The baked goods here show up on a truck," he confided, looking troubled at the thought. "And the coffee is made by machines. It's like a factory, but Sage's—"

"Is like a museum," I filled in bitterly. "No, a crypt."

Kade started to say something, then stopped and looked embarrassed. I felt bad for having dropped that much resentment on him. But it hurt, to be constantly hearing about how great we were while fearing for our future daily.

"Um, to be honest?" He lowered his voice. "I have no idea why everyone is here instead of there. The white mochas are okay, that's the one recipe Elton brought with him from Palo Alto. But I'd never choose to be here if they weren't paying me."

"Really?" I remembered how the ramble juice hadn't worked on Max. Was it possible that Grey Magic didn't work on shifters either? "So, Elton's from Palo Alto, as in Silicon Valley?" That was a bit odd, that someone from all the way down in California would come here to open a store.

"Yeah, told me he pitched his idea for 'the perfect modern café' to a ton of VCs back in the valley and got laughed out of town. But then the weirdest thing happened. Some company up here heard about it and not only offered funding and assistance, but insisted he open up shop in downtown Blue Moon Bay, Oregon."

"Really." That struck me as odd as heck. "What company?"

He gave a hell-if-I-know shrug.

"Does the company ever send over consultants?" Someone had to be performing the Grey Magic I could smell even now. "A businesswoman in a grey pantsuit, maybe, and every time she visits, business is booming afterward?"

Kade shook his head. "Nah, doesn't ring a bell. But really, business is always booming here. You'd think it would make Elton happy, but he's always crying these days, the poor guy. Maybe the place is secretly driving him nuts … it sure drives me nuts."

That made three of us. "I'm sorry you have to work there," I said, realizing it couldn't be easy for a guy with Kade's background to find gainful employment.

"It's okay." Kade flashed a stoical smile that looked more like a grimace. "But that said, I'd rather work for Sage's, if you were hiring."

So that's what Max's original phone call had been about. She'd been asking if there might be a holiday part-time job for Kade. I bit my lip.

"I notice you guys have your tea game dialed in," he added, looking thoughtful. I was surprised to see that underneath the swagger and attitude, Kade was a lot like Max. Observant. Curious. Kinda geeky. "But it's clear you've never thought much about coffee. I've been reading about what it takes to start a roastery and Sage's would be the perfect venue for it. You've got enough room to showcase some of the roasting equipment, makes customers feel like they're part of the process."

That was an intriguing notion. Shoot, maybe it was just my old crush on him rearing its head… "I'll let you know if things pick up."

"Really? Thanks."

Max tossed me a grateful look from the car, but by the time I fastened my belt in her passenger seat for the short ride to the bakery, I was already regretting my words.

Even if Kade turned out not to be a murderer, he was still a thief. Sure, he might be attractive and get our younger female demographic to show up, but could I risk my family's bakery on a known criminal?

Oh well, no need to feel guilty for saying I'd call if things picked up.

Things were never going to pick up.

Not when some big, rich company was about to stomp us out of existence like ants underfoot. Geez, of all the bad luck. Our bakery had to be the established coffee shop in the very town that this company was determined to install its their "perfect café." But why had they picked our town in the first place?

Unless … said big company had it in for us, specifically? Now I was getting paranoid, like Jenna.

Grateful for the distraction of the dream spell project, I ushered Max into the darkened bakery kitchen. Flipped on the florescent light, hung up my coat, lit all four stove burners. And with a snap of my fingers, a large cauldron appeared on the stovetop, full of boiling water. I added my herbs and murmured the spell words I made up spontaneously:

"Kade seems cool, but is he up to his old tricks?
Man, fly, or bobcat, what makes him tick?
We're going to find out how he gets his kicks,
Sandwoman 306, once known as Nyx, gimme the fix."

"That's seriously what you do, make up a dumb little rap?"

I turned, startled. I'd almost forgotten Max was in the room. "For a new spell or a unique one, I do come up with my own rhyming incantations, yeah," I said, realizing it made me feel kinda vulnerable to be doing magic in front of a nonwitch. "Most spells use a standard script, though, and some have pretty old-sounding language. It's kinda fun to vary it."

"Fun," she repeated, shaking her head. "Dang, your witch stuff is so … tame."

She wasn't exactly easing the situation with her smirking commentary.

"We keep our clothes on, if that's what you mean by tame."

Max's laugh dislodged the tension, as she seemed to acknowledge the dig on shifters. "Well, that's just sensible, working around these bubbling cauldrons."

"Speaking of cauldrons." I grabbed her hand and interlaced our fingers. "This is only going to burn for a second or two. Or so I'm told."

"You've got to be kid—*ahhhhh!*"

The dreamscape opened in a forest.

I recognized Corvid Woods Park. Fall leaves formed a colorful patchwork on the slushy, muddy ground. The ground was so far below me, most of what I could see was the canopy. I felt a sense of youthfulness, wistfulness, all across the landscape. Was Kade a daredevil child, climbing a tree?

And what was I in his dream?

I tried to move my hands in front of my face so I could see what I looked like. A feathery grey wing appeared in its place.

"What the hex?" I blurted out, but it came out as "Hoot! Hoot!"

I was an owl.

Next to me on the branch was another owl, who had apparently just realized what she was.

Max made excited owl sounds and flew madly in circles around our branch. She was really getting into this. I tried to tell her we needed to focus on Kade; this was his dream, we were only observers. Unfortunately, being an owl, all I could communicate was "Hoot! Hoot!"

But luckily, being an owl, I had excellent vision and hearing.

On the ground under my tree, a tall, red-haired boy was playing, kicking a soccer ball up against the thick trunk of a three-hundred-foot pine tree. He looked around twelve or thirteen, his expression wondering, full lower lip stuck out the way Max's was when she was deep in thought. I could feel his curiosity about the world, and also his contentedness. Then shadows began to lengthen.

The forest was abruptly darkened as the sun began to set rapidly, replaced by the rising of a huge full moon.

The boy cried out in terror and began bursting out of his clothes, his skin changing into spotted fur. From my owl perch, I held my breath in silent sympathy. The change looked so painful and shocking. Within seconds he had grown a stubby, furry tail. His face was the last to change into a bobcat's short muzzle. His screams became piercing caterwauls.

Something scurried by us in the forest, a small, furry something.

The boy, now a bobcat, went crazy for it. He dived after the furry thing, a pale white snowshoe hare, and began to chase it.

Oh man. I'd paid enough attention in biology class to know what would likely happen next … predation … and I didn't want to watch. I was firmly the type who covered my eyes during the scary parts of movies. What was I supposed to do now, flap my wings and fly toward that moon? Was it even possible for a dream figure to escape its dreamer?

The big bunny dove behind a bush and bobcat-Kade dove after it, letting out a growl.

Please let him wake up before he catches it, I prayed.

I averted my eyes to the tree bark, expecting to hear horrible tearing sounds, but all I heard was a human yell.

I looked down to see Kade, no longer a boy nor a bobcat, but in his normal adult form, standing in front of an unmoving woman's body. Her long blond hair splayed out. Her fuzzy white boots and yoga pants displaying her long slender legs.

Ashlee Stone, who else?

"No," yelled Kade. "No, please don't be dead. Please don't be dead. I didn't mean to hurt you. I didn't know!"

What did he mean he didn't know?

Suddenly the other owl, Max, was circling around him. Hooting at him, trying to get his attention—what was she doing? She was supposed to be observing, letting it unfold. Not interfering. Not trying to get him to stop saying incriminating things in front of me.

Kade ignored the bird and went on berating himself, pleading with Ashlee's body. "Please don't be dead. Please don't be dead. If you're dead, then it's my fault. Then I don't deserve to live."

The Max-owl landed on his head and began pulling his hair, making him yell. A second later we were back in the bakery. The cauldron was bubbling over.

I snapped my fingers to make it vanish. "What the hex were you doing?"

She huffed. "I knew you wouldn't understand."

"That you were trying to get Kade to stop saying incriminating things in front of me?"

"No, I was trying to comfort him!"

"What, by flying around threatening to poke his eyes out?"

"It's not easy to be comforting when you're a bird! Avian states are inherently creepy, who can relate to a tiny flapping dinosaur?" She sighed and grabbed her coat off the hook. "Look, I could try to explain. But you can't possibly understand what people like Kade and I go through growing up. The guilt and confusion we feel. About what we are."

"You think I, a witch, wouldn't understand that?" Not only a witch but a lone Green Witch born into a sea of Beigeness.

"Hazel, I'm not trying to put down your magic. What you do is truly amazing, even with the terrible poetry." She shuddered. "But imagine how I felt when suddenly around age thirteen, I started to sleepwalk ... and wake up in the middle of the forest. As a bobcat. And yeah, plenty of times I'd already killed and eaten smaller animals before my consciousness awoke inside the bobcat. It's not a smooth operation, at first. You lose time. I used to go to bed praying I wouldn't wake up in the woods staring at a dead hiker. Which would have been super unlikely," she added. "Bobcats fear and avoid humans. We're not a menace."

I shook my head. "But you just told me that shifters miss time. And attack while they're 'unconscious.'"

In other words, Kade could be guilty and not even know it.

"No, no, no. Only during the first changes. Not now. He's a grown man. All this dream proves is that my brother was traumatized by his experiences growing up."

The high school version of me, the people-pleasing part, desperately wanted to shut up and nod along. Be agreeable. But a new part of me had been born over the last week or so, and that part cared about clues. Evidence. Facts. That part of me wouldn't let it go. "That's b.s., Max . This dream clearly points to Kade's feeling panicked and guilty. About something to do with Ashlee."

I thought she would argue with me, but her green eyes flashed orange and filled with tears. "I thought he'd come clean, that his big secret was he flirted with my high school bully! He knew how much I hated her, especially after Grad Night. And now he's—"

"Grad Night?" I cut in. "What did Ashlee do on Grad Night?"

"Nothing!" Max bit her lip. "And who cares? She's dead. What matters now is that Kade's still holding out on me. How can I protect him when I don't know the truth?" She shook her head and, without bothering to wipe her eyes, turned to walk out.

"Max." I touched her arm, and she whirled back around. "Yes, he's probably been keeping something from you. But I also think, unlike me and my sisters, you two are honestly close. There's a lot of love between you. If you talk to him, he might tell you the truth."

She squeezed her eyes shut, but when opened them, her gaze was resolute. "I'll talk to him, in the morning. And tomorrow night, same drill," she added, reaching out to poke my upper arm, "but with your fiancé's mind."

"Great." I tried not to groan out loud. Kade's internal landscape had been more intense than I'd expected. Sneaking into a person's head, I now realized, was a way bigger deal than entering their apartment.

Part of me was getting worried about what we might find in Bryson's psyche. Not that he was a murderer, but, well, something might be up with him. I could excuse the sleeping standing up thing as a quirk. As for Max saying I always seemed "tired and depressed" after seeing him, that was perplexing. I had to wonder if she wasn't projecting her own problems with past boyfriends onto me. But then there was the fact that Gran had never made a wrong call. What if Bryson was a perfectly great guy, yet still not right for me and she knew it?

I told the worried part of myself to shut up and press on. Whatever the truth turned out to be, with my friends at my side, I could handle it.

CHAPTER FOURTEEN

THE HARDEST THING about giving Bryson the dream cookie was lying to him. Sure, I was technically lying to him all the time by not sharing the fact that I was a witch. But this was the first time I was going to *do* magic on him.

Was it ethical?

On the other hand, if this was the only way to stay in the supernatural detective club with Britt and Max, and work to clear him of all suspicion, then it was unethical not to. Right?

We were having another stay-in date—I know, I know, but at least this time we'd switched it up and gone to his place instead of mine. Bryson's waterfront studio had a postcard view of the sunset over the water, but we rarely went up to his place because my couch was comfier. Which showed you that we had the right values as a couple.

The gas fireplace in front of the couch looked new and snazzy, but its gleaming mantel was bare. No paintings on the walls. Bryson hadn't added a lot of personal touches yet, I noticed. Even the built-in wall shelf over the mantel contained no books, just the last week's junk mail. Typical guy, he sucked at decorating. Oh well, after we got married he'd probably move into my place. Though tiny, it was still bigger than his.

Bryson paused after his first bite of dream cookie, as if he couldn't believe what he was tasting. "This … is this…?"

I beamed with pride. "Like having faeries gently brush your hair for hours, then snuggling into a soft bed, surrounded by kittens?"

He didn't answer, his face far away as if deep in thought as he chewed. But when he finally looked up all he said was, "I'm impressed, Haze. You're a damn good baker."

Hardly the poetry of Kade's response, but Bryson didn't have to be a poet, I reminded myself. He was a stand-up guy.

There must be a solid explanation for why he also slept standing up.

I ate my half of the dream cookie, savoring each bite, and we settled onto Bryson's pullout futon where he casually threw his arm around me. At his warm touch, I started to feel relaxed, despite the incredibly stressful week we'd both had.

It was my idea to meet up at his place for a change, so he could give me a guided tour of his family photo album. I figured it was past time I got to know his folks, even if only through photos. Since he was about to meet mine in the flesh come Thanksgiving.

Cindra would be away in London for the holiday, but my parents and Bea had agreed to come over. They hadn't sounded especially enthused, but then again, my house didn't have a double oven, soda machine, giant sectional sofa, big screen TV, or video game system like Bea's did. Nor was my home's decor glamour-updated monthly to match the latest trends.

As soon as Bryson and I began to pore over his old family photo album together, I found myself surprised by how … intimate … this felt. Our heads leaning close as he played the entertaining tour guide, wittily captioning photos as the pages turned. Bryson as a baby. His siblings sledding in the snow, rosy cheeks and happy grins. His parents' laughing faces as they posed next to a huge Thanksgiving turkey that dominated their cozy kitchen. Then a photo of Bryson himself, chilling in a recent selfie.

At the back of the book were some older photos of his grandparents and even great grandparents, giving me the chance to gawk at the funky fashions of the 1940s and 50s.

Finally, we came to a tiny old black and white daguerreotype photo that had to be from the early 1800s. Even though the man wore Victorian dress and a formal, old fashioned expression on his unsmiling face, I could still the resemblance to Bryson.

"Oh, hey, you found Archie. This photo's one of my most prized possessions."

"Who is that guy?"

"Just another ancestor." He grinned and flipped over the yellowed photo. "He even fought in the American Revolutionary War when he was a teenager. You'll get a kick out of this story."

"I'm already getting a kick out of his hipster 'stache."

"I know, right? Even funnier is the legend about him. People back then were so backward and superstitious, they believed in magic." He shook his head at the quaint notion. "And supernatural beings of all types."

"Wow." I tried to keep my face blank.

"These idiots actually thought my ancestor was some kind of demon."

A chill ran down my spine. "Archie was a demon? Is what people said?" I added quickly.

Bryson shook his head ruefully. "Can you imagine? He was actually sentenced to death for some ridiculous crime that was obviously not real. Because there's no such thing as the supernatural, of course."

"What a crazy, crazy story," I said, hoping he couldn't hear my heart pounding.

Demons weren't actually evil, I reminded myself. But as beings from an alternate dimension, they were different enough from humans (including witches) that they often did things we would think of as evil. Interaction with such beings functioned best as an interdimensional partnership. With demons staying mainly in their own realms and we humans staying in ours.

Archibald Emory Smythe hadn't stayed in his realm, and so Bryson had a demon in his family tree. That … could explain a lot.

"Hazel, I didn't realize hearing Archie's story would unsettle you." Bryson squeezed my arm reassuringly. "Don't worry, legend has it he escaped from prison and was never seen again." *Poofed back into his own dimension, likely,* I thought. "But he left behind plenty of descendants—like me!"

Demon's spawn, Gran's voice echoed in my head.

"That story didn't unsettle me at all, Bryson," I said. "In fact, I think it just makes you even more interesting."

"Oh good." He smiled. "Those really were some hella good cookies. You got any more of those laying around? I liked the texture."

"And that must be why he has such weird sleep habits," I explained to Britt and Max, who were sipping chardonnay and eating chips around the bakery's corner booth at midnight the same night. "If he's related to a Sandman demon, maybe he's better at resting than a regular human, which is why he can do it standing up. Maybe his people don't need beds." Come to think of it, his demon heritage could also explain why he was so relaxed and relaxing to be around.

"Sounds creepy, yet basically harmless," Britt pronounced. She'd fed on a cute bar customer earlier and was feeling chipper.

"Or, is he harmless but basically creepy?" Max picked up the bottle to pour herself a second glass. "I'm reserving judgment till we see his dream." Her slumped posture and scowl told me she was not in the greatest of moods. Kade hadn't shown up at work today, nor was he answering her texts. I had to wonder if he'd seen the writing on the wall and skipped town.

"Speaking of creepy things." Max frowned at Britt. "Do *you* still sleep like Hazel and I do? Now that you've been turned?"

Britt smirked. "I sleep like the dead."

"So, sleep is when you're most vulnerable to attack. Noted."

"In your rabid kitty dreams."

"All right, let's just go to Bryson's dream." My hands were sweating from the anxiety, and I really wanted to get this over with.

Though I knew Bryson was innocent, it was still scary to go deep into a person's head like that. Even the most balanced people, I reasoned, had jagged places in their hearts. Beautiful but dangerous edges that it might hurt to crash into.

Also, lifting sandy hairs from his brush and bagging them, last time I was over at his apartment, made my soul feel dirty.

"Ugh, must we do this?" Britt made a face as she grabbed a final handful of chips. "His dream's probably going to be super dull, like eating oatmeal while watching golf ... sorry, Hazel."

"Investigating him and Kade equally was your plan, Britt," I protested.

"I know, but thinking about it more, your Bryson's too boring to be a killer."

"Don't be idiotic, Brittany," Max said sharply.

"Thank you," I said.

"Some of the world's most notorious killers were boring S.O.B.s," Max went on.

I sighed and downed my wine.

Five minutes later, we plunged our stacked hands into the cauldron and let out a three-part harmony of a scream. Max was alto, I was mezzo, and Britt soprano, in case you're wondering.

Sunlight. Brightest sunlight. The morning sky in Bryson's dream was three shades lighter than the sea, whose lapping waves died out gently on the sand right in front of us. The scent of fresh baked goods permeated the air, drowning out the salt and surf I knew we should be smelling.

Because the setting of this dream was as familiar to me as my own body. We were on the public beach, just blocks from downtown Ocean Street, watching a huge wedding procession approach.

It was Bryson's wedding, and he looked as serenely sexy as ever walking with his veiled bride to where the surf lapped at their bare feet. As the preacher droned on, Bryson beamed down at his bride.

It was me, right?

Wasn't it?

Frantically I tried to see if I could recognize my own family and friends in the crowd of guests, who unfortunately had their backs to me, but it was hard to concentrate because a Flamin' Hot Cheeto had fallen on the sand.

With a squawk, I reached out to nab it … I was a seagull? Ugh.

Did this particular Sandman have a real fixation with birds or what?

I heard a squawk and two other seagulls appeared, each ready to fight me and each other for the spicy snack. Max and Britt, I presumed.

As the ceremony concluded, Bryson gently lifted the bride's veil … and I gasped with joy (and some relief) to see my own face.

Yes, it was me, and I looked exactly as I do on any given morning or late at night. No makeup. Messy hair covering one eye. But I was grinning beatifically.

So was Bryson.

"I do!" he declared, and the guests roared with approval. While I'd been messing around with Cheetos, our crowd had magically grown to include the entire town. "I love you, Haze, and I am never going to leave you. We're in this to the bitter end, baby. You and me versus the world."

A seagull squawked with joy as Bryson kissed my—well, that Hazel's—lips, and out of the cloudless sky, pink cupcakes began to rain down. The crowd erupted into cheers.

"You guys, he really loves me." Back at the bakery counter, I dabbed away a tear and grinned victoriously. "Woo! I am *loved.* No need to investigate further, this guy is never going to leave me."

Max and Britt exchanged an amused look.

"Told you it would be boring," Britt said.

"Mm, okay, guess we can downgrade him as a suspect." Max scrunched her shoulders and made a "whatever" face, like she didn't take being wrong personally. She paused. "It's a relief to know for sure that he does sleep. Let's start ramping up the effort on Drew and Jenna. After what Jenna's kid, Sophie, said, they're sounding like the strongest leads we've got."

"And don't forget Fred Kensington, who kicks little doggies," I said. After meeting Sophie, I really wanted it to be Fred, not Sophie's mom. "Ya know, I'm glad this went well," I added, "but I must say I'm sick of you two calling my fiancé boring. Not every guy has to be brooding and intense. I dare you to come to my house for Thanksgiving next week and actually get to know Bryson."

Max's eyes widened. "Oh, Brittany, you cannot say no to this. Trust me, she is the hostess who does the mostest. Cooking is to die for … like, you'll die *again.*"

"Sounds tempting, but will there be anything for me to drink?"

I paused, catching her drift. "If you must, my brother-in-law is fair game. I've always found him annoying."

I brushed away the tiniest concern that hanging out with a vampire and a shifter might be nibbling away at my humanity.

The important thing was Bryson loved me, all the way down to his unconscious mind.

Sunday was normally my day off, but I was catering the Kensington's family support dinner tonight, so I had plenty of baking to do.

I pulled on my stompiest, witchiest boots and barged into the bakery's kitchen, where Gran was stirring batter for chocolate caramel mini-waffles.

"I figured it out, Gran. The real reason you hate my boyfriend." I held out my phone, the screen showing the pic I'd snapped of Bryson's prized antique photo. "It's his demonic ancestry, isn't it? You must have sensed it in his aura."

She smiled wanly. "Of course, I did, Hazel dear. You would know too if you were anywhere near ready to take over the bakery. You can't read auras. You can't even teleport. Your magical training has a ways to go, my dear. And you don't seem committed to the task."

"Maybe so to all that ... but right now we're talking about Bryson. Who cares if he has an interdimensional ancestor? I did some research last night, and it turns out a lot of family trees have a demon in them somewhere."

She shrugged slightly and I rejoiced that I'd gotten her to acknowledge a point of logic. "Sure, when you go back a dozen generations. But your Bryson is a different story. His aura contains a pronounced demonic mark. Extremely pronounced. You ... you haven't started learning how to read auras, have you?" Her tone was hopeful.

"No," I admitted. "He was just showing me his family photo album and mentioned the story about his ancestor. Who was persecuted by the Puritans, by the way. Sound familiar?" Our own line had a few members who'd struggled with such issues. "If anything, our two families have more in common than not."

"Truth be told, it's not his family I'm worried about. It's him," Gran said, rubbing a stick of butter on the waffle iron. It sizzled and shone. "His courting you so quickly, combined with what I see in his aura … well, color me suspicious. He may be a perfectly upstanding demon or he may be up to no good. I don't want to take the chance with my favorite granddaughter."

I shook my head in disbelief. "I can't believe you're so prejudiced. He's the best thing that ever happened to me."

She poured dots of batter into the four mini-waffle slots and didn't respond.

"All I want is for you to give him a chance."

Gran snapped the mini-waffle's lid decisively. "And all I want," she said, looking me in the eyes, "is for you to marry a man who's not literally demonic."

I ignored that. "We're hosting Thanksgiving dinner this year." My heart was pounding. The stakes of Gran's approval felt so high. "Will you come, take the opportunity to get to know him?"

Her eyes darted to the right. "Maybe. I'll think about it."

YES!

"But only because I'm so tired of your sister's house. That grand staircase! Big pretentious entryway they call a 'foyer.' Who do they think they are, dukes and earls?"

Great. So, she would come over because my house wasn't as nice as Bea and Grant's place, therefore it irritated her less. That was slightly deflating.

But these days, I'd take my victories where I could get them.

CHAPTER FIFTEEN

I'M NOT A very princessy person.

Like most Green Witches, my hands are always busy, rolling out pie dough or pulling garden weeds.

Nevertheless, when the limo driven by Stephen, the Kensington family's chauffeur, swung by the bakery to pick me up at five, I felt just like Cinderella going to the ball.

And when the passenger side window rolled down and David called out, "Hop in, cake baker!" my heart soared like an eagle.

With Stephen's help, it didn't take long to load the trunk with my brand new Cambro insulated food carriers (a nervous investment in the hope of future catering gigs) filled with fresh pastries. Carefully, I smoothed down my white linen blouse, which I was wearing with navy wide-legged trousers and a matching wool cardigan, and sank into the sleekly curved, black leather couch seating.

I'd had a feeling my Sage's Bakery T-shirt wouldn't cut it for this event. Now that I was riding in a limo, sitting across from the hot photographer no less, I was extra glad I'd taken the time to look nice.

"Feel free to indulge in some treats." David leaned back and gestured to the lit tray compartment between us holding seltzer bottles and elegant snacks. "I always do. I love riding in cars."

"It sure beats driving," I agreed, thinking that must be what he meant. Then I realized "cars" had to be rich-people code for limos. I dimly recalled as much from watching old movies. "Jeeves, would you bring the car around?" Car equals limo. There, I was already picking up the lingo.

Biting into a fresh blackberry and cream cheese toast tip was heaven. So was the seltzer David poured for me into a crystal glass containing muddled mint leaves and orange slices. As we rolled through downtown, I half-closed my eyes and tried to imagine what it would feel like to be one of *those* people, the truly wealthy. But so much of that lifestyle was a mystery to me.

Including David's presence, not that I was complaining.

"Dumb question … what *does* a photographer do at a small, intimate family dinner?" I wondered aloud as our limo zipped up the hills into Blue Moon Heights.

"In this case, take some pictures of cute children," David said. "Estelle's young nieces—well, and Fred's —will be there, so I'm arranging a little shoot in the parlor. Marina sewed the girls ladybug costumes and hung giant felt flowers from the wall."

"Sounds adorable." I noticed he'd almost forgotten to add Fred's name, as if the old man were an afterthought. No wonder, if Fred was that unpleasant. "They're lucky you were available tonight."

"I kind of have to make myself available," David tore into a chocolate-covered strawberry, not meeting my eyes, as if the subject embarrassed him the tiniest bit. "The family has me on retainer."

"Seriously?" My eyes must have about bugged out. "They have their own photographer twenty-four seven?" Such wealth boggled my mind. "Do you … live at the house, too, like the assistants?"

"Ha … no." David laughed, but his suddenly stiff posture told me he was still uncomfortable with this subject. "Hey, I know being on retainer sounds weird, but it's pretty cool. Leeza calls me in whenever there's an event or holiday. I show up and snap a few photos, but I don't stay more than an hour or so."

"Just long enough to enjoy that free champagne, huh?" I teased.

That got a grin. "You know it."

I decided it was okay that I had a tiny, harmless crush on David. Yes, I was engaged ... but I still had a pulse. And it's not like our flirtation was going to go anywhere, even if I wanted it to. He was too gorgeous for me.

Mind you, Bryson was too, but God love him, he was head over heels committed to me. His wedding dream had proved it, though I still felt guilty for invading his privacy.

Stephan pulled the car down a long private road, through a black metal gate that parted automatically to let us in, and into a long, curved driveway.

A stunning and kingly house loomed into view. It was, to my surprise, a rather new construction done in the Northwest style of architecture. With deep overhanging eaves and huge, south-facing window walls that seemed to be rising straight out of the surrounding pine trees and majestic boulders. I blamed Hollywood for my disappointed expectations that the Kensington house would be some stately colonial-style mansion. Yet, though I hated to admit it, since Java Kitty Café had some similarities in its design, I quickly came around to seeing the building's clean, airy appeal. It was modern to a T.

Waiting for us at the roundabout was Leeza, who ushered me straight into the kitchen while David veered off to do his shoot in the parlor. I guessed since he was on retainer he didn't even have to carry his camera equipment with him.

While Landon busied himself prepping king salmon filets with a tarragon rub, his kitchen helper, a teenage girl named Daffodil, helped me arrange my sliders on the beautiful blown glass trays they'd selected for tonight's meal. I'd bet dollars to donuts the glassblower would be a local artist, too. Estelle Kensington—and her human extension, Leeza—left no detail unobserved.

Speaking of Leeza, she was still hovering. "Since it's your first job with us, Hazel, I'm going to lay out the guidelines we use here to ensure a successful catering experience." *Oh boy*, I thought. I hadn't expected her to be laid back, but dang, she was absolutely no-nonsense in her professional element. "Your restroom will be the one between the kitchen and the staff room. Under no circumstances will you use the guest powder room."

"Got it." Who cared about weird bathroom rules? Every morsel of food I'd prepared was dosed with ramble juice. I was excited and nervous to see what truths it would reveal.

"You may greet the family when you serve the dessert pies, they appreciate a personal touch," Leeza added. "But don't linger. You're welcome to rest your feet in the staff room till Stephen comes to drive you home. Are we clear?"

"Crystal," I murmured, thinking how was I supposed to see people's reactions to my ramble juice if I wasn't at the table? Grr, Leeza always seemed to be thwarting my attempts to pick up information.

Hmm, there was a thought.

Curious and suspicious that she was always getting in my way. It was almost enough to make me put her on the suspect list.

After rattling off a half-dozen more insulting "guidelines," she finally bounced out to help wrangle the kids in David's photo shoot.

Daffodil walked out to the dining room to serve cocktails and appetizers, and I was left with Landon, who'd finished seasoning his fish and was washing his hands.

I decided it was an excellent opportunity to gain some info from him while improving the dessert.

"Landon? I'm worried these cherry pies will be too 'one-note' in their flavor profile with cherry ice cream. Can you taste them and let me know what you think?" I put on my best damsel-in-need-of-a-man's-opinion face, with wide eyes and a hopeful expression.

Landon glanced up from the sink and fell right into my trap.

"Oh yeah, your palate's right," he said after the first bite. I let him shove the rest of the mini pie into his mouth. "So, I do have a pure, Madagascar vanilla bean ice—"

"Who do you think killed Ashlee?" I interrupted, knowing we had seconds till he was back on food.

Landon smiled a lazy smile. "I'm thrilled you asked for my opinion, Hazel, because I have a small crush on you."

Er … what? This was not what I expected him to say. People didn't just up and get crushes on me. I was the cake baker, the sidekick. On a good day.

"You're out of my league, though," he said, looking down shyly.

"I—er—about Ashlee," I stuttered.

Landon shrugged. "I don't really care who offed that stuck-up gold digger. I like a woman who works for a living. With her hands, not other parts, if you know what I mean."

"I'm sure I don't," I muttered, blushing.

"You're the real thing, Hazel. Wow, there's even a dusting of flour in your hair." Landon reached out to touch my hair. His meaty hand felt strong, rough, unwelcome.

I pulled back. "Stop it."

Landon seemed to remember where he was. "Oh geez, sorry, I don't know what got into me. Please don't tell Marina. She's been through so much lately already, with that crazy assistant of Ashlee's implying she was having an affair with Drew. She might think I believed it and was getting even, or something." He shook his head like a dog with water stuck in his ears, and I knew the potion was spent. "Vanilla," he cried out helplessly. To him it was probably the last thing we were talking about that made sense. "Let's go with vanilla ice cream for the pies."

"Perfect." I smiled up at him. "I knew you'd come up with a great solution."

Then, to spare us both even more awkwardness, I excused myself to use the restroom.

I stared in the bathroom mirror. Well, I'd done about all the sleuthing I could do in the kitchen—and what had I uncovered?

One: I wasn't the only one nursing a harmless (?) crush.

Two: Before she abruptly quit, Ashlee's assistant had accused Marina of something serious. Sleeping with Ashlee's then-fiancé Drew. Yet, when I saw her right after the assistant quit, she'd showed no signs of being skittish about marrying Drew. Had she not believed it, then? Or was she such an icy-veined gold digger that she didn't care? Or … what if the information had never gotten to Ashlee at all? Was it possible that the assistant had been intercepted and fired before she could tell her boss her suspicions? If you believed Drew, the Kensingtons had never fired anyone in a hundred years.

But I was no longer content to believe Drew, about anything.

I texted Max: At the Kensington's. Got a lead on Drew, possible affair with assistant Marina. Can't believe I'm saying this but … do you think you could "go flying" into his suite to check it out?

The response came instantly: Not a good time. Kade admitted to making fake IDs for Ashlee so she could leave Drew and start a new life. Driving him to a safe location to wait till the killer's found.

Holy goodness. So that's what those papers were in Max's car. And now Max was helping Kade skip town? Things were getting real.

And Britt was at work, not that a vampire's help would do me much good at the moment. I was definitely on my own here at Kensington Manor.

That's when it occurred to me that the little bag of invisibility mints was still in my purse. I could do some spying myself.

Max would be so proud.

I chewed a mint and watched in wonder as my mirror image poofed. Like sunsets and recreationally popping Bubble Wrap, some witch tricks never got old.

Opening the door a crack at first, I made sure the hallway was clear and then tiptoed right into the parlor where David's photo shoot was in full swing.

The kids—three bouncy preschoolers—were indeed cute in their ladybug costumes. David seemed to be having fun photographing them while Leeza looked as driven as ever in her role as his assistant, making silly faces at the children and running in to wipe faces and brush hair. What was her deal, was she just a consummate pro, or was she guarding some big family secret?

I tiptoed into the dining room. The family was gathered at the table, praying in front of the spread.

"Loving God," Estelle's rich voice intoned. "Please cherish dear Ashlee's soul, heal our son's wounded heart, and restore peace to our grieving home."

Beautiful prayer, but I was a little surprised she was the one leading it and not Fred, the man of the house. Were the Kensingtons more progressive than I thought?

"Amen," everyone murmured. Except for Fred, who was busy casting flirty looks in Daffodil's direction as she served him a romaine, blue cheese, tart cherry, and walnut salad. To my horror, he escalated to making kissy faces at the girl—right in front of his own wife, who was snuffing out the prayer candle. Everyone else pretended not to see what Fred was doing. Daffodil looked like a deer in headlights. I wondered if she'd be quitting soon.

Man, that guy was as lower than a snake's belly.

I was relieved to see that Sammy Boy wasn't in the room. Now that I knew Fred was a dog kicker, I felt protective of Estelle's pup.

Suddenly, I realized Drew wasn't in the room either. Wasn't present at a dinner in honor of his dead wife. "Wounded heart" indeed. Where the heck was he, out partying at some nightclub?

His was definitely the first room I'd check for clues.

The house had its own lift, whose doors probably opened right into people's bedroom suites, in an Ordinal person's attempt to be as cool as witches with our dematerialization spells. I saw a uniformed housemaid heading into the lift and tiptoed in after her as quickly as I could, squeezing myself all the way to the edge of the elevator car to avoid bumping into her cleaning cart. She got off on the third floor and pushed the cart into a glam-looking sitting area, complete with a wet bar heavy in its whiskey selections.

Seriously, there were so many potted trees and hanging strings of lights and metallic accents up in here that it looked like a trendy outdoor bistro.

I had to tail the housemaid really close so I wouldn't get stuck in the elevator heading down again. Luckily she knew her business and walked with purpose right up to a closed door.

I knew I'd struck gold when I heard her knock and call out, "Mr. Drew?"

"You can come in, Elsa." It was Marina. "He is out … I was just, ahhh … organizing all of his … things."

Yikes, she sounded nervous. She really wasn't a good liar. Suddenly suspicious that Ashlee's assistant had been right, I pushed into the bedroom after the maid as soon as she'd unlocked the door with a key from her giant ring.

Elsa began to make up the bed, and Marina ducked into the bathroom.

I followed, very nearly getting swatted by the closing door.

Whoa. I was thinking I would have to be super careful where I stood, but this bathroom was the size of my whole house, no kidding.

I lurked at one end of the long sweeping vanity counter. There was a separate door for the toilet, and a big-screen TV on the wall so you could watch from the enormous round tub filled with bubbles.

I looked away as Marina disrobed, flinging her clothes onto the heated floor, and settled into the tub with a sigh of pleasure.

The door to the toilet area opened and Drew Kensington walked out in a tan silk bathrobe, one hand behind his back. "You ready for this, Marina?"

"Always." She smiled like someone who was about to unwrap a present. A big one.

This was not looking good.

For Landon, at least. For me and my investigation, things were heating up as nicely as the steaming tub Marina was luxuriating in.

"Close your eyes and open your mouth," Drew said.

Oh, geez, what was I in for now? I'd have to beg Britt to wipe my mind, assuming her compulsion powers extended that far.

But when Marina obeyed, Drew popped a tiny chocolate into her mouth. "Good old sativa, guaranteed to pump up creativity," he said with a smile.

So, he'd just offered her a pot edible? Those were legal in Oregon, though Blue Moon Bay didn't have its own shop. If they did, our bakery might be doing better what with all the people suffering from munchies.

"Mmm, thanks, boss."

"Well, enjoy your me-time in the big tub." Drew pointed to the side of the tub where a whiteboard sat with dry-erase pens. "I know you always have your best design ideas in here. Investing in employees' strengths is one of the core values of Kensington Industries."

Me-time? Your best ideas? Now I was totally confused. Drew was just pampering his assistant by offering her the spa-like experience of his bathtub? To enhance her creativity?

"You're the best boss ever."

I had to agree with that assessment.

He shrugged off her compliment. "Hey, you're the best assistant ever. Oh, by the way, did you file those reports from—"

"Yep."

"Cool, thanks."

There was zero sexual tension between these two. None whatsoever.

The maid knocked loudly. "Marina?"

"Come back in an hour please, Elsa," Marina called. "I'm organizing … bathroom … things."

Man, I could really see how a rumor could get started that they were having an affair. Elsa muttered loudly to herself as the cart rolled away.

"Coast is clear now." Drew ducked his head affably. "Time for me to go back to hiding from another awkward dinner event, where all the guests are staring at me to see if they think I'm capable of murder. Why does my mother insist on these outdated mourning rituals?"

Marina made a cluck of sympathy as he headed for the door behind her.

I'd just jumped out of his path when Drew turned abruptly and lunged at Marina from behind.

I saw his fangs come out just before he clamped them down on her pale neck. He covered her mouth to stifle her cry of pain and took a long drink. Too long.

Stop it, I thought, realizing I was holding my own breath. If he went on much longer she'd be missing too much blood.

Marina slumped a little, and I was about to scream just to make it all end—though doing so could make my life end—when he breathed out a sigh. Didn't sound like pleasure exactly. Just relief. He must have been super hungry.

What was happening to this town? Was I the only person from high school who wasn't a freakin' vampire now?

He took his fangs from her neck and licked the wound to heal it. "You okay?" he said, as if suddenly remembering she was a human being and not just a can of blood soda. The guy didn't seem to know what he was doing. My respect for Britt went up just watching him.

Britt. She'd fed from Ashlee and Jenna around the time of the wedding, and they'd both had weird reactions to her bite. Because, I now realized, they'd already just been bitten by Drew. The two vampires couldn't sense each other, so they'd unknowingly fed off the same people and caused them to overdose on happy vampire chemicals.

Marina giggled and murmured some words in Russian. Her face looked goofy, like Jenna's had. "That is some potent chocolate you give me, boss."

Drew grinned lazily. "Hey, you should get something sweet out of the deal … I mean…" He retracted his fangs. "Because you're missing out on pie and ice cream."

Crap! Pie and ice cream. It must be almost time for me to serve dessert. I snuck out of the bathroom behind Drew and barely made it out of the bedroom (which Elsa rather pointedly left open) before he closed it.

"So lovely to see you again." Estelle gifted me with a queenly smile when I presented her a cherry mini pie. Topped with vanilla bean ice cream as nature intended.

Her eyes fluttered in near-ecstatic anticipation as she picked up her fork. But before she could load up her first bite, Sammy Boy snatched the whole pie slice off the plate and popped into his little mouth.

"No!" I cried out.

Unflappable as always, Estelle delicately dabbed at her pup's mouth with a white linen napkin. The whole table laughed—not at me, exactly, but I still felt flustered.

If Estelle's dog ate the "ramble juice" dosed pie, I might not gain any info from her. Oh well, I was more interested in what secrets Fred had to leak.

"Please accept my sympathies on Ashlee's passing," I said, hoping it would serve as a prompt to get people to talk about Ashlee.

Fred laughed. "Who?"

Estelle's face was tight, and I had to pick my own jaw up off the floor. I'd expected him to say something crass, but "Who"? Like she didn't even matter? Cold as ice.

Except his tone of voice wasn't cold at all. It was confused. Innocent.

My mind balked at the mismatch between what I was hearing and what I believed about Fred. Was it possible, just possible, Fred didn't remember who Ashlee was?

While I was floundering and considering my next move, Sammy Boy reached out and snapped up a pie that Daffodil was about to set on a guest's plate.

"He can't resist your pies, can uuuuuu, baybeeeee?" Estelle gazed indulgently at her pup, then turned back to address me in her adult voice. "But never mind this silly boy, I'm so delighted to see you at the house, Hazel. Please give my regards to your grandmother."

"I will, thank you, ma'am."

She paused. "How is the bakery doing? Forgive me for intruding if this is a delicate subject, but are you faring all right these days what with the current economic climate?"

"Climate?" I echoed weakly. "You mean the vast economic desert?"

She tsked in sympathy. "That new upstart, Javanese Kitten or whatever they call themselves. Your product is in every way superior. But, alas, in this day and age it seems gimmickry often wins out over craft."

"Alas," I said sadly. "But don't worry, we'll be okay."

She nodded politely.

I squeezed my lips into a forced smile and turned away as quickly as I could. Ouch. It wasn't just that she didn't think our bakery was going to make it. She talked as if it was a forgone conclusion that we were toast.

And I was beginning to fear she might be right.

I decided to cool my jets in the staff room and see if I could pick eavesdrop on any conversations. Landon and Daffodil were there, talking about their respective day-off plans. The atmosphere was chill and congenial, like how I remembered the Thursday beer night. Working here wouldn't be that bad, I thought, if the bakery did go belly up. Then, I was horrified at myself for even contemplating such a thing.

"Out of curiosity, who cooks on Wednesdays when you're out?" I asked Landon.

He grinned. "The Kensingtons order in from Chef Wu's downtown. Yes, rich people get takeout. It's a thing. As a chef who trained for six years, I try not to weep into my *foie gras*."

"Fascinating." I'd much rather eat Chinese food, too. Something else occurred to me, though. "If you're a trained chef, why didn't you make the pastries for this event?"

He wrinkled his nose. "Baking's not my bag. Don't get me wrong, Hazel, I would never denigrate your craft."

I didn't *feel* denigrated. Till he said that. "I was just wondering, who normally bakes around here?"

"Well, it was Velma, David's great aunt, but she passed away a year ago and we've been trying different people out ever since. None have worked out so far."

"So, whose idea was it to try me, yours?" If he had a crush on me, it stood to reason.

"No, no, this came from straight from the top."

"You mean Fred and Estelle?"

Landon gave a wan smile. "Well, not so much Fred."

"The poor guy!" Daffodil's lips curved down sadly. She turned to Landon, blushing. "Sorry."

"Leeza's not in here," Landon reassured her. "We don't have to pretend."

My heart sped up as the realization hit me. The way they were talking about Fred. "He's sick, isn't he?"

"Leeza thinks all hell will break loose," Landon went on, "and it'll be in the papers if we so much as say it out loud but come on. Fred's not the same man he was, and it's messed up that they all try to hide it from the world."

Whoa.

I paused, mentally reinterpreting every action I'd seen Fred take. He hadn't remembered who Ashlee was. He'd flirted with a very, very young woman. He may have even kicked a dog. What if what drove all those actions wasn't nastiness but merely the confusion and frustration of … living with dementia?

If it was true, I needed proof.

And I had a feeling I'd find it in Fred and Estelle's bedroom suite. When my great grandma had dementia, we had to cover all the mirrors, because she freaked out when she couldn't recognize herself. If Fred was really suffering from Alzheimer's or the like, there were sure to be clues in his part of the house.

"Back in a bit," I said, rising to my feet. "Uh, bathroom."

"Really, again?" Landon sounded a little worried about me. "I hope you don't have food poisoning."

I chewed the invisibility mint and tiptoed up the empty staircase.

Through the window wall behind the stairs, a moving shape outside caught my eye when I was nearly to the fourth floor. Sammy Boy was running around in the courtyard, his cute little mouth hanging open in a pant. Estelle must have let him out for a poop. Adorable.

Though I didn't see Leeza waiting outside with a baggie, so maybe he was just out for a quick burst of exercise. The fourth floor, unlike the third, opened up into not one but two landings that functioned as large sitting areas. One on either side of the stairs, divided by a black corner wall.

The first one I ventured into was decorated with elk antlers and tartan plaid upholstery and other over-the-top masculine motifs, as if this part of the house mistakenly believed it was a log cabin. This had to be Fred's space.

And his suite was full of everything I'd expect from a dementia patient.

Tons of bright lighting in the sitting room that looked like they'd been added recently. Covered mirrors in the bathroom. Drawers and cupboards were labeled with the contents. Most tellingly of all, his bedroom locked from the outside. Proving that he couldn't be trusted to safely navigate his own house alone.

No amount of money, sadly, can shield you from growing old and sick.

The only good news for Fred was that he'd been scratched off my suspect list. If he couldn't leave his bedroom unsupervised, it was unlikely he'd masterminded a murder.

Which shifted my suspicion right back to his son. Drew didn't seem like a bad guy, really, but he also sure didn't seem too broken up over his wife's violent death. He also didn't seem to take an abundance of caution when it came to safely biting his employee, Marina. Then again, he was clearly a very young vampire and just learning how to survive—he probably didn't have the energy to focus on much except quenching his hunger. Especially with his main blood doll gone.

Hmm. Was it possible Drew had miscalculated the last time he fed from Ashlee, and accidentally killed her by taking too much blood?

After watching him with Marina, it seemed very possible indeed.

I paused at the top of the stairs to check out the second fourth floor sitting area, mostly out of curiosity about the décor. To my delight, the furniture in here was as big and bold as a 1980s hairstyle. *Dynasty* and *Lifestyles of the Rich and Famous* came to mind. The elegant powder room was done in polished black, with a spideresque crystal chandelier that covered the whole ceiling. Then came a hallway with a locked door. The keyhole was modern but stylized, with a heart-shaped lock pad, the aperture just large enough to let one steal a peek inside.

That had to be the door to Estelle's bedroom.

I hesitated.

Sure, I'd snooped in Drew and Fred's bedrooms, but Estelle felt different. I respected her. Plus, I had no practical reason to enter the woman's inner sanctum. The only thing I suspected her of was possibly helping to cover for her son, going on the theory that he'd accidentally drained Ashlee during a routine biting. She seemed like a good mom, and I could see her doing something that was wrong if it was to protect her son. Not to mention her family's reputation.

But honestly? The retro fancy decor in here was so cool I kinda *had* to check it out, just from a gawker's perspective.

Through the keyhole, I could make out a luxurious bed with cream-colored satin sheets. But I didn't have time to speculate about their thread count or astronomical cost. Because there was a man lying on that bed.

It was a naked man, and the naked man was definitely David.

CHAPTER SIXTEEN

MONDAY MORNING, I felt like I had a hangover from trying to process all the crazy things I'd heard and seen in the Kensington home the evening before.

Unfortunately, Gran wasn't on board with making it easy for me to get through the day. I'd barely handed her her morning cup of Earl Grey when she began pestering me about Bryson's wacky demon DNA.

As if it mattered. I wanted to tell her that compared to the Kensingtons, Bryson and I would be the most average, drama-free, picket fence couple that ever lived in Blue Moon Bay.

The woman was driving me so batty that I forgot to pick up an oven mitt and stupidly grabbed for a hot tray, searing my fingertips and scattering a batch of tahini-pepita-chocolate-chip cookies on the kitchen floor. I'd been so pleased with myself for trying a new, experimental recipe using trendy ingredients, since going all in on our "homegrown, traditional" branding ones wasn't exactly yielding great results.

Sucking on my poor burned thumb, I trudged to the supply closet to fetch the broom and mop.

Gran hadn't even noticed my accident. "And another thing," she called from the till, where distressingly absolutely no one was waiting in line to buy anything. "Have you considered the effects of marrying a demon, on your magical legacy?"

A demon? "Come on, Gran." So, she'd escalated her insults; calling him demon's spawn was no longer enough. "At least you can grant that he's human, more or less."

"Is he, though?"

"One ancestor—"

"One that you know of," she corrected with a shake of her head. "As I was saying, when a witch marries a demon, their offspring may well turn up with demonic magic running through their veins instead of witch magic. That means you'd have no apprentice at the bakery. No magical heir."

I threw up my hands. "And why is that, Gran? Do demons make bitter-tasting cookies or something?"

"Oh, Hazel dear, you can be so naive at times. Demons don't bake. Demons don't cook at all, though they may claim they '*love* to cook' and own a kitchen full of fancy gadgets. That's one of the standard ways you can test to see if a man is actually a demon. They foist all the cooking onto others."

"That's ridiculous." Though, all of a sudden, I remembered the Sandman demon telling me she'd email me the cookie recipe. Would it have killed her to bake the stupid things herself? Then I thought about Bryson's glibly offering my house up for Thanksgiving. Surely he'd help me cook, though … wouldn't he? "What are the other standard ways?" I asked, fearing I'd regret it.

"Well, there's the tongue test. They can glamor the rest of their form to look human, but the tongue never lies."

I swallowed. "Do I want to know what that means?"

"Only if you care about your future children being indistinguishable from iguanas." She let out a wild chortle that made me honestly wonder if she was on the same path to senility as Fred Kensington.

Learning that Fred wasn't the monster I'd thought he was—let's face it, hoped he was—had shifted my suspicions to his vampire son. The sight of Marina's head slumping over in the bathtub would stick with me forever, as would Drew's lazy, fanged grin after he fed off her. He clearly wasn't grieving his dead bride. Had he even loved her to begin with or simply used compulsion to win her over, just so he'd have a dedicated blood doll? And maybe some arm candy too to make him seem more distinguished in a business setting?

The only trouble was, though I could easily see Drew's motives for marrying someone like Ashlee, I couldn't understand his motives for killing her. It had to have been an accident. A careless overenthusiasm in feeding.

The savage way Drew had chomped Marina's neck disturbed me. But seeing David's hot, naked body in Estelle's private suite had messed with me, too.

The two of them being involved had me reeling with shock. Not just because she was so much older (ok, that was part of it). Or even because she was his employer (though that was shady, too).

No, it was the fact that I'd been observing them, investigating them, and still I'd had no idea of their affair till yesterday.

They were sneaky, I'd give them that much. I'd never even seen them interact. Sneaky cheaters who lied about one thing could easily lie about another too, right?

And yet, knowing what I did bout Estelle's husband—that he wasn't really himself anymore—was it fair of me to judge her so harshly for giving in to temptation? Especially since there could well be other stuff in her life causing her extreme stress lately. For instance, her own son was a vampire. And possibly a blood doll killer. Did she know either or both of these things?

And if she didn't, how badly would it break her heart to find out?

The more I thought about it, she would have to be aware of everything going on in her house at all times to be able to hide her affair with David so smoothly. She had to know about Drew's fangs, and any messes he made while feeding. But how far would she go to clean up those messes?

I was in the midst of gloomily sweeping up a mess of my own—the expensive, ruined cookies—into the dustpan when the bell rang to announce a new customer.

In his crisp tan uniform with gun holstered, Deputy Elliot James walked into my bakery for the first time.

At the sight of his undeniably hot profile, all our other patrons looked up with interest. Not surprising, since they were: an older women's book club, two out-of-towners from Seattle, and a young mother with sticky toddlers in tow. Elliot was sexy in that "strong, silent type" way that so many women were still into, despite the recent liberation of men to be chatty monsters.

But what was particularly interesting about Elliot at this moment was how out of place he looked. Surrounded by puffy, round pastries and my rustic pink flower arrangements only made him look more angular. More stark. More serious.

"Deputy James?" Gran smiled. "I don't suppose I can interest you in a butterscotch blondie?"

Elliot's stoic face betrayed a moment of pain. "No, thank you, ma'am."

Figured. His stomach probably lived a monk's life, just protein-packed salads and water with fizzy electrolyte tablets.

His next words didn't surprise me either, though they did make my palms sweat. "Ma'am, I'd like to speak with your granddaughter for a moment."

Gran's smile faded. "Oh, I see. Go on and take your break early, Hazel."

My clammy hands now turning to ice from nerves, I led Elliot into the kitchen and closed the door to the bakery dining room.

His nostrils twitched. "What's that in the oven?"

"Almond-cherry sage muffins."

"Smells really good, wow," he said, almost despite himself.

"Thanks, I dreamed up that recipe last spring. It was a special for our seventy-fifth anniversary." I tried to give him a friendly smile but couldn't manage small talk over my anxiety. "Any updates? About Ashlee's case?"

"If there are, they'd be classified." The sudden harshness to his tone surprised me. "I came by to warn you. You and your friends need to stop sniffing around the case."

I snorted. "Nice impression of a grouchy, small-town sheriff. Practicing for your next role, once you oust Gantry?"

Elliot crossed his sinewy arms across his tan uniform shirt and spoke quietly. "I'm not playing, Hazel."

My heartbeat sped up. What the hex? Also, how did he even know we were sniffing? "Elliot, you can't tell us what to do. It's a free country."

"Yeah, it's free because there are laws. Against interfering with police procedure, for example."

His tone was neutral to cool, not what I was used to from our casual, joking pleasantries. We'd known each other over a decade, but this had to be our longest adult conversation. It was also the first one that you might call *adversarial.*

And I wasn't finding it to be very pleasant.

"Look, your amateur sleuth thing was harmless at first," he added, in a more conciliatory tone. "But now you're getting in my way. So, you're done. Got it?"

My heart was thumping angrily. "Amateur sleuth"? "Harmless"? He was making us sound like idiots. In a bad way.

"Oh, we are far from done," I huffed. "We've turned up a ton of new info. Which I *might* be willing to share if you could stop being so—"

"Ashlee Kensington's case is a matter for law enforcement," Elliot cut in, his dark eyes meeting mine directly. "Not you. And definitely not Maxine."

Hold the phone, did this mean Deputy James was no longer sweet on Max?

Oddly, this flustered me more than anything else he'd said. How could Elliot simply abandon his record-length, unrequited, hopeless crush?

Was nothing sacred?

"Erm, has something changed in how you feel about Max?"

"What?" Elliot narrowed his eyes. The question appeared to throw him off. "No? I mean, what's changed is, I can't trust her with intel. Not if she's going to use it to run a parallel investigation that interferes with mine."

"Well, I wouldn't say Max is exactly *running* it, we're all pretty equal ... wait a minute." It was the second time he'd said that. "How's she interfering?"

He gave me a look.

Of course. Kade.

With all my focus on the Kensingtons, I'd almost forgotten about how he'd admitted to Max that he made Ashlee a fake ID. And how she'd then spirited him out of town, which Elliot clearly hadn't loved.

"But ... you don't really think Kade is the killer." They'd been close friends in high school. Elliot and I were both always over at the de Klaw twins' house. But their paths had diverged sharply since then.

"Of course not but running doesn't make him look innocent." Elliot's gaze hardened and he gave me a significant glare. "Just in case you had any ideas about pulling the same stunt with Goodman. I recommend against it."

My temper, which I sometimes went months without hearing boo from, flashed again. How dare he threaten me, in my own kitchen? Did he not realize this was my place of power?

"Don't go confusing me with Max, *Deputy*. I'm the one with a fireplace mantel displaying all my Good Citizen trophies."

"You're also displaying his ring." From the hard way he set his jaw, I wondered if he secretly agreed with his boss that Bryson and I got engaged too fast. But Elliot didn't seem the type to meddle in other folks' business like Gantry. Perhaps he just didn't think highly of marriage as an institution. To be honest, I'd never had much of a clear idea about what went on in Elliot James's head. He was so reserved, it made him inscrutable. Maybe that's why I always found myself curious about his life. Something told me he was full of interesting surprises.

Except today, when his surprises were just annoying.

"Well, it was great talking to you, Hazel." Elliot was already standing in the doorway. "Stay away from my case, and you'll be fine. Your muffins are done."

"Aaah!" I'd been so engrossed in our battle of wits, I hadn't even heard the oven beep. I ran to get my oven mitts. We weren't operating at such a cushy margin I could afford to ruin a second batch of baked goods.

After he'd slipped out the back door—wise choice, given his adoring female fans in the dining room—I angrily devoured a butterscotch blondie, washing it down with honey-vanilla tea. Then I scarfed another, for good measure.

Elliot had assumed I would fold on his orders because I was gentle, anxious, sweet Hazel Greenwood. But that was the old me.

Actually, the new me was still all those things. Especially anxious. But she was also determined. There was one more suspect I needed to investigate further, much as I dreaded trying to stuff a sinfully delicious dream cookie into her mouth.

That suspect was Jenna Jeffries.

Drew and *Marina* were not having an affair, but Drew and Jenna might well be. They had history. They had chemistry. I had reason to think Drew was habitually snacking on her veins. Plus, Sophie said Drew was giving her money, and Ash had wanted it to stop. That, to me, suggested a relationship.

Problem was, I didn't want Jenna to be guilty now that I knew she had a sweet ten-year-old daughter.

But I'd gotten too far into this truth-discovering business to abandon a lead, even one that made me uncomfortable.

I pulled up the group text I had going with Britt and Max: Ladies, ready to get in hot water together? Tonight, we do the dream spell on Jenna.

No response came. Britt, being a vampire, might have been still snoozing. Max was probably working on her computer, earbuds in.

After another moment passed without comment from either of them, I couldn't stop myself from adding: Get it, hot water? Because of how the cauldron is boiling and bubbling? <witch emoji>

A response posted back from Britt: Woof, do all the living have such a basic sense of humor?

Max: Nah, it's just humans specifically.

Me: See you midnight, you supernatural snobs. <side-eye emoji>

That night, I was waiting in front of the boiling cauldron with Max when Britt zoomed in, looking dejected.

"Welp, I tried, girls," she said with finality. "I went to Swole Jim's Gym and chatted Jenna up, no dice. She absolutely would not eat the dream cookie."

"But did you tell her it was full of chemicals and thus calorie free?" Max said.

"Yes," Britt said impatiently. "I did what you said. But she clearly views any appealing food as toxic. If I'd compelled her to eat it, she probably would have made herself puke it up. Also, this?" Britt held up a silky brown thread, looking doubtful. "Doesn't seem to be real hair, it's all synthetic extensions. Sorry to be the bearer of bad news."

"So then, we're screwed? Dead end on Jenna?" I wanted to cry.

"Absolutely not, here's the plan." Max steepled her hands like the mastermind she clearly dreamed of becoming. "We pile into one car and go spy on Jenna, old-school. I go flying, witch goes invisible."

Britt nodded thoughtfully. "Okay, what about me?"

"Since you have no skills to contribute, you'll drive the getaway car."

"Did you have to phrase it that way?" Britt muttered. "Your leadership skills are the worst, Maxy."

Things started to look up for us when Jenna's SUV was parked in the first place we thought to look: in front of her house, and so was another car. A royal blue Ferrari that I was betting belonged to Drew Kensington.

Britt sat waiting across the street in the idling car while I snuck into Jenna's small backyard, which contained a swing set for

Sofie and a couple of neglected flowerboxes. Max buzzed annoyingly in my ear, and I had to bite my tongue to keep from crying out with a curse when she occasionally crashed into my invisible body, because, ew, fly. The moment I spoke aloud, I'd turn visible, and I didn't have that many mints left.

Like a moth drawn to light, I wandered toward the back window, lured by the blue glow of a TV screen. As I got closer to the slightly open window, I could hear people talking inside the room. The sound on the TV was down almost all the way.

A sudden squeal from inside the room made me jump.

Max flew into the room, disappearing into the dark woodwork. As I leaned over the flowerbox to peek through the screen, a man's voice said, "Jen, you're so tight …"

"That feels good …" Jenna moaned. "Harder, please."

When my eyes adjusted to the dim light, Jenna was lying facedown on the carpeted floor of her own den, squealing and moaning. Drew sat over her, his big hands digging deep into her hamstrings and glute muscles. She was fully clothed and he was giving her a massage.

What was with this guy? He could be having flaming hot affairs with tons of women but instead he chose to have close, supportive friendships with them?

Though, it's not that there was a dearth of romantic tension between Jenna and Drew. It's just that the tension seemed remarkably … stable.

The big-screen TV in front of them, which neither appeared to be watching right now, was playing *When Harry Met Sally.*

"Jen, you really need to take the time to get a professional massage," Drew lectured, his voice mild. "Your job keeps you so active, all those spin classes. For Sophie's sake, you really need to take better care of yourself."

"I'm helping Sophie right now, I'll have you know."

"Uh, how?" Drew sounded amused and indulgent. I wanted to know the answer, too.

"She'll be able to pay for a great college," Jenna said proudly, "thanks to my weekly blood donations." She eased herself into a sitting position and turned to face Drew. Then she did a duckface pout and tugged on the collar of her simple blue cotton top, baring her slim neck seductively.

"You are such a dork." Drew laughed and reached out to tickle her stomach, which made her squeal again. "You *know* I'd fund whatever you needed, whether or not you 'donate.'"

"Yeah, but I like to pretend I'm earning it this way. It's kinda dark and seedy, kinda hot … oh come on, humor me. I have no life anymore, I'm a mom!"

He chuckled and pecked her cheek. "No, you're right, I guess it could be seen as hot. In a certain goth way."

They smiled at each other and for a moment I thought they were finally going to kiss. But instead, they held hands and watched the romcom for a few minutes. They were moving slower than Meg and Billy. I really hoped Britt had turned off the car, to save gas.

When it got close to the movie's romantic ending, Jenna turned the sound down once more. "So, how's it going on the home front?" she asked Drew, her face tight with sympathy.

"Same old." Drew groaned. "I'm trying to establish myself, but no one takes me seriously. Dad's losing his mind, literally. Mom's trying to 'control the message' about that, about Ashlee, about everything."

Jenna shook her head sadly. "Well, she's always been like that."

Estelle had always been a control freak? I thought. Now that I thought about it, she'd pushed that wedding invite on me hard despite Ashlee's clear reluctance. Not to mention mine.

"I hope you talked to her about sending all those PIs after us? Though it turns out I was wrong about there being one at the wedding." She cringed and looked embarrassed. "I wasn't feeling well that day and got things wrong." Okay, good to know that she wasn't normally paranoid. I felt myself softening toward Jenna. Estelle sent private eyes to spy on her and Drew's handholding?

"The person I thought was spying on us," Jenna went on, gazing at the floor in mortification, "was totally innocent, just this mousy chick I went to high school with." *Thanks?* "Kind of an oddball," she went on, "physically uncoordinated, but harmless." *Triple ouch*, I thought. So much for softening. "Her name escapes me. Rose? Tulip?" *Those aren't even trees, idiot*, I wanted to shout. "Oh well, who cares?"

Aaaand good to know Jenna and I would not be striking up a friendship anytime soon.

"I did confront Mom about those PIs she hired," Drew's brow was furrowed with concern. "I've definitely seen them tailing me other times. But she denied it. No big shock; she still denies trying to break us up in high school. When I press her it's 'I always want what's best for you, son.'" He rolled his eyes. "No matter what I do, she still sees me as a kid. Even getting married didn't change that."

Geez. The more I heard about Estelle, the less she sounded like a protective mom and the more she sounded overprotective and controlling. Suddenly I was seeing Ashlee's simpering deference to her at the bakery in a new light. What if Ashlee believed she had to manage Estelle and be the perfect fiancée or Mother Kensington would declare her not good enough for Drew? Ashlee had already seen it happen to her friend Jenna back in high school.

And if Estelle was willing to go to such great lengths to save her son from dating the wrong woman, it wasn't that much of a stretch to imagine she would do far worse to protect his freedom.

If, say, he happened to drink too deeply and drained a girl.

Tomorrow, I'd—well, not tomorrow. Thanksgiving was fast approaching, but as soon as the festivities were over, I was going to make sure Estelle received either a dream visit or a spy session. Or both for good measure.

"Do you ever wonder if your marriage was, like, cursed?" Jenna asked, not realizing she'd just stabbed an invisible witch in the heart.

"I don't know." Drew sighed. "I guess I didn't really know her as well as I thought I did? I met her again at such a weird time."

"I know." She squeezed his hand. "You'd just been turned."

"That's a big part of it, sure. I was scared I'd starve to death without someone at my side all the time. But the other thing is, she was so vivacious and fun and beautiful, she reminded me of a simpler time."

A sad look entered Jenna's eyes. "People used to describe me that way." *Sure*, I thought, *people always described mean girls that way.* "But now..." Her shellacked fingers rushed to her cheeks. "Do you think I should have fillers done? At the wedding Ashlee said I should."

Drew stroked Jenna's hair. "Jen, I think you're even prettier now than you were in high school. And you're a great mom. Sophie's a lucky kid. Speaking of my other favorite girl, next time I come over, we should all watch *Matilda*. I think she'd be into that one." He paused. "I keep hearing a fly buzzing. Where's your fly swatter?"

On second thought, I hoped that getaway car was ready to go.

CHAPTER SEVENTEEN

BY TEN P.M. on the night before Bryson and I would be hosting our first Thanksgiving, I was a nervous wreck.

Cooking up a storm under pressure was something I was used to, but I'd always turned to magic to help me multitask. With Bryson in the house, though, busily rushing around fluffing couch pillows, giving me back rubs, and reading funny Buzzfeed listicles aloud to me, I couldn't exactly sneak off and whip up a brew or incantation.

Supposedly he'd come over to help me. And he was being his usual sweet self. But when he started playing relaxing music on his phone and tenderly hand feeding me sliced strawberries, straight from the bowl I'd just prepped for tomorrow's salad, I cracked.

"Hey. Do you think you could mince this garlic? Or prep these mushrooms for the stuffing?"

"You sound stressed, Haze." Bryson smiled his perfect, warm smile. Which looked a little goofy since he was wearing a chocolate mustache from having licked the chocolate-squash tea bread batter bowl. "I'll do whatever needs doing to help you feel better."

"Great, thank you!" My sudden relief made me realize part of me had been freaking out internally about Gran's whole "demons don't cook" standard test thing. Bryson's willingness to cook *proved* he was human, didn't it?

Well, basically human. A touch of demon DNA was no dealbreaker. After all, I wasn't your standard issue Ordinal myself.

"Here you go, babe." To my surprise, Bryson set a stemmed glass full of red wine in front of me. He must have poured it from the open bottle in the fridge. "I could tell from your tone that you needed some pampering."

Instead of picking up a knife and cutting board like I'd asked, he began to knead my shoulders from behind. Even though my anxiety was literally about him, his touch relaxed me instantly. As it always had.

"That does feel good," I said grudgingly.

"Course it feels good, Haze." At the hypnotic cadence of his voice, my shoulders dropped lower. "I always know what you need. We belong together, like caramel and—"

"What is your fixation with caramel?" I snapped, whirling around.

Bryson's wounded expression made me squirm with guilt. But, I mean, he was the one who wanted us to host Thanksgiving, so why wasn't he helping?

"Sorry," I said, mostly because it seemed like someone should. "It would just really reassure me to see you do some cooking. Because I'm feeling stressed," I added quickly. "My parents are going to be comparing this holiday to all the ones at Bea's. Her house is palatial, and she's practically Martha Stewart and…" I paused as a giant yawn overtook me. Yikes, it was already 10:15. I was getting super tired and I hadn't even browned the mushrooms. "Do you think you could possibly help–"

"Help lower your stress? Of course." He gave me a look of loving indulgence. "And if you prefer, I'll say we belong together like peanut butter and … chicken." Lazily, his tongue darted out to lick off his chocolate mustache, and I stared. "What?" he said. "Like Swimming Rama. Come on, it's a flavor combo we both love."

His tongue. How had I never noticed how extremely long it was? It was downright flickable. Lizard-like.

Would our future children also sport gecko tongues?

The smell of burning onions hit my nose, just as I heard water boiling over and sizzling onto the stovetop. I ran to remove both pots from the heat. Hadn't I turned those burners off already? I stared at the knobs. After a certain point of exhaustion, it was hard to recall with certainty.

And if I couldn't trust my memory, I had to wonder if my other senses were suspect. Had Bryson's tongue really been abnormally long, or was it Gran's voice in my head, making me paranoid that he was a demon?

Bryson was not a demon. Couldn't be. No, damn it. Bryson was perfect for me.

Too perfect.

Get out of my head, Gran.

But even as my little house began to smell like sage and thyme, fried onions and green bean casserole and candied yams, like Thanksgiving, I couldn't help but notice with a nagging sense of worry that Bryson never lifted a spoon, spatula, or tongs.

It was sometime after midnight. Bryson had biked home and I was in the kitchen area again, obsessively checking every dish and mentally comparing it to my planned menu. Double-checking that everything was as ready for tomorrow as it could be.

A feeling of incompleteness dogged me. I was missing something obvious, but what?

Then I realized all the foil and Saran Wrapped platters in my fridge were filled with nothing but caramel.

A knock on the wall roused me from my mounting panic.

"Yoo-hoo?" called a sonorous voice. It was the Sandman demon, Three Hundred and Six. "I hate to be a bother, but you owe me a few more minutes of your presence. I emailed my invoice but it must have gone to spam … whoa." Her perfectly smooth blue face furrowed into a rare frown. "Never mind, I'll collect later. You're dangerously low on energy."

I yawned reflexively. "You can read people's energy levels? Wait … are you saying you get *paid* in energy?"

"You hired a demon without knowing that?" She looked amused by the ignorance of humans. "Energy is like food for us," she explained, "and witch energy is far more potent than that of Ordinal humans. But it'd be unethical to collect from you now, Hazel. Goodness me, you appear to be running on sheer adrenaline! Even in your sleeping state you're exhausted."

Sleeping state? "This is a dream?" As I asked the question, the foil and Saran Wrapped platters began to levitate, then one by one poofed out of existence.

"Oh, ha, you didn't know that either?" I was getting sick of her amusement at my unenlightened condition. "Yeah, absolutely, I'm just projecting in—it'd be illegal for me to show up in your dimension without being summoned. Plus, this is way easier, since I don't have to go through customs. Such a bother. I don't suppose you travel much?"

"Not the way you do. In fact, not at all." I yawned again. "How could I be so tired even in my sleep?"

"I'm no human doctor, but it's probably not a *good* sign." She hesitated. "There was something odd about that last job you had me do. The beach wedding."

A warm feeling spread through me at the memory. "That's where I realized how much my fiancé loves me ... also I fought other gulls for a Cheeto."

"Yeah. Sorry about the bird thing, I was having a hard time getting a grip on the landscape. It felt like someone else was driving."

A chill ran through me. "What do you mean? Who?"

She sighed. "Hate to be a bummer, but I've been around long enough to see this checks all the boxes, so..." She threw open her right hand and with a sparkle of magic a scroll appeared in it. "Here you go."

I unrolled what appeared to be some kind of public service brochure.

The heading read: **"Are you a witch being preyed on by a rogue Sandman demon who's stealing all your energy?"**

Underneath was this sensitively written paragraph:

> *It can be hard to admit you've allowed a thief into your magical life, but such criminals are charming by nature, and you're not the first or last witch to get tricked into exhaustion. At this stage, many victims become lulled into complacency and trapped in a state of denial even as the perpetrator leeches them dry of energy. But your future wellbeing, and perhaps even your life, will depend on you finding the strength to face reality. You must cast the demon out. Forever.*

Below that were the lines of a spell called Good Riddance.

I skimmed them, my mind flashing back to the golden summer day that Bryson waltzed into my bakery. His charming smile when he first caught my eye. He'd known exactly what he was looking for. On our sweet early dates, he'd been so extra attentive. Learning my favorite foods and shows. How to keep me comfortable and relaxed, how to kiss me so I'd forget everything else around me. And when things looked dicey, he whipped out the ring. He played me like a cheap ukulele.

I was going to marry that demon. I was going to donate my life force, unknowingly, to feed him.

"Why?" I wiped the tears from my eyes. "Why couldn't I see what Bryson was from the start?"

"He didn't want you to see," she said gently. "And you didn't want you to see, either."

"I feel so stupid." I groaned. "My friends kept trying to warn me, too."

"Oh, dear, that never works."

I took a deep breath and held up the scroll for validation. "I am not stupid. He targeted me. It could happen to any witch, right?"

"Absolutely," she breezed. "And having said that, a friend in denial *is* one of the most frustrating experiences to be had in your dimension. To be frank, I'd have muted your texts."

"Um, thanks…?"

"But it's not your fault. Your species places a premium on romantic love, and witches tend to have a hard time finding a mate. Your desperation makes you vulnerable to con artists from all dimensions."

"That sums it up perfectly." I sniffed. "Hex my life."

"There, there, it'll be okay. Probably." She handed me a dream-handkerchief to wipe my eyes. "You know, living in denial can chew up one's energy in and of itself. Hopefully you'll start to feel better right away…"

"Thank you." I dabbed at my tear-soaked face. The handkerchief was softer than a spun cloud. "No, really, thanks for every—"

"So that I can get paid," she finished. "Otherwise, I'll add late fees and interest charges to your bill. My credit rate is twenty-four percent APR. Measured in Standard Witch Vitality Units, of course. And next time, do your homework before you hire a demon."

I decided, on second thought, not to give her a hug.

At three p.m. the next day, my whole family—plus Britt and Max—sat at a crowded Thanksgiving table composed of several card tables jammed together with a giant tablecloth of Gran's over them.

My dad and Bryson—who at this point I could barely stand to look at—greeted each other with a hearty shoulder clap, then burst spontaneously into the Oregon football chant, "Let's go Ducks, let's go!" Causing Dad to beam at me and declare that I'd finally found myself a good one. Dad was going to take the breakup hard, which was part of the reason I was delaying the inevitable till after the holiday.

Bea sat between my mother and the highchair containing Maren, Bea's cute eighteen-month-old daughter. Mother, who couldn't bear to eat in public as the act of chewing squinched up her cheeks, cut up all the food I served her into tiny chunks which she eagerly fed her granddaughter. She chatted happily with Bea as if they were the only ones in the room.

"Oh, Beatrix!" Mother gushed. "I saw the most darling valance the other day and thought of you immediately."

"One of those frouffy waterfall ones?" Bea asked, topping up Mother's chardonnay. "I'm loving this season's neutrals."

Mother nodded happily. "This one was griege."

"Is griege a word?" I ventured, too ashamed to ask what a valance was.

They ignored me.

Listening to their fluent discussion in a language I didn't understand, I felt the same frustration I'd felt my whole life. Bea and Mother got each other, effortlessly. They didn't get me.

Bea's beefy ex-football playing husband, Grant, was parked in front of the TV watching the game along with his twin three-year-old sons, my nephews, Connor and Cameron.

Meanwhile, Cindra, though physically in London—*as far we knew*—enjoyed her own place at the table in the form of a video screen on my dad's laptop. Dad enthusiastically interacted with her rather than striking up conversations with others at the table, like me.

"You look amazing, Star." His nickname for Cindra. What was his nickname for me, you ask? Slowby. Because apparently I'd moved slower on my tricycle than Bea before me. "Your glasses look dope. See, Daddy's not too old to be hip. Keep on inspiring us, baby. Namaste."

I'm pretty sure Cindra had the call on mute much of the time, though she waved to us occasionally from a trendy-looking flat party.

I sat between Bryson and Max, who'd already scarfed so many appetizers I couldn't believe she had room for the turkey she was piling on her plate.

"Was it always like this with your family?" Max said quietly, and I nodded. "I guess I'd forgotten how weird they act toward you."

"It's the Green Magic thing," I murmured. "They never got over my magic being stronger than theirs. Mother doesn't like Gran for the same reason."

At my insistence, Gran sat at the head of the table. Britt sat at the foot, partly because she was tiny enough I could scoot past her chair to get to the kitchen. Also, Britt could easily slip out and intercept Grant for a bite, when he finally had to pee after drinking all that beer.

Gran cleared her throat, then spoke. "Hazel dear, this spread is scrumptious. A real treat. But I cannot bring myself to celebrate or be grateful for the supernatural company you keep. Not you two girls, you're lovely," she added to Britt and Max. "Just him." I didn't need to look at Bryson to know his eyes would be wide with feigned innocence and confusion. "Welp, I'd better be off."

"Wait, Gran." Well, shoot, I was going to wait till after the party, but here went nothing. I stood. "I have an announcement to make."

Bea gasped and grabbed my hand holding up my ring for all to see. "Is that what I think it is—a garish estate ring with a marquise cut diamond?"

"Doesn't matter." I took my hand back. "I'm not marrying this man after all. Or should I say, this demon."

"Haze?" Bryson threw me a look of stunned bewilderment. "What are you talking about?"

"Don't give her that kicked-puppy expression. You know what you did." Britt turned to me. "Actually, *I* don't know what he did. But I can't wait to find out!"

Bryson appealed to the rest of the table. "We all know she's sensitive, but I love her and I know we can work it out. Hazel and I belong together like popcorn and—"

"Lies," I cut him off smoothly. "All you ever loved was leeching my energy. My vitality." Standard Witch Vitality Units. "Being with you was slowly killing me. But no more." I yanked the ring off my finger, but it got stuck for a minute which was a bit anticlimactic. Still, point made.

Bryson no longer looked innocent or confused. He looked halfway between annoyed and homicidal. "So, this is the thanks I get. For being your ideal boyfriend. Putting up with all your quirks. Listening to your inane stories. And don't get me started on the endless foot rubs I've given."

My mother looked peeved, and I dared to dream that it could be on my behalf. "Hazel, this is embarrassing." Nope. "At this point, I wasn't expecting you to marry anyone. But couldn't you wait for the young man to break things off as usual, instead of making a scene at the table?"

"Slowby? What's the problem here, honey?" My dad implored with wounded eyes. "I thought you finally found your better half. Bryson's a catch, and he accepts you, warts and all. Don't you understand how hard it is to find that?" He glanced reverently at my mother. "Don't you get how lucky I am? I mean, how lucky *you* are?"

"Wait, somebody tell me what happened?" Tinny Cindra yelled from the video screen. "Did Hazel pull a Hazel at Thanksgiving?"

"She's breaking up with her demon fiancé right here at the table," Bea called, the righteous outrage in her voice barely containing her glee. "It's super awkward. Text you all the tea later!"

I ignored them and turned to Bryson. "You almost had me. I wanted so badly for you to be a good man, like your name says. Did you pick the name Goodman just for me, or have you pulled this same scam on other young witches still reeling from their toxic childhoods?" Ignoring the scandalized murmurs from my family, I went on, "You knew Gran must have read your aura, so you tried to throw me off claiming you just had a little bit of demon DNA. But that photo of your great grandpa's really a photo of you, isn't it? What's your Sandman number?"

"What's Hazel saying?" Cindra yelled. "I've never seen her talk for that long. Do you think she's drunk or possessed?"

"You did everything you could to trick me into thinking you loved me," I went on, "but you were just going to leech me dry the whole time."

"Aw, don't be so dramatic, Haze." He ruffled my hair affectionately, and I recoiled. Then right in front of my eyes his skin turned a deep, cold blue. Because that's not dramatic.

"Awesome," Britt said under her breath.

"Told you!" Max reached for another drumstick. "Humans don't sleep standing up with their eyes open."

"Dear God, what am I seeing?" My Ordinal dad rubbed his eyes, sounding hysterical. "Are there drugs in this turkey breast? *Did Slowby drug me?*"

"Honey, don't act like it's a big deal." Mother laughed nervously. "Lots of witches are powerful enough to summon demons. I could summon demons if I wanted to."

Dad fainted into his mashed potatoes, and Bea had to scramble to clear his nose and mouth of spuds.

"Great, first you almost killed me," I said. "Then you almost killed my dad."

"Silly bear, I was never gonna kill you." Bryson sounded hurt that I had come to that conclusion. "You've got a surprising amount of magic flowing through you for a common baker. With the human energy I get from clients as a side dish," he went on, "I'd never need to drain you fully. If we went through with the wedding—I was on the fence—you'd only have spent the rest of your life exhausted and never quite knowing why. Big deal, half the humans in America feel that way."

"Hold up, you hadn't decided if you were really going to marry me? But you had that happy dream about … oh my God, you can control dreams." I gasped in realization. "Because you're a Sandman demon. You know how to make yourself soothing, relaxing. When I gave you the dream cookie, you must have recognized the ingredient that came from your own dimension. Your reaction was a clue, but I was too deep in denial."

"Yeah, you were. To be honest, I'm surprised you got wise to me. But it's no big. I'm a bit relieved to move on." He stood and wiped his mouth with the cloth napkin. "You were a killer source of energy, but you're not that great a catch."

Max groaned. "Unbelievable."

"How can you have the gall to say that to her?" Britt demanded.

"Oh, come on, she's a huge dork. Look at her socks."

"What?" I glanced down at my whimsical alligator socks, which opened to a toothy green snout that appeared to be snapping around my ankles. "They're quirky and adorable. Like me."

Bryson—or should I say William—laughed a deep, evil laugh. "Sure, that's what you want people to think. That you're this sweet, happy-go-lucky witch … but don't forget, I've walked your dreams. I know the inside of your head." He turned to the others. "She's riddled with anxieties. Hates herself. Guilt is her middle name."

"We know," Max said.

"That's just Hazel," Britt added.

Looking a bit frustrated, he gestured toward my parents and Bea. "But did you know she's still angsting over *those* idiots, with their stupid valences?"

"A pity, but it's understandable," Gran snapped. "Those idiots raised her."

Mother glared at Gran, who stared her down, then looked away, sniffing with contempt. Bea blinked over and over, a hurt look on her face. Eh, they could both deal.

The more time I spent around supportive friends like Britt and Max, and Gran, the more my family's nonsense drained me. They were *exhausting*.

Why did that sound familiar?

"Honestly, Bryson, you're just like them," I realized. "I don't need you. I'm good with being me … and someday, maybe I'll meet a man who's good with the real me too."

He chortled. "Oh, get some cats already."

"All right, out of my house." Grabbing my blue crystal pendant that I used for demon summoning, I chanted the spell for Good Riddance. Before my speechless family appeared a uniformed escort of six blue-skinned Sandman demons. Their navy linen tunics were topped with grey cloaks that fastened at the shoulder with a shiny opalescent button.

"Honored Witch." Their leader gave a ceremonial bow. "You called on us to rid you of a menace from our distant realm of—oh, dude, check it out. It's William."

I blinked. "Wait … you know him?"

"Haven't seen this scoundrel in a while, ma'am." Another demon said with a disapproving shake of his blue head. "But yes, you could say we know William Haverford Smythe. Sandman One Thousand Three Hundred Twelve. He's borrowed ale money from quite a few of us and never paid it back."

"Fellows, I was leaving the building anyway." Bryson attempted a bro-ish shoulder clap to the leader, but the other demon brushed off his uniform where Bryson's hand had touched him. "There's really no need to cast me from this dimension."

"Not up to us, man," another demon called out. "You know the witch calls the shots."

"Damn right she does." Britt crossed her arms over her eternally perky chest.

"Hell yeah," Max echoed, fixing Bryson with a dirty look that would freeze a snowshoe hare in its tracks.

"Haze," Bryson begged, "we had fun, right? Face it, I was the best boyfriend you'll ever have."

"If you cast him out, will it take him centuries to be able to return?" I asked hopefully.

"Nah, sixty months is average," the leader replied, a bit sheepish. "You could be lucky and get a few more. But the most I can guarantee is thirteen months."

"Hmm." If I cast him out, would Bryson soon be back for revenge? Course, if I didn't cast him out, he was liable to prey on more witches right now. "Do your thing, boys."

"Take good care of yourself, Haze," Bryson/William said ominously, while the blue-skinned demons wrapped him in a net of ice, leaving the lower half of his handsome face free for breathing. And, unfortunately, ranting. "Because when I'm back in your dimension, and I will be back," he said, "I'll be sure to swing by your neck of the woods for a little chat."

"Not if I set up an anti-demon ward first." Pure bravado. I was shaking underneath, and I had no idea if anti-demon wards were a thing, let alone how to construct one.

At least I wouldn't have to worry about it for a year.

The demon crew dematerialized. Leaving most of my guests with their jaws on the floor. In Dad's case, he slept with his mouth wide open.

But Gran was smiling from the bottom of her soul. "Outstanding party, Hazel dear. Made my year." She raised her glass and drank deeply of the wine. Then she whispered a few words and poofed.

I turned to Britt, who was beaming at me, too. As was Max.

"Tell them to forget all of that, Britt," I said, then remembered I was telling a vampire what to do and added, "Please."

"I totally will," she began, and grabbed my hand. "And I'm so, so proud of you, Hazel…"

"Thanks!"

"But also?" She took a drooling glance across the room where Grant was still laser focused on the game. "Do you think, once I've cleared their memories…?"

"Sure. You can have seconds of Grant." Unlike those skinny little sticks Jenna and Ashlee, my brother-in-law could handle getting one more bite.

Besides, it was a feast day, after all.

CHAPTER EIGHTEEN

"CAN'T THINK OF a delicate way to put this," Max said, "but right about now, I'd claw your eyes out for a white mocha. From you-know-where."

She and Britt and I were lounging on my couch, minutes after my family had walked to their cars—politely, quietly, and bearing foil wrapped leftover platters. Britt's vampiric compulsion had not only made them forget the supernatural drama of my breakup with Bryson. It also made them more docile, if only temporarily.

I'd have to keep that trick in mind.

"How could you possibly cram in a mocha, or anything else, after the feast I just fed you?" I shook my head in wonder at Max's shifter metabolism. She ate more than any woman I knew. "Anyway, it's Thanksgiving. No café's going to be open."

Britt and Max looked at each other, as if silently drawing straws for who should be the one to break the news to me.

"Oh, what?" I said. "Even if Java Kitty were open on Thanksgiving, it would be short hours. This ain't exactly New York."

Britt must have pulled the short straw. "They're now open 24/7, 365 days a year."

"Ughhhhh. Fine." I stood with a sigh and grabbed my blue peacoat off its hook by the door. "I guess I can take the smell for a minute or two. I've been meaning to ask the owner, Elton, a few questions."

"You two girls have fun, I'm gonna head home." Britt dug into her stylish clutch purse for her keys. "Grant's blood was so filling, all I want to do now is sleep for the next three days. I think his triglycerides are high."

Max shuddered. "You say creepy undead things like that, and you don't appreciate how hard I have to fight my shifter instincts."

Britt waved goodbye with an exaggerated bared-fangs grin.

"That's vampire trollface, is what that is," Max muttered, then glanced doubtfully around my trashed house. "Maybe I should help you straighten this place up before we go? I'm no Mrs. Doubtfire, but I could shift to cat-mode and lick some dishes—"

"A world of no. I got this." I snapped my fingers and recited a spell I'd been getting better at lately:

"Mop the floor, without my hands.
Clear this room of every smudge.
Wash the dishes, scrub the pans,
Life's too short to be a drudge."

Max's eyes widened as, one by one, the nasty plates in the sink obligingly lifted themselves into the air to be cleaned by a hovering, soapy sponge. A broomstick swept crumbs off the floor on its own, while a hot, wet rag erased muddy shoeprints and shone the tile to a sparkle.

"Man, sometimes I wish I had your magical gifts," Max said.

I shrugged. "Sometimes I wish I had yours."

Ten minutes later, I felt a burst of smug relief when Java Kitty's lot turned out to be empty except for a black Tesla.

"VIP parking, woot woot," Trixie announced in her cool, polished voice, and dove into the spot next to the Tesla.

Inside there was no coffee line. Weirder still, there appeared to be no one working the cash register or taking orders. Max and I exchanged looks of confusion.

"Welcome, friends." A robotic voice piped up through the wall speakers. **"What are we drinking today?"**

I froze, and Max looked ready to bolt. This was too weird for me. I had enough trouble dealing with Trixie, and she at least had a soul.

"Just a moment, hang on!" called a warm but melancholy baritone from the back. Elton popped out, wearing a white apron with the Java Kitty pink cat logo over his street clothes. "Please, allow me to serve you personally … two white mochas, on the house?"

"Yes, yes, yes!" Max banged her fist on the counter with embarrassing fervor.

"None for me, thanks." I folded my arms across my chest. "But I wanted to ask you a couple of questions about the store if you don't mind?"

"Not at all." Elton smiled. "I love to talk shop."

It was a decent pun, but I didn't want to give him the satisfaction of a groan, so I just nodded.

"Elton?" Max's face looked hopeful. "If you still wanted to make two mochas, I'd totally drink hers."

With a wink, Elton set each of Max's cups in front of a sleek-looking steel coffee machine and pushed a few buttons. *Beep boop.*

"So, couldn't get anyone to work the counter on Thanksgiving, huh?" I asked Elton smugly, once Max had walked out beaming, with her two free mochas. She'd declared it the best Thanksgiving ever and declined my offer of a ride home, deciding to walk.

"Those lovely baristas would have come in any day I asked them to," Elton said with a sad smile. "But I had to fire everyone yesterday."

"*What?*"

"The board said it didn't make sense for us to be paying workers now that the Automagick machines are fully up and running."

"Automagick?" The word stopped me. "Is that, erm, a brand name?"

"I guess so. That's what our investor's representatives call them in their emails."

My mind was racing. Of course. All this time I'd been picturing some Grey Witch in a business suit stopping by on the daily, but even that wouldn't explain the constant stench of magic pouring out of Java Kitty. No, the machines here were running Grey Magic themselves, all the time now.

Perhaps I'd been wrong to assume the coffee robot had no soul. A continual flow of concentrated magic was more than capable of animating a primitive spirit in the cogs of a machine. My own familiar, Trixie the car, was proof it could happen. It was a little funny, now that I thought about it, that Trixie ran on Green Magic. Man-made objects tended to be more susceptible to Grey Magic.

If Grey Magic was unstable and dangerous, wouldn't these machines be too? Would they be evil?

"As you can see, these new smart machines are real game changers." Elton's melancholy voice roused me from my thoughts. "They handle everything from greeting customers to making drinks, and of course taking money. Your coffee-buying experience runs smoothly every time, reducing anxiety."

"Um yeah, but it also reduces jobs," I pointed out. "And spontaneity. And human connection." Sure, I felt like a hypocrite, having just made my kitchen sparkle with magic instead of elbow grease. But this? Was a bridge too far.

Elton's thin shoulders slumped. "Yes, you're right. I don't know what to do. The community may overall be worse off because of me and my company. But I make bank."

"Excuse me?" Was he bragging about the profits his café took from my grandma and me? No, bragging would imply some sort of petty joy. Elton was joyless.

"The money I get paid as CEO of Java Kitty is off the hook," he confessed miserably. Two fat tears rolled down his cheeks. "I'm living the dream."

"Elton? Sorry if this is too personal." I didn't know how to say this. "But none of your, um, success seems to be making you very happy."

"I can't even remember happiness." He wiped his eyes. "It's the strangest thing, Hazel. I was all fired up when I got here this summer. Now I'm achieving all my dreams, and yet … my world is so … so…"

"Grey?" I offered, holding my knuckle under my nose to keep out the stink of burning grass.

To my surprise, Elton looked like a thunderclap had just struck him. "Yes!" he cried. "It's so grey here. Every damn day is cloudy. Blue Moon Bay seemed like a paradise in August. But now, it's a grey hellhole."

My mouth dropped open. "Dude, you have a raging case of SAD."

"SAD?"

"Seasonal Affective Disorder. It hits a lot of people in the Pacific Northwest. We're so far north we don't get much sunshine in the winter, and some folks can't handle it."

"What…" He sniffed, then sobbed. "What do all those SAD people do? Kill themselves, I suppose?"

"No! Sun lamps can help, I hear. Vitamin D can help, and exercise, or antidepressants. Or." I leaned in. "They go back to the sunny lands they came from. Like, say, California."

At the mention of his home state, Elton wept openly. "I have to go. I have to leave this beautiful, cloud-cursed place forever."

He did? I blinked. Was it really that easy all along to destroy my competition?

"Well, you do what you have to for your health." I patted his back.

Why hadn't I had this nice little talk with him weeks ago? Answer: because I was too tired—and too deep in denial about my problems.

"Money or no money, this place is a failure for me." Elton tore off his apron and tossed it on the floor. "I need to hop on the first flight back to California and get some sunshine, stat. Once I'm over this SAD thing, the idea for my next company will come to me. Or maybe I'll run for president."

"Ooh, I'm getting chills." A lifetime of responding to dumb stuff men said with smiles and encouragement had made me very convincing. But then again, I really *was* getting chills. Was Java Kitty about to run out of lives?

"Wait a sec." Something occurred to me. "If you leave, won't the machines just keep running without you?"

"Good catch." He pressed his thumbprint to a panel in the wall. It opened to reveal a digital power grid. "To address liability concerns, I'll turn off the power to the machines before I go. If the investors want to turn it back on and run the place without me, that's up to them. After they negotiate a buyout price."

"Right." I barely understood what he'd just said, but it didn't matter.

Because I knew what it meant when Elton, with newfound vigor, slid his finger across every glowing green digital switch. Within ten seconds, the hum in the café went dead silent. The whole place seemed to shrivel a bit, as if the walls themselves had grown sags and wrinkles.

Most importantly, the smell of Grey Magic was gone.

I breathed a sigh.

"Hey, I have an idea." A nostalgic grin spread across Elton's lean face. "You want to help raid the supply room? Since I have a plane to catch, I can't take much with me."

"Raid?" Like a pirate? "You mean steal stuff from Java Kitty?"

"It's a time-honored tradition where I come from. In Silicon Valley, whenever a dodgy start-up fails, the founders take home valuable stuff from the office. If they're confronted, they blame the general chaos. You want anything? Bags of coffee beans? That guy Kade who was in charge of ordering beans for us really knew his stuff. It's all top-shelf." He did a chef-kiss.

I hesitated. As appealing as the offer sounded, "Doesn't your investor take inventory?"

"Nah. They've never been on-site."

"Who *is* your investor?" I asked after Elton had helped me load twenty jumbo bags of coffee beans into the back of my car. Along with a box of designer honey spoons, purple ceramic individual teapots, packs of plain white napkins, and tons of other cool loot.

"Blue Moon Bay Venture Partners," Elton answered.

"Oh. I've never heard of them." Not that I'd heard of any VC firms. That kind of stuff simply wasn't on my radar. But I made a mental note to look them up so I could be aware of any other Grey Magic "ventures" they had going on around town.

Hopefully, I could encourage the others to shut down peacefully as well. Blue Moon Bay wasn't an Automagick kind of town, and I didn't want that to change.

Not on my watch.

Elton gave me a jaunty wave, hopped into his Tesla, and peeled out without looking back.

It was getting dark, and I was legit tired after a long day.

I turned on the ignition. "Let's go home, Trixie."

"Ooh, looks like you scored some swag." Trixie must have noticed all the stuff in the trunk and backseat. *"Suh-weet, what's the occasion?"*

"Oh, no big thing, just raided my former competition, like you do." I couldn't help but crow a little. It was the least Goody Two-shoes thing I'd ever done. Max and Britt would be so proud. And I'd outsmarted the venture capitalists who almost shut down our bakery. "That reminds me, I wanted to research something."

Whipping out my phone, I plugged "Blue Moon Bay Venture Partners" into a search engine. There were very few sites mentioning them, not even a full page. I clicked on the first link.

And was stopped cold by six words.

"Wholly-owned subsidiary of Kensington Industries?" I read aloud to myself in disbelief. "Wholly. Owned. Subsidiary … holy crud." I needed to talk to Max and Britt *now*. Also, I needed to drive home. Home was the safest place to a Green Witch. Our magic even worked better there. I would be looking up a barricade spell as soon as I walked in the door. "Home please, Trixie," I said as calmly as I could.

"You know it, girl."

But Trixie turned and drove in the opposite direction from Filbert Road.

CHAPTER NINETEEN

"I SAID HOME, TRIXIE, not work," I said, groaning.

"You know it, girl."

Her voice in my head sounded tinny and strained.

"Um, Trixie … I don't know how to say this, but I think your internal compass is broken. Are you by any chance glitching?" Did we need to get her back into the shop? Then again, it may have been that shop that had turned her personality upside down to begin with … or had that happened when she shut down?

Trixie was weaving in traffic, driving faster than ever. She was driving north into the hills, toward Corvid Park. The sun was setting on my left, making me squint.

"I need you to stop and turn around."

"I'm sorry, all operators are busy assisting other VIP clients."

"Trixie, this isn't funny." I tried to unlock the door but the button did nothing. "Take me home!"

"Home is an idea. Home is a core profit concept. Kensington Industries curates concepts and develops them for domestic and international markets."

"Oh dear Gods." Suddenly, I was panicking. "You didn't shut down randomly or because you're old. The Kensingtons are behind it all. They messed with your mind using Grey Magic. Just like they used it to sabotage my bakery." I paused to catch my breath. My heart was like a drum in my ears. "I don't get it. They were so nice to my face, but it's like they wanted to exert total control over me. My life. My future." A chill ran through me. Control freak. "Estelle."

She'd been nice to Ashlee's face, too.

"Girl, I wish I could say you were way off. But you're almost totally 100 percent right! Bottom line, we are not *going home tonight."*

The panic grew like a heat in my chest. "Where … where are you taking me?"

"To die in the woods, gal pal of mine. This is like the big finale, no encore. So sorry, but to be frank you kinda did it to yourself."

"How can you say that?" Tears rolled down my face. "You're my familiar. You're supposed to be on my side. A cat or owl would never betray me like this!"

"Okay, so, first of all, I hear where you're coming from. But like did you ever think maybe you should have paid more attention when I first started acting cray-cray? Didn't you miss the old me?"

"Um … well, of course," I lied. The old Trixie could be annoying, like dealing with a person. A quirky person. The new Trixie was smooth and polished like a machine.

It wasn't hard to see the parallels between our bakery and Java Kitty. How had I not suspected Grey Magic all along?

Answer: because I couldn't smell it. The machines doing the magic must not be physically in the car. Even now, a remote Automagick machine must be sending signals through her electrical components. The Trixie who was talking to me was an unholy mixture of Green and Grey Magics.

In other words, the Trixie I knew was dead.

"I just didn't think it was a big deal," I finished lamely.

"Like you didn't think that Grey Magic stink from Java Kitty's litterbox was a big deal?"

"I did! But I had other stuff on my mind."

"Like what, your silly investigation into the Kensingtons? Girl, they were vetting you for hire. You could have had a career and bought a small boat. Instead, you had to go and start suspecting Drew."

"How do you know that I suspected Drew?" I whimpered.

"Come on, girl, get with it. I've been hacked. Snap, I've been spying on you for over a week. Anything you say in here goes straight to Mama."

"You mean Estelle Kensington?"

"Finally got it. What's that old, dated expression, better late than never? Don't see much difference in this case, but what do I know? I'm just a dumb car. Whose whole personality can change, and her person won't even notice or care."

Ouch. "You're right Trixie. I've been neglecting you." I swallowed. "Neglecting myself, too. I put all my energy into Bryson. Spending time with him, which of course leeched my energy. Protecting him with this investigation. Trying to get my friends and family to accept him … even denying the obvious, that he was a demon, took a lot of energy. I see now how badly I screwed up, though I don't suppose it helps much."

"No, that totally does make me feel better." Pause. *"Though now I feel bad about your imminent, grisly death."*

"Thanks."

The gorgeous views of the Pacific told me we were entering the park. The sun was almost finished setting, which meant the park was closed.

The only other car in the lot was a black Porsche with the license plate B0KEH. I'd taken exactly one art class and dimly remembered that was a photography term. It meant blur.

My whole perspective on him had been a blur, until today.

Estelle Kensington stood waiting for us by the trailhead, dressed in hiking boots and a high-end athletic suit with the hood up. Sammy Boy was in her arms, wearing an adorable doggy sweater.

A backpack lay at her feet. I assumed it contained a change of clothes for David, once he shifted back into human form.

Also, whatever weapon they were going to use to kill me must be in there too.

"Delivery completed, self-actualization achieved," Trixie said smoothly. Then, a touch of her old Jersey accent returning, she added, *"Been a great ride, doll face. Catch you on the flip side."* She glitched for a moment, juddering, cabin lights flashing. Then her engine went dead.

Goodbye, Trixie.

"Evening, Miss Greenwood," Estelle greeted me pleasantly. "I must say I'm eager to tie up this loose end—meaning you—so we can all move on with our lives. Except you."

"So, you are the mastermind behind all this," I said. "At first I thought you might be covering for Drew accidentally draining his bride. But you killed her yourself, didn't you? She didn't pass your vetting process. You didn't think she was good enough to be part of your family. Just like you didn't think Jenna was good enough for your son all those years ago. But what really ticks me off is how you tried to sink my bakery … probably so you could hire me as your personal pastry chef. That's gross, lady. You're the worst person ever. You act all super sweet and well-meaning, like I do … but in your case it's b.s."

She smiled grimly. "With all due respect, it's mostly b.s. for you, too."

"What are you talking about?"

"I'm rather glad we're not hiring you after all. You may be a skilled baker and witch, but you don't meet our class standards. Much like the unfortunate Ashlee. I've been overhearing what you say when you're inside your car—"

"Oh, come on, lady," I burst out. "No one's at their nicest whilst driving a car! Which you would know if you ever had to do anything for yourself."

I was met with a cool, composed smile. "The things I've had to do myself would make you weep, little Green Witch."

That got me. "So, you killed Ashlee, personally? You didn't sic David on her?" In either of his forms?

Estelle sighed. "I did what any loving mother would do to a woman like Ashlee. My dear, silly boy Drew had been using her as a blood doll for a few months when she talked him into an engagement. He's not the brightest bulb, though he means well. I immediately knew it was about money, so I met with her—months before the wedding—and tried to be generous, reasonable. I gave her fifteen million reasons to stay away from my son."

I blinked. "You mean you offered Ashlee fifteen million dollars to leave Drew?"

"And she took it," Estelle said, chin defiant. "As I predicted she would."

That must have been when Ashlee had paid Kade de Klaw to create a new fake ID for her so she could truly disappear.

"But then…" Estelle sighed. "She came back again, greedy. Wanting more. Tried to blackmail us. Apparently her assistant had seen something she shouldn't have and reported it to Ashlee shortly after she quit."

"Oh, geez, which highly inappropriate thing did she witness?" I said. "Was it Drew chomping on the staff, Fred acting demented while everyone pretends he's just a jerky old man, or David here turning into the lapdog he is at heart?"

Estelle rolled her eyes. "I have no idea what you're—"

"Yeah, I figured out that he's a shifter," I said. "It explains how he was able to eat so many of my truth serum candies at the

Drunken Barrel and never reveal his secrets." All he'd done was gripe, as usual, about what a bad husband Fred was and how spoiled and irresponsible Drew was. His perspective was about what you'd expect from someone who worshipped Estelle and believed she could do no wrong. "But David must have noticed," I went on, "that everyone else who ate my candies was being too honest, because on Sunday night he snapped up the cherry pie before you could taste it and incriminate yourself. He's pretty devoted to you. My guess is you two have been together for many years. He might be around your own age, but his domestic shifter genes make him look youthful. He's also the perfect partner for a woman as controlling as you, because he's also your possession. A purse dog. With no power, no voice—"

"Oh, he most certainly has a voice, Miss Greenwood." Estelle looked amused at my having figured out David's secret. "I'm sure he has much to say to you, in fact."

Sammy Boy began to bark, then to shimmer as he shifted into a naked David.

"Hey, cake baker!" Without an ounce of self-consciousness, he grinned at me and started pulling on black boxer briefs from one of the backpack's compartments. "I was really hoping you'd give up on your investigation and come to our side." Then argyle socks. "I liked you." Then jeans. "You seemed like someone who really knew her place in the world, like me. I recommended you as a strong hire."

I whirled back around to Estelle. "So, you really were trying to 'hire' me … by taking away my family business. Taking away my options. Is that the extreme vetting process that's the reason you've never had to fire anyone?"

"Well, yes," Estelle said. "Though sometimes we've had to nudge someone along the path to retirement. David's aunt Velma for example, hadn't been up to producing pastries with her trembling old hands. I offered her a generous retirement package but she wouldn't accept it, so..." She shrugged.

"You offed her?"

She gave me a look of pure indignation. "How dare you? I loved Velma. I had her put down, humanely."

"She went over the Rainbow Bridge," David said cheerfully. "I will too one day. It's fine."

"How can you honestly be happy being some rich woman's lapdog?" I was sincerely curious. "I mean, dude, you're a pet."

"I'm someone's best friend," he shot back. "I'm in my proper place in nature and society. You could never imagine the ecstasy that comes with being loyal and true and ... and—"

"And such a good boy?" I was unable to suppress a giggle.

"Laugh it up, Miss Indie Baker. I don't expect you to understand. Look, the world is a hard place, and I chose to be taken care of. Loved. Cherished. I'm living my best life, if you want to know the truth." He turned to me, anger dancing in his eyes that I'd glimpsed hints of in our conversations. Only I'd never imagined it was directed at me. "The only awkward thing about it is talking to people like you. Having to pretend I'm still like you. Still clinging to my precious, special independence when I surrendered happily long ago. All those irritating, judgmental questions about 'art' versus 'keeping the lights on.' Estelle would have offered you a great wage and a life without worries, but you chose death. It's on you, cake baker."

I ignored him and addressed Estelle, as if he was just her dog or something. "So, that's your MO. When you want something, offer people money, then if that doesn't work, kill them?"

"I don't have to answer to you, Miss Greenwood. I've added more value to the world than you ever will."

"My gran's added more value to this world than *you* ever will," I shot back. "But even if you did fund the new library wing, you don't get to go around murdering people. And yes, it still counts if you made David do the dirty work."

"How presumptuous of you." Her nose in the air. "Our partnership may be nontraditional but I do *not* assign dirty work."

"I just held Ashlee in place," David said proudly. "It was Estelle who applied Ashlee's special lipstick. Crimson Cyanide."

Geez. It was getting real now. My heart began to pound wildly. "And is that what you're going to do to me, too, poison me with cyanide?"

"No, dear," Estelle said grimly. "Your mode of execution will be … death by frenemy."

"Did you say frenemy?"

"This is gonna be so cool, cake baker." David motioned to me to follow him. "Can't wait to show you what fun we've got in store. Your last breath's going to be a scream."

David ambled to the black Porsche and popped the trunk. Britt was lying inside, bound and gagged, with silver weights attached to her wrists that clearly had her writhing in pain. I could hear Max's yowls from the backseat. Actually, she was in human form, but in a cage, her feet tied together.

I tried to stay calm. My friends were still alive. That's what mattered. Wait, why were they alive? "You could have shot Max and driven a stake through Britt's heart," I said. "Are you saying you kept them alive in hopes they would decide to kill me?"

David beamed. "Yep, that's the beauty of this plan. Estelle and I don't have to do all the work for once. You three are *all* gonna kill *each other.*"

"Why on Earth would we do that?" We were actually getting along pretty well for once.

"Boy oh boy, I'm so glad you asked. I love showing off the cool toys Estelle gives me."

Like you love riding in cars and eating treats? I thought as he pulled an MP3 player out of the car's glove compartment.

"This digital music player has been Grey Magicked to detect and amplify levels of interpersonal tension. And it looks like the three of you have all kinds of baggage to work with. Going *way* back. It'll play exactly what you each need to hear to go homicidal."

I watched as he lifted Britt out of the trunk and abruptly dropped her small form onto the ground. The harsh landing made her groan through her gag. He opened the cage that held Max and grabbed her by her tied ankles, dragging her out of the car and through the dirt of the trailhead until she was beside Britt. As he untied her ankles, Estelle tapped my shoulder.

"Cell phone, please. There's no reception here in the woods, but why take chances you could reach out for help?"

"How are you going to explain that we all died without our cell phones?"

"Simple, you and Max decided to throw them into the ocean. Says so right here in your suicide note. Oh, you also apologized for killing your former bullies, Ashlee and Britt. And for hiding Britt's body in a place it'll never be found. Since Britt will, of course, turn to dust. I'll be returning in an hour to toss your bodies into that ancient POS car of yours, douse it with gasoline, and set the lot of you on fire."

"Huh, then where are you going to leave our suicide note?" Max had stopped her unearthly yowling long enough to listen to their murderous plan and poke holes in its logic. "Just by a tree or something? It's supposed to rain tonight, plus the wind will blow it away."

David and Estelle exchanged a look.

"Did you have a plan for…?" he began.

"I was thinking we could … never mind, what do you want to do?"

Max snorted. "You idiots are totally winging this."

"There's no need to be disrespectful, young lady," Estelle said mildly. "None of us here are professionals. We're all muddling through as best we can."

"Oh, I know!" David said. "I'll drop it off at the bakery."

"My gran's bakery?" I burst out, shaking with anger.

"Ooh, yes, good boy, good boy." She reached up and patted his head. He opened his mouth as if to pant.

"Grossness," Britt muttered.

So not only were they killing us, they were leaving a cruel, horrible note for my grandmother to find? No doubt that would kill her, too. "I will never stop haunting you," I growled at them.

"Oh, that's nice my dear, but we have haunting insurance," Estelle said smugly, still patting David's head as if he was, well, her pup. Blech. "Comprehensive, naturally. It's a no-brainer, in our situation. So sorry to burst your bubble. All right, girls, time to go! We'll leave you with a lovely song." She almost curtsied, then turned on the evil MP3 player and handed it to David, who tossed it up onto a thick tree branch about eight feet off the ground.

Music began to play, softly at first and then screaming right into my soul. A jagged, painful song. A *familiar* song. It made me want to cry for reasons I could not explain … until I could.

"You guys, don't you recognize the song?" I said. "This is the song that was playing on grad night, when it all went down."

"Holy crap, you're right." Britt stopped to listen. "Well, grad night is the last thing we should talk about if we're supposed to be trying not to kill each other."

"Don't you see, we have to talk about it." I said as the grim realization hit me. "The only way to stay alive is to work out our interpersonal tensions."

"Never gonna happen," Max said. "Guess we're dead. But hopefully I get to kill Brittany first."

"Not a chance, you whiny bobcat."

"Whiny?" Max puffed herself up. *"Whiny?"*

"Yeah, why were you yowling incessantly in the car?" Britt snapped at Max. "I was embarrassed for you. Have some dignity."

"Brittany, I know this is hard for your small, dead mind to get," Max said in her most condescending tone, "but I wasn't making those sounds to express distress at our situation. Or rather, I was. But only in a formal sense."

"Okay, you lost me," I admitted, wincing as the music tore up my soul some more.

"It was a distress call to communicate to my allies."

Britt scoffed. "Oh, right, your allies all over the woods? Come on, we both know you were just posturing with that."

"I really do have allies," Max snapped. "But they've gone to roost already."

I gasped. "The crow shifters? You know them personally?" I'd been watching that flock with fascination since I was ten.

She nodded. "Some of the corvid shifters who live in this park are ordinary people by day. Others stay in crow form nearly all the time and live in the wild. When Kade and I were abandoned in these woods as babies, they're the ones who found us. Some wanted to eat us, but others thought we were cute or we might be useful someday. So, they scheduled a meeting to decide whether to eat us—crows are always having meetings—but by the time it came up, it was too late. They'd already fed us carrion and groomed our fur and sort of considered us … family."

Britt looked thoughtful. "That's a lot like how it works with vampires too."

"But crows move their roosts around," Max said, though she had to shout to be heard over the music which had gotten louder. "And I've been so busy with all this investigation stuff that I haven't kept up with where the roost is. I haven't checked in with the fam in too long."

I opened my mouth to tell her it was okay, that my priorities had also gotten out of whack during this whole investigation thing, but the music was cutting me up like a magical machete and all that came out was a yelp of rage.

Britt and Max exchanged a look of concern.

"If even Hazel's feeling it, you and me are probably going to throw down soon," Max deduced. "Nice knowing you both … well, Hazel anyway."

"Ha, so you admit that you'd lose a fight with me," Britt said.

"Without crow backup, yes." She let out another series of distress yelps, and her horrible sounds did me the service of shutting out the music for long enough to let me think.

"Look, maybe we can't work out all of the tension between us," I ventured. "But at least the stuff from high school. It's old and festering. We never talk about it, because it hurts … even after all these years … at least for me it does."

"For me too," Max looked down.

Britt shrugged. "I was a little freaked out that night but whatever."

"No, not whatever." I wasn't going to let her Britt her way out of feeling stuff. My life—all our lives—depended on it. "You were traumatized the first time you ever saw magic. Yes, traumatized. Look, I'm afraid of tons of things that the two of you scoff at. But I'm not afraid of feelings."

Max covered her eyes and moaned. "Augh, you sound like that sap Elton. I wanna kill him, too."

"Elton's not a bad guy. He just had Seasonal Affective Disorder and, okay, maybe he needed a therapist—a good one," I added quickly before they went to the obvious zinger about my ex.

"Bryson was a bad therapist because he never helped people get their feelings out. He just fed off their energy, made them feel calm and relaxed. But they never got better at understanding themselves or their relationships. If we can do that, then this song won't have any power over us."

"Don't take this the wrong way, Hazel, but your voice is grating on me like a mosquito in my ear," Max said. "It would be fun to claw your face. No offense."

"Yeah, well, if we're confessing what we want to do to Hazel," Britt said. "I really want to take a bite of you and just fill up the tank. Drain you."

"Not if I stake you first." Max snapped a large twig off a nearby tree branch.

"No staking, no draining, just talking," I insisted, and they both hit me with homicidal glares. Which I ignored. Because this was my moment. "Grad night was supposed to be fun for everyone," I began, speaking as quickly as I could. "It was like prom for those of us who couldn't get a date to save our lives. It was like friend prom, where you stayed up all night with your besties and partied for the last time ever as classmates."

"Oh, that's weird," Britt interrupted. "I thought grad night was just another opportunity to get dressed up, look hot, party with my friends, and make out with fine guys. You know, like any Friday night. But on the school's dime."

"Okay, but I'm just saying for *me* it was special." I shrugged. "Max and I were right in the middle of the crowd for once in our lives, fast dancing to some silly song, having the time of our lives. We stopped to grab some punch, and before you know it, a slow song came on, a really romantic one. This one."

"No, no, I'm not hearing a slow song at all!" Britt said.

"Me either." Max looked impressed. "This magical tech is really sophisticated. We're each hearing totally different things."

"Well, I'm hearing the romantic slow song and it hurts. Because I remember what happened when this song came on. A boy asked me to dance for the first time in my life. It was Elliot, and I'm sure he was only asking out of politeness. But I knew I should say no because he was … you know … Max's."

"What?" Max began to laugh. "Me and Elliot?"

"Yeah, don't play dumb. I know you two have always had a special relationship, even if you never dated. But you insisted you didn't mind if I danced with him, and he was a really good dancer. I liked the way he held me, and he smelled amazing. Then midway through the song I looked up and saw that you'd ditched me." I was getting angrier and angrier just thinking about it. So much for talking things out. "You. Ditched. Me. All because I dared to shine for a moment. I dared to dance with the boy you liked." I shoved Max hard, and she was caught off guard and stumbled back.

"Whoa … Hazel … is that what you've been thinking all these years?" Max shook her head in wonder. "Elliot and I are like family. That's the special relationship we have. It's not romantic. We're like siblings."

"Huh?" My mouth had dropped open. How had I jumped to the wrong conclusions about Max and Elliot all along? Now that I thought about it, the protective way Elliot looked out for her, and also his annoyance with her antics, felt more sibling-like than romantic. But that left me even more confused. "But … but if you weren't jealous of me and Elliot dancing, what happened that night?"

Max sighed. "So, one minute I was dancing with a cup of punch in my hand. The next minute I was a scared animal, trapped in an extra-large dog crate behind the school."

"Whoa," I said. Someone threw Max in a dog crate?

"Ashlee Stone was peering in at me through the bars." Max's gaze had grown distant, like it had that night at the Drunken Barrel. "Like I was her own private zoo animal."

"Ashlee roofied you?" Britt spat the words. "And locked you in a cage?"

"I was so panicked," Max went on. "I banged my head against the walls of the kennel trying to escape. But every time I did that, she'd squirt bear spray in my eyes. It hurt so much, I kept screaming. Then she'd say my name and laugh. She knew exactly who I was. She was torturing me on purpose. I think she'd been planning it for months."

"Ashlee knew you were a shifter?" I asked.

Max nodded. "She'd seen my brother shift, one time, behind the school—he had even less control over it than I did—and put two and two together that I was one, too. Then she said she would tell our parents unless I did everything she told me; she would basically destroy the peace in my family. So, I shifted back and told her, sure, I'd do whatever she asked."

"Ugh. You did?"

"I had to. Was afraid if I didn't, she'd never open the door and let me out. I could hear the music from the gym, a fast tempo that felt like it matched my own panicking heart. I can hear that stupid song playing now." She balled her hands into fists, then seemed to catch herself and released them. "I shifted back to human form. I groveled, naked, in a cage, to Ashlee not to tell my parents about Kade and me. A memory that still makes me want to barf to this day."

"That's awful, Max," I said. I didn't have to ask to know it was the first time she'd told anyone what happened.

She smiled ruefully. "Anyway, I really sold it. Much as I detest lying, I'm good at it. She opened the door with a big smile … then I shifted *again* and jumped on her throat."

"Holy goodness. You could have killed her." Just picturing the scene made me want to faint.

"Don't actually remember what happened after that. I woke up in the woods three days later."

"Oh, I can tell you what happened," Britt said. "I was coming outside for a drink and a smoke—back then I smoked to keep my weight down from the drinking—when I saw a wild animal go for Ashlee's throat. I tore off the paper bag off my bottle of booze and started beating the animal on the head with the glass bottle. To save my friend. And also because I had a lot of aggression in me back then. Anyway, it ran off toward the woods."

"Oh, that was *you* who caused the big bump on my head?" Max looked pissed off again.

"You're welcome, I kept you from being a teenage murderess. And imagine how I felt seeing a freaking wildcat attack my friend!"

"Your friend deserved worse," Max growled. "Honestly, of all the bad things Estelle did, killing Ashlee was the least offensive. I mean, what else can you do with a compulsive blackmailer?"

"Be that as it may," Britt said, fangs out, "you can't just go around killing people. If you could, my meals would be a lot more satisfying. Anyway, we were all jerks in high school."

"Speak for yourself," I cut in. "After Max ditched me, I didn't lunge for any throats or brain anyone. I just sat there and cried my eyes out."

"Oh Hazel, *blech*." Britt mimed shoving her finger down her own throat. "Face it, you were a sniveling wimp in those days, which is just another form of jerk if you ask me. And anyhow, you did not just cry. You also erupted into magical green flames in front of the punch bowl."

"Uh, what?" Max blinked. "Why would you do that, Hazel?"

"I wasn't trying to. You disappeared, remember? And I thought it was my fault for dancing with Elliot. So, I did a simple reunion spell to locate you. But since I was just a little baby apprentice witch, I didn't realize those only work if the subject is *seeking* reunion with the spellcaster. Or thinking about them at all, in any way. I tried the spell over and over but since Max apparently had zero thoughts about me—"

"Are you really still mad at me for that?" Max shook her head in disgust. "I was either screaming my eyes out from bear spray or running through the woods with a concussion."

"Regardless of your *reasons* for not being there for me," I said huffily, "all the energy from my spell boomeranged back in my face. It hurt, too. It could have killed me."

"But then," Britt remembered, a thousand-yard stare in *her* eyes. "Then you yelled some crazy rhyme, and the flames were doused. I think the bad rhyming traumatized me, more than the burning, to be honest. I may have called you some things, in the heat of the moment..."

"A freak, a psycho, evil witch." I recited ten more things that were R-rated.

"But for me, the worst moment came afterward," Britt admitted. "When I gave Ashlee a ride home at the end of the night, she showed me Max's clothes and tried to convince me she'd left them behind when she turned into an animal, the animal that attacked her. Normally I'd just think Ash was drunk. Which she was. But after what I'd just seen Hazel do, it actually seemed plausible. To my last day, which could well be today, I'll never forget how I felt that night. I remember looking up at the moon from my convertible and thinking that our town, Blue Moon Bay, was chock full of magic … and I had no magic in me at all." Britt looked forlorn, like a lost kid. "And *this* stupid song was playing on the radio, kind of a midtempo new jack swing revival thing—"

"Wait, wait, wait, *you* felt left out?" I said. "You, Britt, the queen of the school?"

Britt nodded sadly. "I think maybe that's why I got together with my sire so soon afterward. Maybe I wanted to be special, too, like you guys." Britt sighed. "Yeah, well, I'm sorry I was friends with people who tortured you with bear spray. I'm sorry that I kind of tortured you, too."

"That's really big of you to admit, Brittany," Max said. "And Hazel, I'm sorry I never caught up with you and explained what happened. I shouldn't have ghosted you. Once I was convinced it was all finally behind me, I just wanted to move on … and I wanted to forget everything about high school. Even you. I'm truly sorry about that."

"Thanks for saying all that," I said, reaching out to touch her shoulder. "As for me, I'm sorry I didn't take either one of you seriously when you warned me not to settle for Bryson. I thought you were both bitter singles, so I discounted your perspective."

"Oh, I may be single but I'm not bitter," said Britt. "Girl, I play the field. Let me be your teacher."

"And I may be bitter," Max said, "but I'm not single. More on that once we break out of here. Hey, did anybody notice that the music stopped?"

Max and I had just removed the silver chain bracelets from Britt's wrists—they left behind a nasty black burn line—when we heard a golf clap ring out.

"Nice job girls." Estelle was back, standing right outside David's Porsche. "I guess you were all more emotionally well-adjusted than I gave you credit for." She turned to David. "Well, it's riskier and messier than plan A but I think we need to do it."

From her powder-blue REI rainproof puffer jacket, she pulled out a pistol.

Screaming, I ducked behind the nearest spruce tree. Max shifted to cat form and began her pointless yelping thing again.

Luckily, Britt moved to knock it the gun of Estelle's hand, but David shoved her before she could. Estelle fired once, shooting her in the chest.

I knew a bullet couldn't do more than slow the vampire down for a moment, but while the hole in her chest was closing up, David managed to slap a silver bracelet on her again.

Now we were screwed.

Over and over again, the bobcat that was Max yelped, a terrible wailing animal sound. Suddenly from the air above us, a responding caw rang out. Then another, and another. An angry chorus filled my ears, and I looked up to see that the sky was filled with black shapes mobbing the moon overhead. Swarming like angry bees, straight for us.

"The crows!" Britt yelled with relief and some surprise. "They're really here. She wasn't making it up about the crows being her friends. Well, I'll be damned."

"Er, aren't you?" I asked. "The whole vampire thing?"

"*Rude,* Hazel." Britt rolled her eyes. "That's just an urban legend. Probably. Anyway, looks like I won't have to find out today. Phew."

The entire murder of crows swooped down, surrounding David and Estelle, pushing them to the ground.

"Ew, they're going to peck their eyes out," Britt muttered. "You might want to look away, Hazel. You don't seem like you could deal with seeing that."

"Thanks, yeah," I said. "There's not enough therapy in the world."

Before the crows could do anything gross, though, Elliot's squad car zoomed up, lights flashing. He and another cop jumped out, guns pointed at Estelle's head. David immediately put his hands up.

"Stop, sisters and brothers," Elliot commanded, and the force of crows reshaped itself to surround him like a dark, feathered mantle. I stared at him as if it was the first time I'd really seen him while he handcuffed David first, then Estelle.

Elliot was part of the murder of crows that I'd watched since my childhood. He was a shifter, and he was letting me see it for the first time.

"No one hurts our sister," he said sternly to the pair.

The crows cawed in angry agreement.

"Oh what, seriously? How could you crows call this bobcat sister?" David spat. "That's not the natural order of things."

"Yeah, well, nature's overrated," Elliot said, calmly setting a large blanket on the ground in front of the bobcat, who shifted back into Max and wrapped herself up cozily. "If you don't agree, feel free to stay here and have your eyes pecked out."

Strangely, neither took him up on the offer.

"Told you I had family in the woods," Max said dreamily, snuggling into her blanket while Elliot led the two criminals to the back of his squad car.

"Thanks, Crow Bro." She kissed Elliot on the cheek.

"Anytime, little sister. Next time, loop me in before you go and try to solve a murder, will you?"

"You mean before *we* crack your case," she bragged.

Elliot rolled his eyes and for a moment looked exactly like the teenage boy I used to crush on, slouching in the back row.

Again, I stared, this time in wonder at how I could have missed their obvious sibling vibe. He'd never been into her as a girlfriend. Which meant ... well, what did it mean? Anything?

Elliot tossed a glance of concern at me and Britt. "These two know everything, right?"

"Yes, but it's okay," Max assured him. "They're my friends." She glanced at Britt, who looked as if she was really wanting to argue that point. I sort of did myself. Yes, we'd been friends while solving this mystery. But what would happen now? "For the moment, anyway," Max amended.

"Either way, your secret's safe with us," I said.

"Good." Elliot's tone was light, yet I had that weird sense again that there was an "or else" behind his statement. The more I learned about him, the more I realized there was still more to know.

A second squad car pulled up behind him.

"My buddies'll give you each a ride home," Elliot said. "Unless you want to take Hazel's car?"

I shuddered. "No thanks! My car died. I mean, she's really *dead*."

Poor Trixie. We'd never really meshed the way a witch and familiar should. Yet if I ever got another, I vowed I wouldn't take them for granted the way I had her.

Really hoping for a cat this time.

"Hey." Elliot gestured to my feet.

"What?" I shrieked. "Did I catch a stray bullet? Am I bleeding?"

"No, I just noticed your alligator socks. Those are cool." He shrugged and turned toward his own car. "See you around."

Britt shot me a look just as I was processing that *Elliot liked my socks*.

"I'll see *you* around," I said, with a new smooth confidence. "Or no, maybe I'll see you later, croca-gator. Get it?"

Britt was shooting me a very different kind of look now, but I didn't care.

We'd outmaneuvered the murderers. I'd survived the breakup. And also, Elliot was already walking away and never heard me say those idiotic things.

I was ninety percent sure.

Today was *my* day. The best Thanksgiving ever.

CHAPTER TWENTY

THE TOWN OF Blue Moon Bay was not exactly rocked to its core by the murder of Ashlee Kensington.

Most people who knew her hadn't much liked her, even if they'd pretended to in high school.

From early in life, she had a talent for extortion, and was a shallow, scheming, mean, and generally unpleasant person. She was pretty, though. Through nature and hard work and cash. She could be charming, too, when she wanted things. These gifts opened shiny golden doors for her, for a while.

But in the end, she was garbage.

Still, we were a town that cherished its traditions. The Kensingtons were among our founding pillars. And as unsettling as it was to have the peace disturbed by a dead woman's thousand-dollar shoes pointing toward the cloudy night sky, I worried that the arrests—especially Estelle's—might shake people's faith more than the murder itself.

How would Blue Moon Bay recover from seeing a much-admired leader of the community brought low?

"Mornin', Hazel." Margaret waved her copy of the *Blue Moon Bay Gazette* toward me. As usual this morning, she and Helen were the first ones in at seven a.m. on the dot. "You hear the news," she crowed, "about that awful Kensington woman being indicted for offing her own daughter-in-law?"

"All I can say is, thank goodness our sheriff caught that hussy," Helen yelled at her companion. "Thought she could pull one over on Bill Gantry, but nothing gets by that man. He's got Columbo beat for smarts."

I gritted my teeth as I served up their twice-baked chocolate almond croissants.

Predictably, Gantry had stepped up to accept full credit for cracking the mystery and nabbing the bad guys. To my immense disappointment, Elliot told us to let him. I wondered if that meant he was close to collecting the proof he'd needed to oust Gantry—hopefully for good. In the meantime, it was hard to keep mum about the truth while Gantry strutted around like he was the town hero.

As if on cue, Sheriff Gantry walked in, with Elliot at his side. The police were among the first to come back to our bakery when Java Kitty abruptly closed its doors on Thanksgiving night. Granted, they needed coffee early in the morning. But I told myself it was more than that. They missed us. We were, ourselves, a Blue Moon Bay tradition, and unlike Estelle, we hadn't overplayed our hand.

Elliot becoming a regular, however, had been a surprise. I could only assume he was tailing Gantry pretty closely if he'd deign to enter a bakery on the daily. Or maybe he *really* liked my socks? Whatever his motives, I'd learned how he liked his coffee and looked forward to seeing his gorgeous face first thing in the morning.

Though, he was no longer the only hot guy whose face I'd be seeing bright and early.

"All right, Kade." I turned to my brand new barista, who'd been in the back restocking herbs on high shelves that neither Gran nor I could reach. "That'll be a double latte, easy on the foam, and one dry cappuccino."

"Done and done."

"Hold on, who's this handsome man?" Margaret purred.

Kade's tersely muttered hello told me I would have to be the one to introduce him. Man, he made one amazing cup of coffee, but I was discovering that he wasn't much of a people person.

Then again, neither was I when I first started here, so many years ago. You start where you start.

"Ladies, meet the fabulous Kade. He's going to make you the best cup of coffee you ever had." Seriously, he'd helped us step up our espresso game.

"Where should I tuck his tip?" Margaret's tone was creepily suggestive.

"In this jar," I said quickly, placing a clean mason jar on the counter before she or anyone else could make bigger fools of themselves.

Max walked in, laptop case under her arm, at the same time as Sophie Jeffries.

"Sophie!" I greeted the kid like an old friend. "Grab yourself a stool."

"I can only stay seventeen minutes before I have to run to make the first bell," Sophie informed me earnestly. "I just wanted to say I heard the news. Now that they caught the killer, maybe I don't need my nightlight anymore."

"I'm glad to hear it. Let me get you an orange raisin scone on the house and we can chat a little before you have to run."

Max's eyes widened. "Cool, you're giving away free stuff? Then I'll take four chocolate croissants—"

"Oh no, *you're* not getting so much as a free napkin." I attempted to give her a stern look, but it only turned into a crooked smile. I was so happy to have her back. "You're not even a real customer, Max,"

I teased. "More like a tenant. You gotta pay me to rent that corner booth all day as your blog office."

"You know, you're starting to sound just like your grandmother," Max said with a twinkle in her eyes. "Where is Miss Sage anyway?"

"Oh, she's been setting her own hours lately. Waltzes in at noon most days." It was on the tip of my tongue to add that Max would know that if she wasn't so deep in her worky-work trance at noon. But just at that moment, a limo pulled up in front of the store. "One second..."

Leeza, Estelle's assistant, was walking toward us, looking serious. Feeling nervous, I dashed out from behind the counter to open the door for her.

"Hazel." Leeza gave me a cool nod. "This is the last time I'll be talking to you, since I no longer work for Estelle."

Well, that made sense. "Because Estelle won't need a personal assistant in prison?"

"Because I don't want to work for a murderer."

"That was going to be my next guess." Not really, but it was refreshing to hear. "Sorry, I should have given you more credit."

"It's okay. I did consider overlooking it, because of the benefits package. But the thing is, Estelle's also a liar, a cheater, and possibly, I really hate to say this but, a dog killer. Sammy Boy's disappeared. I don't know what to think anymore about that household, I just know I'm peace-ing out."

"What about Landon? And Marina?" And Daffodil and Stephen and all the others. Would The Help all be heading out en masse? I was surprised that the thought made me sad.

"Oh no, they're staying on to work for Drew."

I found myself relieved to hear that. Even if *I* never wanted to work for the Kensington family, it was clear those folks thrived in their positions.

"Everybody loves him," she went on. "He's a great boss. With Estelle gone, he's really come into his own. He's also hiring a full-time nursing staff for his dad. Says it's time we all stop pretending Fred is okay and get him the care he needs."

All that was a *huge* relief.

"Sounds like Drew has turned out to be a responsible adult?" I asked, wondering if the wealthy vamp was just another late boomer, like me.

"Well, *sort* of." Leeza frowned, wrinkling her forehead. "Drew's latest venture is to open an upscale nightclub downtown and build a moat around the house. Because he likes moats."

"I see. I think you're smart to move on," I said, realizing there was no way she could have stayed, knowing what she knew about the family. The others—well, except for David—had always maintained a healthy perspective. Perhaps they were a bit cynical about their employers, but it protected them. Leeza had been a true believer.

"Thanks." Leeza paused. "I probably shouldn't say this, but I think you're undisciplined as a baker and a businesswoman. And your funky little shop is so fifteen years ago. And sugar is the devil."

"Wow, don't hold back," I muttered, a bit shocked she'd come out with all that.

"But you're a truly honest person, Hazel. You're exactly who you appear to be. I admire you for it. And that's why I came to say goodbye."

"Thanks." Though, *was* I who I appeared to be, really? I sure didn't advertise the fact that I was a Green Witch. Or a magical detective, for that matter. Maybe no one was exactly who they appeared to be.

At least not in Blue Moon Bay.

"Well, my bags are packed," she said. "I'll be taking on a new job in LA, supporting a much more wholesome family. The Kardashians."

"Good luck with that."

We shook hands.

As she turned to go, I saw that Max had settled into work, earbuds in, fingers clacking at the keyboard like a madwoman. Tapping her foot to the music only she could hear.

Margaret had wisely given up trying to flirt with Kade, for the moment.

Helen, though, was making googly eyes at Gantry. "Great detective work, sir," she purred. "You should get some kind of award. Say, is that a bacon and sausage sandwich you're eating? Genius."

Well, they say everyone is someone else's idea of a catch.

Elliot's dark, deep-set eyes caught mine, and amusement creased his normally stoic face, sending an unexpected thrill through me.

The crow and I had a secret together. I liked how that felt.

I settled in to chat with Sophie. "So, any progress on trying to get your mom to let you have a cat?"

"Not really." Her glum face perked up. "Hey, I was wondering if maybe you'd talk to her? You just have this way with people…"

My laughter cut her off. "Sorry, it's just no one's ever said that to me before in my life."

"Oh." Sophie's brow furrowed. "Then maybe you shouldn't talk to her."

"No. But I know who should." Compulsion for a good cause? "In fact, go ahead and start thinking up cat names. This plan's foolproof, kid, trust me."

So, this was my clientele at seven a.m.: My oldest friend. A ten-year-old hungry for conversation. A pair of cops—one good, one bad. And two feisty old ladies who'd long ago lost the ability to sleep in.

No, the bakery wasn't hopping in the same way that Java Kitty had hopped. Maybe it never would be. But I was no longer afraid we were heading for the dust bin of history.

Or the dumpster.

Sophie had skipped off to class and I was setting out sample slices of thick-cut walnut bread, spread with fig and Kalamata olive dip, for everyone to try, when Britt walked in wearing dark sunglasses. Her hair was wrapped in a head scarf.

"What are you doing out in the sunlight?" I stage-whispered once it was just her and me at the counter. "Wait, is this because now that Java Kitty's gone bye-bye you're forced to wait till morning to satisfy your junk food cravings?"

"No." She slapped a page of printer paper down on the counter in front of me. "My only craving is to know who wrote this."

Someone had typed a note on the paper, with an actual typewriter.

UNNATURAL CREATURE OF THE NIGHT:

WE FORMALLY BESEECH YOU TO DO THE RIGHT THING AND STAKE YOURSELF AT 12 O'CLOCK MIDNIGHT TONIGHT.

WE KNOW WHERE YOU LIVE. OBVIOUSLY.

WE HAVE PERSONNEL GUARDING YOUR PORTLAND RESIDENCE AS WELL, SO DON'T TRY TO RUN.

JUST GO DIE, PEACEFULLY, OR WE WILL BE FORCED TO TAKE MATTERS INTO OUR OWN CAPABLE HANDS.

SINCERELY,

THE BLUE MOON BAY VAMPIRE HUNTER'S SOCIETY

"This reads like a nasty bank letter," I muttered. "Maybe even a shade nastier."

"I know right? Maybe it's a practical joke." Britt glared daggers at Max, who was now doing a little butt-wiggle and head-shake dance in her chair as she typed. "I bet she'd like to see me sweat."

"Sure, but it's not her style." I nodded politely to Gantry and Elliot as they got up to leave. "Dropping off a letter is too long an effort. She's an off-the-cuff jokester. Plus, she doesn't own a typewriter."

"Who does these days?"

"Hipsters? The very old? Aspiring authors?"

"So, you're saying it's not someone I need to take seriously," Britt said hopefully.

"No, I'm saying we need more information. For example, did Drew Kensington receive a note like this? Or your sire, assuming they're local?"

Britt rolled her eyes and I remembered she didn't think much of her sire. "I don't know about Drew, but my sire's unlikely to be receiving much mail. He was local, but when I tried to contact him, I found out he's dead. Died about a month ago. Not that he was providing the slightest bit of support or guidance—"

"Uh … Britt? That's not good that he just died a month ago. Means these guys might have gotten to him."

"Oh crud. I see your point." Britt lifted up her arms and made a face. "Now I'm officially sweating."

"Take a seat, I'll be right back," I said, trying to hide my excitement at having a new mystery to solve. Ever since Estelle and David had been arrested, life had been calmer … but also not as interesting. Who would have thought I'd get so hooked on sleuthing? "I'm going to make us a nice pot of Irish breakfast tea and put together a plate of pastries to help us think."

"And I'm going to go separate that dweeb of a shifter from her computer," Britt declared. "If someone's targeting vampires in

Blue Moon Bay, it's going to take all three of us to stop me from becoming their next victim."

It's not that I wasn't worried about Britt. As tough as she was, she wasn't invulnerable. But a little thrill shivered up my back, one that had nothing to do with anxiety.

"Booyah, we're getting the gang back together!" At Britt's shocked glare, I hastily fixed it. "I mean, boo ... Yeah ... someone's hunting you. I want to validate your feelings of fear, and support you in this time of—"

"Just go get the goodies already before I bite you!" she said with a laugh. "I'll get the bobcat, assuming she can currently be reached from Planet Earth."

"Mini chocolate chip teacakes, coming right up," I sang, and ran into the kitchen.

NOTE FROM THE AUTHOR

Dear Reader,

Welcome to Blue Moon Bay!

If you're already looking forward to your next visit, you can join my newsletter to receive new release info, sales, sneak peaks, and bonus content.

When you sign up at my website, www.sierracrossauthor.com, you'll receive the free audio version of A Green Kind of Witch, a prequel novella about Hazel, brilliantly narrated by Joanna Roddy.

Happy reading—and listening!

xo, Sierra

Printed in Great Britain
by Amazon